"You still didn't ar...
Were you asked to...

"Get you to stay by using whatever means necessary?" Fiona sat down hard on the edge of the bed, dragging her hand through her long, thick dark hair. "Yes. Leigh used those exact words with me a little while ago."

Jake's heart sank. The rest of him still had not registered the stand-down order.

"But that's not why I'm here," she breathed, her eyes locked on his. "I'm here because I'm incredibly attracted to you. I want you, Jake Anderson. Nothing more than that."

Every part of him wished he could believe her. He cleared his throat, willing away his unrepentant arousal. "Leave with me," he told her, desperate to give her one more chance. "Let me take you away from here, get you some help. Then we might revisit this."

"I can't." Her sensual mouth twisted. "I can't leave. I have a very real reason for being here."

"Then tell me."

* * *

Book twelve of The Coltons of Mustang Valley

* * *

If you're on Twitter, tell us what you think of Harlequin Romantic Suspense! #harlequinromsuspense

Dear Reader,

I know I've said this before and I'll say it again—
I love the Coltons. This family, with all their locations
and intrigue, has always fascinated me. Reading
how they find love amid turmoil, murders and
suspense is one of the highlights of my reading
experience. Yours, too, I think! Working with all
the other authors and the fabulous editors makes
writing these stories a dream.

This story, the last of twelve books set in Mustang
Valley, a fictional town in Arizona, had all my
favorite things: a cult; a handsome, sexy rancher; an
undercover female FBI agent; and suspense—lots
of suspense. I so enjoyed telling Jake and Fiona's
story and wrapping up this particular installment
of the Colton saga. I hope you are as entertained
reading this book as I was writing it!

Karen Whiddon

COLTON'S
LAST STAND

Karen Whiddon

HARLEQUIN

ROMANTIC
SUSPENSE

Special thanks and acknowledgment are given to
Karen Whiddon for her contribution to the
The Coltons of Mustang Valley miniseries.

Recycling programs
for this product may
not exist in your area.

ISBN-13: 978-1-335-62657-8

Colton's Last Stand

Copyright © 2020 by Harlequin Books S.A.

This edition published by arrangement with Harlequin Books S.A.

For questions and comments about the quality of this book,
please contact us at CustomerService@Harlequin.com.

Harlequin Enterprises ULC
22 Adelaide St. West, 40th Floor
Toronto, Ontario M5H 4E3, Canada
www.Harlequin.com

Printed in U.S.A.

Karen Whiddon started weaving fanciful tales for her younger brothers at the age of eleven. Amid the gorgeous Catskill Mountains, then the majestic Rocky Mountains, she fueled her imagination with the natural beauty surrounding her. Karen now lives in north Texas, writes full-time and volunteers for a boxer dog rescue. She shares her life with her hero of a husband and four to five dogs, depending on if she is fostering. You can email Karen at kwhiddon1@aol.com. Fans can also check out her website, karenwhiddon.com.

Books by Karen Whiddon

Harlequin Romantic Suspense

The Coltons of Mustang Valley

Colton's Last Stand

The CEO's Secret Baby
The Cop's Missing Child
The Millionaire Cowboy's Secret
Texas Secrets, Lovers' Lies
The Rancher's Return
The Texan's Return
Wyoming Undercover
The Texas Soldier's Son
Texas Ranch Justice
Snowbound Targets

The Coltons of Roaring Springs

Colton's Rescue Mission

The Coltons of Red Ridge

Colton's Christmas Cop

The Coltons of Texas

Runaway Colton

The Coltons of Oklahoma

The Temptation of Dr. Colton

The Coltons: Return to Wyoming

A Secret Colton Baby

Visit the Author Profile page at
Harlequin.com for more titles.

Once again, this book is for my husband, Lonnie. He eagerly awaits each book release and reads every single one. I'm so happy to have him in my corner always.

Chapter 1

For the first time in her life, undercover FBI agent Fiona Evans truly understood how someone became indoctrinated into a cult. Ever since arriving at the Affirmative Alliance Group center, she'd been bombarded by a relentless onslaught of information, all presented in such a smiling, feel-good, we-only-want-the-best-for-you way that she felt guilty asking for a break. There were seminars and classes, films and audio recordings that were piped into her room at night under the guise of helping her learn while she slept. The other members, so earnestly pleasant and cheerful, were supportive, telling her over and over again that they—and AAG's founder, Micheline Anderson—only wanted to help her become the best person she could possibly be.

Luckily, Fiona considered herself strong and capable, well trained and not the slightest bit susceptible to either criticism or brainwashing. If she weren't, even she might have bought in to the relentless indoctrination of nonsense by AAG.

Teeth aching from all the saccharine, Fiona smiled and nodded and pretended until she thought she would scream, which she did sometimes inside her head while smiling back at them.

Even Micheline, a woman Fiona thought of privately as the cult's supreme ruler, went out of her way to show an interest in her group's newest arrival, sending a personal note of welcome along with fresh flowers. "An honor," whispered Leigh Dennings, one of Micheline's protégées. "So rare. True proof of how special you are."

With difficulty, Fiona kept from snorting at that. Gullible she wasn't, though she definitely wanted Leigh and the others to believe she was. In fact, she'd taken great care to make sure she appeared to be exactly the kind of vulnerable person they sought out as recruits. They'd found her, destitute and alone, on the streets of Mustang Valley, asking where she might find a shelter to get a free meal.

Instead, one of the AAG members had found her and taken her to its lovely and welcoming center, ten miles from downtown Mustang Valley. It had a long, tree-lined dirt drive leading in from the main road, an always open, hunter-green gate, and big potted plants in front. Fiona had stared at the woodsy, yet fancy log cabin exterior, large triangular roof over two sprawling stories, before being led into the large, open lobby. She'd been served complimentary beverages and a light lunch and told someone would be out to speak with her soon.

Affirmative Alliance Group had been founded forty years ago by Micheline Anderson, formerly known as

Luella Smith. Ever since the FBI had been given an anonymous tip hinting Micheline's involvement in numerous crimes, including money laundering, they'd researched her. A gifted nurse, Micheline promoted herself as a healer and self-help guru. These days, her followers numbered in the hundreds of thousands, most of those via the internet. Locally, members were only in the hundreds, most of those living in their own homes. Only about twenty people lived in the AAG center full-time, mostly Micheline and her inner circle as well as new recruits who were in the process of being converted.

Like me, Fiona thought grimly. She'd bear it—she had to. As long as she kept her eyes on the big picture, the reason she'd come here, she would survive.

Trying to grab some alone time, Fiona hurried from the crowded room where she'd just attended yet another seminar on becoming your best you—or some variation thereof—and rushed toward the ladies' room. She'd learned early on that around here, the only place they'd leave you alone was either in the shower or the toilet.

Just as she reached the door, someone grabbed her arm.

"I've been looking for you!" Leigh gushed. "You're not going to believe who asked about you."

With difficulty, Fiona kept from rolling her eyes. "Micheline?" she guessed.

Clearly astonished, Leigh giggled. "Wow, you *are* amazing. Smart as well as lovely. Come with me. Micheline asked me to bring you around to talk with her."

Though Fiona actually considered refusing, she reminded herself of her task and nodded. For such a petite and delicate person, Leigh kept an awfully firm grip on Fiona's arm as she steered her down a long hallway, through some double doors marked Private and into a part of the center where Fiona had never been.

Here, plush carpet softened their footsteps to a hush. Elegant mahogany tables displayed expensive-looking vases and statues, matched with clearly valuable artwork hung under muted lighting. Fiona felt as if she'd left the Old West and stepped into the corporate offices of some über-rich CEO.

Giving herself a mental shake, she made a show of gaping around her at everything all at once. Seeing, Leigh laughed, the sound like bells tinkling. "It's something else, isn't it? I remember the first time I saw it. I was overwhelmed, too."

They stopped in front of an intricately carved mahogany double door. Spine straight, like a soldier standing at attention, Leigh knocked three times, the staccato sound sharp.

"Come in." A warm voice, inviting confidences. *Micheline Anderson.* Finally. Playing the role of everyone's friend. Fiona's gut tightened. Funny, in this place, her gut was the only thing she trusted.

Stepping inside, Fiona eyed Leigh, half expecting her to bow. Instead, Leigh murmured something that sounded like, "Here you are," and turned to leave.

"Wait." With a benevolent smile, the leader of the AAG waved Leigh to a chair. "You may have a seat also, Fiona," she offered, making it sound as if Fiona actually had a choice.

"We are to have a special visitor this afternoon." Bright blue eyes sparkling, Micheline pushed back a strand of her well-coiffed blond hair. "My son, Jake. I haven't seen him for twenty-three years. I would appreciate if both of you helped in making sure he feels welcome."

Immediately, Leigh nodded. "Will do," she chirped. "If you could provide me with some sort of list of his likes and dislikes, I'll have staff get to work immediately."

Micheline's broad smile faltered. Just a tad before she had it firmly back in place. "Honestly, I have no idea. The last time I saw him, he was only seventeen."

Fiona looked from one woman to another. "I'm sorry, but I have no idea why you wanted to talk to me."

Leigh snapped her head around to eye Fiona, her perfect brow creased in a frown. But then, so quickly Fiona wasn't sure if she might have imagined it, Leigh smoothed her expression in a return to the ever-pleasant, eager-to-please beauty queen she was. "Patience, Fiona," she said, folding her hands neatly in her lap.

Micheline watched them interact with the same compassion that had endeared her to her followers. A slight smile curved her red-painted lips as she waited. "You're new here," she told Fiona. "Tell me, what do you think of the AAG?"

Heart skipping a beat, for a split second, Fiona found herself at a loss for words. She recovered quickly, remembering all the hours of intensive research she'd put in. "It's a bit overwhelming at times," she volunteered softly. "I can see so much happiness, so much good. I'm just not sure I could ever be worthy of belonging." There. Textbook. No doubt exactly the sort of thing Micheline had hoped she would say.

"Of course you're worthy," Micheline purred. "I see great potential in you. Which is why I'm going to assign you to my son. Show him around, keep him company while I'm in meetings, and make sure he has a good time."

"She's giving you a great honor," Leigh prodded when Fiona remained silent.

Not sure how she felt about this, Fiona pasted a smile on her face and nodded. Best to play along. "Thank you, ma'am," she stammered, hoping she appeared dazed enough. Her role was to play a grateful and zealous convert while obtaining concrete proof of even one of the crimes Micheline was suspected of being involved in. She already had substantive leads on Micheline's varied schemes, including running a fake marriage counseling center outside town, and scamming people out of money with phony self-help seminars.

Apparently, she did. Micheline leaned back in her chair, her expression satisfied. "You and Leigh will meet him when he gets here. He's driving down from northern Arizona, and I expect him sometime between two and three." With that said, she picked up a stack of papers from her desk and began reading through them, a clear dismissal.

"Come on." Leigh took Fiona's arm. "Let's go up to your room and see if we can find you something suitable to wear."

Allowing herself to be led away, Fiona glanced down at her fashionably torn jeans. "What's wrong with what I have on?" she asked.

Leigh only shook her head.

Once they reached Fiona's room on the second floor, Leigh followed her inside. "Micheline has great plans for you," she announced the moment the door closed.

Every instinct on alert, Fiona turned. "Really? What kind of plans?"

"She's grooming you to become a welcome coordinator like me, to help find people just like yourself who need help and could use the AAG's warm and welcoming family."

"Wow." Pretending to be awestruck, Fiona waited to hear the catch. One thing she'd picked up early on here was that AAG did nothing out of the simple goodness of its hearts. It was all about getting money out of its followers.

"Wow is right," Leigh gushed. "She wants you to focus on Mustang Valley College. Mainly on one particularly lonely, wealthy freshman named Theodore Royce the Third, whose money hasn't brought him happiness."

"But AAG will," Fiona finished, her tone bright, even though her stomach churned.

"Of course. He's already sought us out, attended a few seminars and talking to one of our counselors. You will take over for her." Leigh had begun riffling through Fiona's closet. "You don't have many dresses."

Fiona crossed her arms. "I'm not really a dress-up kind of person."

"Why not? You're so pretty and you have an amazing body," Leigh gushed. "Why not use that to your best advantage and show it off to prospective members? How do you think I became Miss Mustang Valley?"

Weighing her options, Fiona decided to play along. "Such an amazing accomplishment."

"It is, isn't it?" Leigh wrinkled her nose. "Now I'm going to help you. We're going to do a makeover."

"When?"

"Right now, silly." Patting the desk chair, Leigh picked up Fiona's admittedly small makeup bag and looked through it. "This won't do at all," Leigh muttered. "I'll be right back."

And she dashed off, leaving Fiona staring after her. A moment later, Leigh returned, carrying a much larger makeup case. "I want you to pay close attention to what I do," Leigh instructed her. "So that you can replicate the look on your own. I'll let you borrow some of my makeup even, since I have tons more."

As Leigh began rummaging through her stuff, Fiona put her hand on the other woman's arm to stop her. "What's the point?" she asked, honestly bewildered. "Why are you having me change the way I look?"

Batting her long—surely false—eyelashes, Leigh sighed. "To help you attract Jake, Micheline's son. No offense, but Micheline feels you might need just a little help in that department. And I agree with her."

"Attract Micheline's son?" Fiona felt as if they'd entered an alternate universe. "Why would I want to do that?"

"Because he's quite the catch, I hear." Leigh leaned closer, meeting Fiona's gaze directly. "And Micheline has given her blessing."

Ewww. Creepy. Wisely, Fiona kept these thoughts to herself. Everything Micheline Anderson did had a reason. So what hidden motive might be behind her using Fiona as bait for her son?

"You're a beautiful woman, Fiona," Leigh continued, not noticing. "But honestly, you present yourself as stern and serious and strong. Men don't like that sort of thing, you know."

Resisting the urge to gape at the other woman, Fiona widened her eyes instead. "I'm proud of being strong," she said quietly. "And any man who doesn't like that doesn't need to be hanging around me."

Her comment had Leigh giggling. "You're so funny." Even though Fiona hadn't been joking. "Now sit still and let me show you how to enhance what the universe gave you."

Fiona sighed. Why not? If this was the worst thing that happened to her while here, then she'd take it. Though she already knew how to apply makeup, it'd be interesting to get Leigh's take.

She sat unmoving while Leigh, humming tunelessly under her breath, applied foundation, blush and powder before moving on to her eyebrows. Fiona didn't balk until Leigh came after her with a pair of spidery-looking false eyelashes.

"Please." Fiona held up her hand to ward her off. "How about we just use mascara?"

"They're magnetic," Leigh explained, as if that made all the difference in the world. "I just put a little bit of special eyeliner on you and they'd attach right to it."

"No, thank you." Keeping her tone polite, Fiona shook her head. "I have some great mascara that I'd prefer to use instead."

Leigh heaved a disappointed sigh, but she put the lashes back in a box. "Fine. You won't look as dramatic, though."

Fiona nodded. "I understand." She did suffer through letting Leigh apply three painstaking coats of mascara.

"There you are," Leigh finally cooed. "Look at yourself and see how stunning you are."

Half curious, half dreading it, Fiona strolled into the bathroom to take a peek in the mirror. As soon as she caught sight of herself, she froze. Leigh was good, she had to admit. She'd used the makeup to highlight Fiona's cheekbones and make her eyes appear huge. Even her lips, painted a reddish-purple color, appeared plumper, more sensual.

In short, she didn't look like herself at all. In fact, Fiona thought, if anyone at the Bureau were to see her like this, she'd get laughed out of the building. But thankfully, she wasn't in the office—she was undercover.

No one would see, she reminded herself, willing her heart rate to slow. Since here she'd been playing a role, she might as well embrace a new look along with it.

"Well?" Leigh demanded, poking her head in the door. "What do you think?"

"I love it!" Fiona enthused. "I don't even recognize my face. You're amazing."

Leigh smiled at the compliment. "See, I told you with a little work you'd be gorgeous. Now all you have to do is get Jake Anderson to look at you and he's a goner."

"I see." Though Fiona didn't. "I'm still not sure—"

"Failure is not an option," Leigh cut her off, her normally breezy tone turning emphatic. "I need you to get super close to him, as close as possible." Unexpectedly, she pulled Fiona in for a hug. "And then since we're BFFs now, you can tell me everything about it."

Fiona hugged her back, pretending to be hugely grateful for the other woman's friendship. Her cover had just gotten even more perfect. "Of course I will. You don't know how long it's been since I had a real friend."

Leigh's bright blue eyes got a little misty at that. Either she was a master actress, or her emotions were easily swayed. "I'll always be here for you, girlfriend," she declared. "Now let's go downstairs and wait for Micheline's son to arrive."

* * *

Battling a strange mixture of anger, hope and frustration, Jake Anderson finally turned onto the long driveway leading to the AAG center. He hadn't seen his mother in over two decades, and really hadn't cared to. Now, at forty years old, part of him couldn't help but wonder if his seventeen-year-old self's perception of her might have been slightly tainted by his youth. Nah, he didn't think so. Micheline Anderson might be beloved by her thousands of followers, but inside she was a monster to the core.

And, if she was to be believed, now dying of some rare form of fatal cancer. Somehow, she'd tracked him down and called him, tearfully begging him to come see her so they could reconcile before she left this earth. What kind of a man would he be to deny the woman who'd given birth to him his presence in the last moments of her life?

The sad thing was, he didn't believe her. From his earliest recollection, his mother had done nothing but lie.

When he'd escaped her clutches right after graduating high school early, he hadn't bothered to change his name, since Jake Anderson seemed so common. He'd worked hard, managed to erase the scars of his past and built a life for himself. After putting in several years as a ranch foreman, he was now the proud owner of a small but growing property of his own, a couple hours north of Mustang Valley.

He didn't know what Micheline had planned, but he knew for certain he wanted no part of it. He'd go visit her, stay a couple days and get out. Hopefully untouched and unscarred.

Pulling up to the building, he parked and got out of his truck. Though he'd seen photographs of the place in a few newspapers, he allowed himself to admire its clean, woodsy lines. Welcoming and neat, the renovated ranch house seemed the perfect place to allow Micheline to ply her trade.

None of his business, he reminded himself. Still, every fiber of his being clenched in dread as he forced himself to walk through the front door.

Blinking at the change in light, he suddenly came face-to-face with the most beautiful woman he'd ever met. Wide, dark eyes met his, and a graceful hand came up to push back silky black hair away from her face. He couldn't help but let his gaze roam, from her slender shoulders to her full bust and narrow waist.

"Excuse me," she said, her voice throaty and sexy as hell. "Can I help you?"

"Yes." He managed to rapidly collect his wayward thoughts. "Sorry. I'm Jake Anderson. I'm here to see Micheline." Damned if he could bring himself to call her his mother.

She blinked and extended her hand. "Oh. Welcome. I'm Fiona Smith." She used her fake name rather than real since AAG had tech experts. "I was asked to show you around until Micheline's schedule clears enough so she can see you."

Figured. He suppressed a flash of resentment. Micheline couldn't even bother to make sure her afternoon was open enough to see her own son.

For a moment, he seriously considered turning around, getting back into his truck and heading home.

But then Fiona took his arm and leaned close, bringing a tantalizing feminine scent with her. "Please," she whispered, distress shining in her eyes. "I'm new here. Showing you around is the first task I've ever been given. I don't want to fail at it."

What could he do but go with her? Still, she might be attractive, but what kind of person could she be if she belonged to his mother's cult?

She led him down a long hall into a large room dominated by a huge stone fireplace. A fire blazed cheerfully, despite the relative warmth of the Arizona day. People were seated on various couches or at tables, some reading, a few talking, and he even saw one or two playing a board game or doing a puzzle. Almost, he thought, as if he stood in the lobby of some fancy hotel.

He eyed them as he passed, trying for casual but wondering if he'd be able to see something on their faces or in their eyes that might reveal what had made them ripe for Micheline's indoctrination. When Jake had been younger, she'd talked about someday starting her own church. In fact, she'd managed to create her own group of followers.

He wanted no part of it.

Fiona continued on, her hips swaying as she led him to a door on the far side of the huge room. Just as they reached it, an overly made-up young blonde woman rushed over.

"Hello there," she murmured, looking him up and down, her predatory manner reminding him so much of the way his mother used to act that he nearly took a step back. "I'm Leigh Dennings, a welcome coordinator here at the AAG. And the reigning Miss Mustang Valley," she chirped.

Not sure how to respond to that, he settled on "Congratulations."

"Thank you." She smiled sweetly at him before turning her attention to Fiona. "If you need anything, anything at all, just ask someone at the reception desk to call me and I'll be right there."

Fiona nodded. "Will do." She checked her watch. "Do you have any idea what time Micheline will be available?"

Good question. Eyeing Fiona, Jake waited to hear her answer.

Leigh shrugged. "I know she's booked solid all afternoon. I'm sure she'll be out here as soon as she can."

"You know what?" Jake decided he'd had enough. "Take me to her. Right now."

"I… I don't think she'd appreciate me doing that," Leigh stammered, eyeing him as if he'd suddenly sprouted a pair of horns and a tail. Fiona, on the other hand, looked at him with what he'd swear was approval. In fact, she appeared to be struggling not to laugh.

"I don't care," he told Leigh. "Not only is she the one who called and asked to see me, but it's been years. If today is not a good day, then I'll be heading home and you can tell her if she really wants to see me, she's welcome to make the drive to my place." Which he knew she'd never do in a million years. Micheline preferred to remain in her place of power.

Still staring, Leigh finally nodded. "Give me five minutes," she said and then rushed off.

Both he and Fiona watched her go.

"I take it your relationship with your mom is strained," Fiona drawled. She sounded completely different than the nervous, uncertain acolyte she'd resembled a few minutes ago. Was it because Leigh was gone?

"Strained doesn't even begin to describe it," he replied, flashing her a sideways grin.

Her dark eyes widened, and then she grinned right back at him. "I like you." She jerked her thumb over her shoulder. "Here comes Micheline. Give 'em hell, cowboy."

Stunned, he barely managed to collect himself in time to turn and watch as his mother barreled toward him, her high heels clicking on the wood floor.

"My boy," Micheline boomed, causing more than a few heads to turn. She held out her arms, clearly expecting him to rush into them.

Since he didn't want to cause a scene, though he stayed in place, he allowed her to hug him, hoping the grimace on his face looked more like a smile than it felt.

"Let me look at you." Pulling back, Micheline made a show of pretending to take in every detail of his appearance. "Wow, son. Forty sure looks good on you." The slight edge in her voice told him how little she liked the idea of having a child so old.

Already bored, Jake thanked her. "Is there somewhere private we can go and talk?" he asked.

To his disbelief, she actually checked her watch, a flashy designer thing that cost more than several head of cattle. "I don't live too far from here," she mused, considering. "But I've got a magazine crew arriving in thirty minutes to do a photoshoot and feature on me for *Mindful Living* magazine." She shook her head, sending her artfully styled blond hair swinging around her perfectly made-up face. "I know." She brightened. "We can chat in my office."

Chat. He'd driven all this way so she could squeeze out thirty minutes to chat with him.

"Follow me." Without waiting to see if he would, Micheline spun around and marched off in the direction from which she'd come. Leigh trailed along after her.

Fiona put her hand on his arm, as if she understood exactly what he was thinking. "I don't know what's going on here," she said. "But maybe it wouldn't hurt to give her a shot."

Jaw clenched, he nodded.

When they reached Micheline's office, the double mahogany doors were wide-open. Jake stared as he realized several other people were already there. In addition to his mother, Leigh and Fiona, a big blond guy with a crew cut and a physique that screamed *bodyguard* stood with his arms folded.

Moving with all the grace of a queen, Micheline sailed around to the other side of her massive desk and settled herself in her luxurious leather chair. "Have a seat, Jake," she said. "And then we'll talk."

Instead, Jake took his time looking around the room, taking care to make eye contact with every single one of them. "Could we have some privacy?" he asked the room at large.

Fiona actually took a step toward the door before apparently realizing no one else had moved. They all looked to Micheline, clearly waiting for her approval.

An expression of shock crossed her face. But then she slowly nodded. "Everyone out."

"Even me?" the muscular guy asked.

"Yes, Bart," Micheline said, smiling. "You can stand guard outside my door." She looked at Jake, one perfectly shaped brow raised. "He's my bodyguard."

"I figured."

As soon as the door closed, Micheline came around the desk and took Jake's arm. He didn't jerk away, but he felt himself tense up even though he knew better than to show any weakness around her. He let her lead him over to a small, overstuffed couch in a little sitting area to one side of her office.

"Sit." She patted the space next to her. "When I'm gone, all of this will be yours."

He didn't bother to hide his distaste. "I don't want it. Any of it. Micheline—" damned if he'd call her *Mom* or *Mother* "—you said you were dying."

"Yes." She looked down, hands twisting in her lap. "Stage-three bone cancer. I'm not sure how much time I have left."

"Tell me about your treatment," he asked. "I assume you're doing chemo and some sort of radiation?"

Grimacing with distaste, she waved her hand. "I don't want to talk about any of that right now. We'll have plenty of time for that later. How long are you staying?"

He didn't have the heart to tell her he had planned on heading home in the morning. The less time he spent under her roof, the better. The things he'd witnessed her do to others when he'd been a boy still made him shudder. He'd seen her order beatings when someone defied her and once, he seriously wondered if he might have witnessed her disposing of a body she'd murdered. As for himself, he guessed he'd been lucky that she'd pretended he didn't exist.

"I'm not sure," he replied instead. "I definitely don't want to intrude on your busy schedule." Said without even a hint of sarcasm.

Micheline's expressive face fell. "I have so much to make up for with you," she mused. "Before…you know." She waved her hand vaguely.

By that, he deduced that she didn't want her assistants, or whatever they were, to know about her cancer. None of his business, he thought. "The question is," he said, deciding to be blunt, "are you going to have time? It's clear you're insanely busy."

Eyes narrowing slightly, she regarded him. While he waited for her answer, part of him wished she'd just dismiss him and let him go. Another part, a tiny kernel of the child he'd once been, hoped she'd put him first for once.

"Can you give me a couple of days?" Micheline pleaded. "Too many people depend on me for me to just drop everything. If I can tie up some loose ends and delegate a few things, I'll be free to spend a day or two with you. Will that work?"

This from a woman who hadn't ever seemed to care if her own son was lonely. And when he'd craved a father figure, she'd told him coldly that she had no idea who his father had been.

"We'll give it a shot," he responded, his expression as neutral as his voice. "I've got people taking care of my livestock. Let's play it by ear and see how it pans out."

Was that surprise that flashed across his mother's face? Surely not, especially when she let out a cry of pure joy and wrapped him in a hug. "Thank you, Jake. Thank you. I promise you won't regret it."

He couldn't shake the feeling she was playing a part. But then again, what did he know? He hadn't seen her in years. Maybe she'd changed. Doubtful, but who knew?

Micheline released him, pressing a button on a walkie-talkie on her waist and summoning Fiona and Leigh back in. A moment later, the door opened and the two women entered. Micheline turned to Fiona and smoothed her face into a benevolent look. "I'm entrusting him into your care," she said, patting the younger woman on the shoulder. "Looking after Jake is to be your only task while he's here, and he's to want for nothing, you hear?"

Slowly, Fiona nodded. "Yes, ma'am."

Micheline and Leigh exchanged a look. Jake wasn't

sure what it meant, but it clearly made Fiona uncomfortable.

"Are you all right with that, Jake?" Micheline asked.

Glancing up, he saw both Fiona and Leigh watched him expectantly. He had no idea why it mattered, but he suddenly didn't want Fiona to think him heartless.

"That's fine," he replied.

"Perfect. Fiona, be your best you and take good care of my son," Micheline reiterated, taking Leigh's arm and sailing away.

Chapter 2

Be your best you. AAG's stock phrase and one of many catchy little sound bites Micheline fed like pap to her followers. They set Fiona's nerves on edge. She swallowed, willing away her embarrassment and hoping Jake didn't pick up on his mother's underlying message. Did Micheline and Leigh seriously think she'd fall into bed with Jake simply because the head of AAG wished it?

Undercover while undercover could be a tricky thing.

Luckily, Jake appeared to be oblivious. He watched his mother go, his hard expression at odds with the hurt she could swear she saw briefly flit in his gaze. His broad shoulders and narrow waist filled out his western shirt well and the way his brown hair had started graying at the temples gave him a look of distinction. But his compelling blue eyes were what attracted her the most. Despite his guarded manner, they glowed with warmth.

"What now?" he asked, noticing her staring.

Improvising, since she truly had no idea, Fiona figured she'd first need to find him a place to stay. "Let me get you a room. I imagine you need some time to freshen up after your long drive."

"That sounds great." Jake glanced around. "Will I be staying here or somewhere else?"

Crud. Though Fiona had hoped she would, Micheline hadn't mentioned letting him stay in her house. Despite decreeing that he'd be bunking in the center, Fiona couldn't imagine a mother wanting her son to stay elsewhere. Still, she knew better than to offer up something that might be wrong. "As far as I know, you'll be staying here with us. But let me check with Leigh. She's one of Micheline's right-hand people."

He nodded. "Thanks."

Fiona fingered the walkie-talkie Leigh had given her earlier. Taking a deep breath, she thumbed the unit on, bringing it up to her mouth and murmuring Leigh's name.

"On my way," Leigh said. A moment later, she appeared, striding through the room with her usual exuberant self-confidence. Her silky blond hair gleamed, and her long, perfectly toned legs flashed beneath the hem of her short skirt.

When she reached them, Leigh flashed Jake a flirty smile before turning her attention to Fiona. "How can I help?"

Tamping down an irrational flash of jealously, Fiona briefly wondered why Micheline hadn't chosen Leigh to fix up with her son. This thought stung so badly that Fiona wondered at herself. He might be handsome as all get out, but her job came first. Centering herself, Fiona managed a smile. "Since Jake is going to be staying a few days, I thought I'd find out where he's—"

"I've had a room prepared for him," Leigh interrupted with a small laugh. "Right across the hall from yours, as a matter of fact."

It took an effort, but Fiona managed to appear happy about that news. A quick look at Jake reassured her that he didn't appear to notice Leigh's innuendo. Thank goodness, because the last thing Fiona needed was fighting off a man who believed he was entitled to anything solely due to being Micheline's son, even if he really wasn't.

Though so far, Jake seemed the opposite. Almost as if he too saw through all the BS. Nah. She knew better than to make quick assumptions about anyone, most particularly someone related to this cult.

"Here," Leigh chirped, batting her false eyelashes. "Take this." She handed Fiona a one-hundred-dollar bill and a card key similar to the room keys used by hotels. "The two of you go out to dinner tonight, on Micheline, of course. There are several excellent restaurants nearby. Enjoy yourselves and get to know one another." She simpered prettily. "And if you need a recommendation, please let me know."

Then, with one more pointed glance at Fiona, Leigh sashayed off.

Every male in the room watched her go.

Except Jake. When Fiona looked up, she caught his gaze fixed on her. Her lips parted, and her heart skipped a beat. "What?" she asked, hating how breathless she sounded.

"I'm just wondering at the difference in my mother's choice of aides," he said, shrugging. "You and Leigh are like night and day."

If only he knew. Handing him the hundred-dollar bill, she flashed an impersonal smile. "If you follow me, I'll show you to your room."

He stared at the money as if it was tainted. "I don't want this," he said, holding it out. "Please. Take it."

Instead, she looked up at him, frowning. "Why not? Micheline is your mother. I don't feel comfortable accepting her money."

"Neither do I." Once more, he thrust the money toward her, his jaw clenched. Again, she ignored it.

With a grimace, he tossed it on the floor. Horrified, she eyed it, torn between not wanting to be wasteful but also not wanting to let him win. Finally, she couldn't stand it anymore, so she retrieved it and jammed the bill into her pocket.

"Let me show you to your room." She turned and walked away, not bothering to look behind her to make sure he followed. When she reached the second-floor hallway, she headed toward her own quarters, stopping right outside the door. Checking the room number on the card key, she saw he was indeed directly across from her. This knowledge caused her stomach to swoop alarmingly, since under any other circumstances she'd be teasing him about sneaking into each other's room.

"Here you are." She used the card to unlock and open the door. "I'm right there," she said, pointing at her door. "Knock if you need anything."

Following her inside the compact space, he looked around with interest. "Not bad. Not what I expected, but still…"

She dropped the card key and the hundred-dollar bill on the dresser. "I'll see you later," she said, her voice as stiff as her spine.

"Wait." He caught her arm. She tensed, not sure what she expected but hoping she was wrong. When she glared at him, he released her. "Sorry. But please, can we talk a minute?"

"Sure." Aware crossing her arms would be a defensive posture, she kept her hands down at her sides. "If you want to know where I want to go for dinner, it doesn't matter. I'll eat whatever you're in the mood for."

"I don't want to talk about dinner." He gestured to the room's lone chair. Once she'd taken a seat, he sat down on the edge of his bed. Elbows on his knees, he studied her.

"Why are you here?" he asked, the intensity in his voice matching his eyes. "Leigh, I can understand. But you? You seem like a levelheaded person, someone who considers her options carefully and deliberately before making a choice. What made you choose to join the AAG?"

Her cover story stuck in her throat. For whatever reason, she couldn't lie to him, this handsome man she'd just met and barely knew. Something about him… He appeared to be the first genuine person she'd met since arriving at AAG, though she really didn't know enough about him to reach that kind of a conclusion. She settled for a shrug instead of telling her story.

"You know this is a cult, right?" he continued, his expression fierce.

Making sure to act alarmed, she made a sound of indignation. "Do you truly expect me to sit here while you say bad things about AAG? Your mother is practically a saint."

He laughed at that. "You clearly don't know her, then." He held up both hands in a defensive posture as she deepened her frown. "Never mind, Fiona. I didn't mean to upset you. Forget I said anything."

She nodded, careful and cautious. Still smiling, he looked at her, rugged and masculine and the sexiest damn cowboy she'd ever met.

"I'm looking forward to having dinner with you later." He jumped to his feet, dusting his palms off on the front of his jeans. "But right now, I'm going to get my bag from my truck, shower and unpack, and maybe even take a quick nap."

Considering him, she stood. Ignoring the insistent tug of attraction she felt when she looked at him, she nodded. "I'll see you later, then," she said, her voice clear and steady.

He followed her toward the main entrance. As she turned to walk away, he called her name. "Fiona."

Her heart skipped a beat. "Yes?"

"Seven tonight?"

"I'll be ready," she said, her heart racing for absolutely no reason whatsoever.

Back in her room, she shook her head, making a face at herself in her mirror. Now was definitely not the time to be acting like a teenager with a crush. Especially since putting her and Jake together was something Micheline wanted to do. That alone made Fiona want to do the opposite.

In her five years working in the Phoenix FBI office, she'd been jockeying for a prime undercover operation like this one. She'd known in advance of coming here what kind of woman led the organization. She'd spent hours prepping, learning everything she could about Micheline Anderson and the AAG. Naturally, she'd also read quite a bit of material on Micheline's estranged son, who actually was Ace Colton.

For all intents and purposes, Jake appeared to be the polar opposite of the woman he apparently still believed to be his mother. As if when he'd left home, he'd asked himself in every situation, what would Micheline do, and then done the exact opposite. Of course, that made sense. Jake wasn't Micheline's biological son.

He led a quiet life, running a small cattle ranch north of here. At first, Fiona had suspected Micheline had asked him to visit with the intention of bleeding him dry, but judging from bank records, every penny Jake made went right back into his ranch. He wasn't exactly flush with cash.

Unlike the head of AAG, who spent money as if there wouldn't be a tomorrow. Which explained why Micheline was behind in her personal income taxes and appeared to be struggling to juggle all her bills. She booked speaking engagements and even organized a few crowd-funding events, lining her pockets with donations, fees and contributions from people desperate to live their best lives. Despite that, she managed to stay cash poor.

Fiona planned to take her down. She wouldn't rush, she'd be careful, her methods above reproach. But she would stop her. The money laundering was bad enough, but her some of her investment schemes had bilked a lot of people out of cash.

During her training at Quantico, Fiona had learned to trust her instincts. Her gut told her that Jake wasn't involved in Micheline's scams, ongoing or pending. As far as Leigh, who appeared to honestly believe in her boss and her mission, Fiona thought the young woman might have been blinded by what she viewed as altruistic behavior. Either that, or Leigh was a very good actress.

Intelligence had indicated Micheline had something big coming up, though no one had been able to learn what exactly it might be.

Before taking this assignment, Fiona had gone over every possible scenario with her colleague Holden St. Clair. He'd recently spent some time undercover investigating a killer who targeted beauty pageant contestants—the same beauty pageant Leigh Denning had won. He'd even fallen for, and gotten engaged to, a contestant—a distant Colton cousin named Isabella. Appearances were definitely deceiving when it came to Micheline and her people. No one had known the prodigal son would return, but she'd been prepared just in case. She hadn't expected Micheline to try and push them together or her own, visceral reaction to Jake's rugged masculinity. In the past, Fiona had been drawn to more clean-cut, law enforcement types. Jake, with his wavy brown hair and easy, relaxed attitude, seemed the exact opposite.

Cowboys had never been her type. Until now, apparently, when she needed to stay focused on her job—digging up information that would expose Micheline. Maybe it wasn't too late for some of these poor, deluded people.

At least Jake appeared levelheaded and unwilling to put up with any nonsense. Yet one more thing she liked about him.

Whatever Micheline was plotting involved Jake and, to a lesser extent, Fiona. Not for one second did Fiona believe Micheline had cancer. She'd lied to get her son to come visit, and she lied to her followers, not just seeking donations, but stripping people of their entire savings by getting them to invest in her schemes. While gathering proof of this, as well as investigating allegations of money laundering, the Bureau had been unable to find even one recent instance where Micheline had visited a doctor—any kind of physician at all. Not a general practitioner and certainly not a specialist like an oncologist.

Thinking of the Bureau had Fiona grabbing the untraceable cell phone she'd been issued when she'd taken this assignment. She had a text from Holden, saying he had news and to text back when she could talk. They'd settled on a basic sort of code in case someone else managed to get ahold of her phone. If she texted back anything but the number 1, he knew not to call.

She texted 1 and waited. A moment later, her phone rang.

"Big goings-on at Colton Oil," Holden said. "Seems Micheline paid them a little visit recently. She's still claiming she's dying from stage-three bone cancer."

"Okay." Since this wasn't news, Fiona waited. She also had to be careful what she said, just in case someone might be listening in via a hidden bug or recording device in her room.

"She told Ainsley Colton and Ace Colton about her son Jake Anderson's upcoming visit," Holden continued.

"Yes, he's here now. He got in today."

"Wow. Then things are about to get really interesting. Does he know? I mean, rumors have swirled about a Colton baby switch for months."

"He doesn't appear to know, actually," Fiona responded. "He's never mentioned anything about Micheline switching babies in the hospital when both Ace and Jake were newborns." If Micheline had done this, she might be guilty of additional crimes, too.

"That's really odd, since the entire Colton family does, and they raised Micheline's birth son, who grew up as Ace Colton. My fiancée, Bella, has gotten closer to Marlowe throughout all of this, and of course I'm old army buddies with Spencer, and they shared this with me."

"Then what game is Micheline playing?" she asked.

"That's for you to find out," Holden replied. "How are you and Jake getting along?"

Rubbing her now aching temples, Fiona sighed. "For whatever reason, I felt an instant connection to Jake."

"Micheline instructed you to cozy up to him?"

"Yes. We're going to dinner tonight, on her."

Holden laughed, a short bark of sound. "Have fun with that. Remember, stay out of trouble."

Ending the call, Fiona stashed the phone back in her pocket. Its compact size made it almost undetectable, and she kept it on her at all times. She wouldn't put it past Micheline and her crew to periodically search her room.

Replaying the information Holden had given her, she kept circling back to Jake. Did he know? Could that possibly be the reason he'd stayed away all these years? Right then and there, she knew she had to do what Micheline had asked of her—get close to Jake and find out exactly what kind of information he had.

All the way to his car, Jake gave himself a mental tongue lashing. Fiona Smith might be one of the most beautiful women he'd ever met, but she certainly didn't need rescuing. As an adult, she'd clearly made a conscious choice to join his mother's "self-help" group. He barely knew her and did not have the right to try and change her mind. However, that didn't stop him from wanting to.

Hefting his bag over his shoulder, he gave a quiet groan. He'd never been able to resist attempting to right a wrong, especially when said wrong involved children, animals or women. Micheline was a parasite, preying on vulnerable people, using them for her own ends and twisting their minds. He couldn't stand to see Fiona meet that sort of fate.

Since he didn't intend on being here long enough to have time to persuade her, he figured he'd sound her out at dinner tonight to ascertain her true thoughts about the AAG. One thing he'd noticed in particular was that many members didn't even seem to be aware it *was* a cult. If he could get her to admit that, she might be agreeable to talking to one of his friends who worked to deprogram cult members. It was worth a shot.

Back in his small room, which seemed just as antiseptic and impersonal as that of any chain motel, he walked to the window and pushed aside the curtains. Instead of a view of cement and parking lots, he saw a lush garden filled with vibrant flowers of every color. A large metal bench made an inviting place to sit, and he could have sworn he saw a koi pond on the other side of the bench.

For just an instant, he allowed himself to enjoy the restful beauty of it all. And then he remembered who had most likely arranged that lush garden, and why. Micheline would do anything—anything—to get what she wanted. She'd move people around like chess pieces, manipulate their emotions and their surroundings, as long as she thought it would benefit her in some way. She cared nothing for the wreckage she left in her wake. Collateral damage, she'd always said, as if the wording made it right. The garden no doubt played some role in her schemes. She never did anything without a reason.

At thirteen, he'd come to the realization that if she found a way to use him, she would. As a kid, he'd been forced to charm elderly couples into investing with his mom, aware his mother only wanted their money. Back then, she'd marketed herself as a skillful investor, but secretly priding herself on taking every cent of people's life savings. She also lured in a rotating crop of men in her personal life, all wealthy, training Jake to make them all feel as if she might be a doting mother and a wonderful girlfriend. Of course, once she'd managed to use them, she'd dump them and move on to another, uncaring that her young son might have just been happy to have a father figure around.

At seventeen, having seen far too much of the awful things she did to people, he'd taken off before she could.

Shaking his head, he reminded himself not to focus on the past. Yet, even now, with his mother claiming to be dying, he had difficulty believing anything she said. In fact, he couldn't help but suspect she had an ulterior motive for wanting him to be here. She never did anything without a reason, usually one that benefited her.

He took a hot shower and then stretched out on his bed with the intention of dozing. But images of a doe-eyed woman with a sleepy smile had him tossing and turning. He finally abandoned the idea of a nap and decided to go for a walk instead. Might as well explore the AAG headquarters and grounds.

Managing to slip through the lobby unnoticed, he headed in search of an exit that went to the back and the garden area he'd viewed from his room. To his annoyance, Micheline's overly chipper minion caught sight of him and made a beeline for him, her heels tapping a staccato beat on the floor.

"There you are!" Leigh beamed at him as if she felt so delighted to see him. "Where are you going?"

He explained he'd decided to tour the premises, which appeared to distress her.

"Alone?" she asked, her tone appalled. "What happened to Fiona? She was given the task of escorting you anywhere you wanted to go."

"I told her I wanted to take a nap," he clarified, not wanting to cause trouble for Fiona. "She has no idea that I've even left my room."

"I see." Still frowning, Leigh thumbed her walkie-talkie and spoke a few words into it. When she met his gaze again, she'd smoothed out her expression. "Fiona will be here momentarily."

With an effort, he kept from groaning out loud. "I really didn't want to disturb her," he said.

Leigh's brightly painted lips widened into a smile so false, it made him want to grimace. "For the time that you're here, Fiona is to devote herself completely to you. Micheline has given her that assignment, and it's in her best interest to make sure she does what she's asked to do."

Was that a threat? The words seemed to indicate it was, though Leigh's vacuously pleasant expression told him she wouldn't see it that way.

Fiona rounded the corner, hurrying toward them. The first sight of her caught him like a punch in the stomach.

Dark eyes troubled, she swung her gaze from him to Leigh. "I'm so sorry I wasn't here to help you," she began. "I had no idea."

"Why would you?" he asked, watching her for the

slightest indication that she might be afraid. There. That slight tremble in her lush lips. So help him, if Micheline dared enact some sort of punishment on Fiona, he'd have her hide.

Leigh watched Fiona, her eyes narrowed, her expression hawkish. Suddenly, he realized what he had to do. "I apologize," he said, softening his tone. "I give you my word I won't go anywhere without letting you know."

Fiona locked gazes with him. Finally, she gave a quick nod. "Whew. Glad we got that sorted out."

"Me, too," Leigh chirped. She patted Fiona lightly on the back and then marched away, her task clearly completed.

"What was that about?" Jake asked. "Did I get you in some sort of trouble for going off without you?"

"Of course not." Her small flash of a smile contained no humor. "I imagine your mother is just overly concerned with making sure you have a good time."

"That has to be it," he agreed, even though he knew damn good and well it wasn't. "I saw a beautiful garden area from my room. Would you take me there?"

Though she gave a confident nod, she leaned in close. "I'm new here, so I'm not exactly sure what you're talking about. But unless you want me to call Leigh, how about you and I try to find it on our own?"

The warmth of her breath tickled his ear, sending a shiver down his spine. Her scent intoxicated him. Resisting the urge to reach out and touch her hair, he managed to agree. "No Leigh. You and I will just wander around until we find it ourselves."

"We'll just go out back. Since your room faces that way, I'm sure we can manage to happen upon it." She shrugged. "I've only been outside a couple of times, but

I remember how to get back to that walled-off area. I'm sure that's where the gardens are."

It turned out she was right. They followed a pebbled stone pathway bordered by lush plants and flowers. When they turned one corner of the building, he saw the bench he'd spotted from his window.

"Wow." Fiona stopped short, one hand to her chest. "I can't believe I never knew this was here."

He took a seat on the bench, gesturing her to sit beside him. Moving gingerly, she did, leaning back and stretching her legs out in front of her. She sighed. "This is nice."

Chancing a glance sideways at her, he admired the way her dark hair gleamed in the sun. *Sensual*, he thought of her expression, and then pushed the thought away. Not going there. With her eyes half-closed, she actually appeared relaxed, no longer vibrating with tension.

Because of this, he allowed himself to let go of some of his own stress. He hadn't wanted to come and he didn't like being here with the knowledge that his mother somehow was manipulating him, but for this small moment in this peaceful garden, he could release all that.

They sat for a few moments in companionable silence. He liked that she didn't feel compelled to fill the silence with chatter. Again, he found himself wondering what it was about this woman. One look at her and he'd known immediately that he wanted to get to know her better. She fascinated and intrigued him, made him ache in ways he hadn't since he'd been a teenager. Of course he'd dated, but he'd never allowed himself to get serious. After all, he didn't want to take a chance on loving someone like his mom.

Yet here he was, fighting his attraction to this woman who clearly didn't understand the evil behind the head of AAG's smiling façade. Fiona seemed too innocent, too trusting.

And the thought that she was under Micheline's thumb galled him. Clearing his throat, he broke the silence. "Tell me, what appeals to you most about AAG?" he asked.

Slowly, she opened her eyes and focused on him. "I like the idea of evolving," she said, the answer seeming to come easily. "Of becoming the best person you can be."

Micheline's stock phrase. *Be Your Best You.* She'd developed it when he'd still been a teenager, living with her. If she'd even once thought her behavior to be the best version of herself, he shuddered to think of what the worst might be.

"Is that what you think Micheline and Leigh are doing?" he asked, keeping his tone mild. "To me it seems like they're awfully concerned about money. Even more than truly helping others."

She blinked. "We all have to find ways to use the talents we've been given," she said, once again parroting his mother. "The AAG has to have an influx of cash to support itself. All Micheline is doing is taking her talent for helping others and soliciting donations to keep us going." She shrugged. "You honestly can't blame her."

He could and he did, but knew better than to say that out loud. Did Fiona honestly believe that crap?

Though he knew he'd probably get nowhere, he'd hate himself if he didn't at least attempt to help save her. "Are you aware that many people consider AAG a cult?"

Something—Surprise? Dread?—flashed in her eyes. "Many people?" she asked, her tone dry. "That's kind of vague. Who exactly do you mean?"

Unable to help himself, he covered her hand with his. "What I'm trying to say is that I know someone you could talk to, if you want help trying to make sense of all this. He's a therapist who specializes in this kind of situation."

She'd gone absolutely still, her beautiful eyes still fixed on him. *"This kind of situation?"*

"Cults," he finally admitted. "He deprograms people who've been indoctrinated into a cult."

Though she looked down, he could have sworn her mouth twitched in the beginning of a smile.

He squeezed her hand once before releasing her. "You don't have to decide right now. All I ask is that you think about it. There'll be no cost to you—I'll take care of all that. And if you need a place to stay, I've got that covered as well."

When she finally met his gaze again, her face had gone expressionless. "Thanks for your kind offer," she said. "But none of that is necessary. I'm fine where I am. Right now, at this point in my life, this is where I need to be. I belong here."

Her words made his heart ache. "Fiona, I know we've just met, but I'm attracted to you. The thought of you under Micheline's thumb is…unpalatable to me. Please, at least say you'll think about it."

"I need to get ready for dinner," she stammered, the heat appearing to simmer in her eyes matching what thrummed in his blood.

He opened his mouth and then closed it. With a curt nod, he pushed to his feet and turned to head inside and up to his room. "Just knock when you're ready to go. I'll be there waiting."

She didn't follow.

All the way back to his room, he cursed his impetuous words. She must think him a complete idiot. He definitely felt like one. He couldn't help but wonder if Fiona might run to Leigh or Micheline and tell them what he'd offered. That would definitely be...interesting, to say the least.

Back in his room, he checked in with Tom, the hand he'd pegged to run his ranch while he was away. Though he hadn't expected any trouble, he couldn't help but feel relief to hear that everything continued to run like clockwork in his absence.

Though he only planned on staying two more days at the most, he went ahead and unpacked his suitcase, hanging his clothes up in the closet. Wherever they ended up going for dinner tonight, Western shirts, blue jeans and boots would have to work, since that's all he had.

He turned on the television to kill time and watched the evening news, glad of the sense of normalcy in a place that felt anything but.

The tap on his door came just as the news program ended. He shut the TV off and opened his door.

Fiona stood there, wearing a form-hugging dress of pale yellow and a pair of killer stiletto shoes. Somehow, she managed to look both virginal and sexy as hell. His body responded immediately.

"Are you ready?" she asked, clearly unaware of the effect she had on him.

"I am." If he could walk. "You look...amazing."

Instead of smiling, she grimaced. "Thanks. Leigh picked this dress out and brought it to me, along with the shoes. Micheline bought it. Your mother told her that yellow is your favorite color."

He gaped at her for a moment, and then everything clicked into place. "Did Micheline ask you to get close to me?" he asked.

She blinked. "Yes," she finally answered, surprising

him with her honesty. "For whatever reason, she thinks you and I would be a good match."

This both infuriated him and intrigued him, even without knowing his mother's reasoning. "Then you know what? You and I ought to give her a good show."

"Excuse me?" Clearly startled, Fiona eyed him. "What do you mean?" A slow, sultry grin spread across her face as his words sank in. "Are you saying we should… pretend?"

Careful to keep it casual, he shrugged. "If you're up for it, sure. I'm not planning to be here that long anyway, so…"

Slowly, she nodded. "Okay. I think that's a great idea." Again, she flashed that smile, lighting up her dark eyes. "It's easier since you're so hot."

"Hot?" It took a moment for him to understand. "You think I'm hot?" The thought was so unbelievable it made him laugh. He realized she'd already begun playing her role. He held up a hand before she could respond. "No need to explain. I get it. And for the record, I find you hot, too." She didn't need to know he truly meant it.

They exchanged grins. Again, that pull. Leaning toward her, he found himself fighting the urge to kiss her.

Later, he thought. When necessary to help with their acting. Fiona didn't need to know how much he'd enjoy it.

If only he didn't get the sense she was hiding something.

Chapter 3

Fiona loved the idea of playing along with Jake to fool his mother and Leigh. And who knew, Micheline might be so pleased with her apparent success with Jake that she'd accidentally reveal something that might help the FBI build their case against her.

And, since Fiona always tried to be honest with herself, the notion of getting all up close and personal with the sexy cowboy made her entire body hum.

Even if Jake did happen to believe she needed a deprogrammer's help to get her out of the cult. He'd simply have to continue to think that. She had no choice in the matter, at least until she had enough evidence to secure an arrest.

As they strolled arm in arm through the now-crowded lobby, she felt as if she floated in her pretty dress and heels. With her chosen career, she rarely if ever got to dress like this. And the appreciation she'd seen glowing in Jake's blue eyes made her feel feminine and beautiful. In her line of work, if she wanted to be taken seriously—and she did—she'd learned to underplay her feminine side. She couldn't even remember the last time she'd dressed like this.

"They haven't yet rung the dinner bell," Fiona mused. "You should see these people move when they do. They all jostle for a good place in line. It's amazing and sometimes slightly scary to watch."

Jake nodded. "What kind of food do they serve here?"

"It depends." She shrugged. "I think they mostly try to keep it healthy." She grinned. "Though everyone seems happiest when they have pizza night."

When they reached his truck, she stopped and studied it, letting him see her appreciation. "Latest model Ford F-250," she mused. "With a lift kit, custom wheels and a bed cover. Not at all what I expected."

He unlocked the doors. "I'm almost afraid to ask, but what did you expect?"

"A farm truck." She got inside, running her hand over the soft black leather. "You know, big and kind of beat-up. Not a beautiful new truck like this."

"You sound as if you know a lot about trucks," he said, pushing the start button.

"All vehicles, actually." She smiled slightly. "I'm a bit of a car nut. I've been that way ever since I was a pre-teen. My dad worked for a dealership in Phoenix, and he sometimes let me go to work with him."

Jake nodded. "Does your family still live there?"

"Yep." Sticking to the truth, without elaborating. Less chance of slipping up, or giving herself away.

He waited a heartbeat and then nodded. "Where to?"

"Do you like sushi?" She braced herself for him to decline. Even before she'd gone inside AAG, she never could find anyone willing to eat sushi with her.

"Sometimes." He shrugged. "Only if it's really great. Is there a good sushi place around here?"

Nearly humming with anticipation, she nodded. "There is. Turn left on Fifth Street."

When they reached Purple Sushi, she barely restrained herself from bouncing up and down in her seat like an excited child. "It's been so long since I got to have sushi," she said, not bothering to hide her glee. "Thank you so much for agreeing to come here."

Eyes gleaming with amusement, he watched her. "I'm guessing AAG doesn't ever serve it."

Just like that, she sobered. "No, they don't." She supposed she should thank him for reminding her of the reality of her life right now. She couldn't let her love for a good tuna roll make her forget the entire reason she was here in Mustang Valley.

"Don't." He lightly touched her shoulder.

"Don't what?"

"Dim your joy just because I mentioned AAG," he said.

Since she couldn't tell him that wasn't all of it, she simply nodded and got out of the truck.

Once they were shown to a booth near the back, a waitress came and gave them menus and took their drink orders. Fiona stuck to water while Jake ordered a beer.

"It's been so long since I had sushi, I'll let you order for both of us," Jake said, pushing his menu away.

She narrowed her eyes. "Have you ever even *had* sushi?" she asked.

His sheepish grin was answer enough. "I'm game to

try it," he said. "Since you're such a big fan, it can't be all that bad."

This made her laugh. "You know what," she mused. "I like you."

"I like you, too." He studied her for a moment. "I just can't help but wonder what my mother's motivation is for wanting us to get together. She never does anything unless it's going to benefit her in some way."

Here was where she should rush to Micheline's defense, as any good little disciple would. But right now, Fiona didn't have the heart. She just wanted to enjoy her meal and the company. She'd go back to her role once they'd returned to the AAG center.

Right now, she just wanted to enjoy a couple of good sushi rolls and the company of the handsome cowboy sitting across from her.

Instead of responding to Jake's statement, she smiled at the waitress, which brought her over to see if they'd decided. Fiona ordered an assortment for them, wanting to give Jake a chance to sample several of her favorites.

Through it all, Jake sipped his beer and watched her, his expression contemplative.

Once the waitress had gone, Fiona eyed Jake. She wanted to see if she could find out how much he knew. "Since we're getting to know each other, what's the deal with you and your mother? Is it true you haven't seen her for years?"

"Yep. All true." He eyed her. "I'm sure you probably won't agree with me, but Micheline is not a good person."

Now they were getting somewhere. "Why do you say that?" she asked mildly, clasping her hands on the table in front of her.

Instead of answering, he leaned across the table, his

intense stare locking on her. "My turn," he said. "What made you decide to join AAG?"

"They found me roaming the streets," she said simply. "They offered me a place to stay and a hot meal. They were kind to me when no one else was. I owe them for that."

He took another sip of his beer, clearly considering what he should say next. She could tell he badly wanted to talk to her about leaving the cult, getting some help. While she found this admirable—hell, it was something she would do herself were the situations reversed—she couldn't tell him the truth and risk blowing her cover.

Luckily, their food arrived. Happily, she eyed everything, enjoying the colorful artistry of the two elaborate sushi towers. Jake eyed them, too, his expression a mixture of curiosity and confusion. "Do we eat those?" he asked. "It seems a shame to mess up the artwork."

This made her laugh. "It kind of does, doesn't it? Just wait until you taste it."

They passed the serving platters around, taking samples of each. She waited for Jake to try one, wanting to see his reaction when he had his first bite. In her experience, people either loved or detested sushi. She had to see in which camp Jake would fall.

He chose a crab roll. "Good choice," she said, nodding in approval as he popped it into his mouth.

Chewing slowly, he appeared to be savoring the taste. He swallowed and inclined his head. "That was pretty good, actually."

"Only pretty good?" she challenged. "Try the California roll. Most people like that one."

"Why aren't you eating?" he asked instead.

"I wanted to see your reaction." Shrugging, she began

to help herself to her own plate. "Fresh," she managed, speaking around mouthfuls. "So, so delicious."

Together, they finished off all the food she'd ordered. To her delight, as he sampled various rolls, Jake ate with gusto.

"Dessert?" the waitress chirped. They both shook their heads.

After paying the check with Micheline's hundred-dollar bill, they walked out to Jake's truck in a food-coma silence.

"I enjoyed that," he said, smiling at her across the seat.

"So did I," she responded.

"Clearly." He made no move to start the truck. "Before we head back, I wanted to talk to you about the AAG. Did you happen to do any research before you joined them?"

Though she knew where he was going with this, she pretended not to. "No. I needed help, and they offered it. Right now, I owe them a debt, and I'm working to repay it."

When he started to speak, she held up her hand. "Please. I can see that you have issues with the organization. But don't project them onto me. I promise you, my head is clear. I completely understand what I'm doing. Okay?"

After a moment, he nodded. "Okay," he agreed. "Let's head on back. Just promise me one thing?"

Brows raised, she waited.

"If you ever need help, no matter what time of the day or night, you'll call me." He reached into the center console, extracted a business card and handed it to her. "This is my ranch, but my cell phone number is on here, too."

Accepting the card, she slowly nodded. "Thanks,"

she said. If he noticed she made no promises, he didn't comment.

As they turned onto the long driveway leading to the AAG ranch, the tall streetlamps Micheline had installed came on.

Though the sun had begun to sink below the horizon, the sky had not yet fully darkened. This, the gloaming, was Fiona's favorite time of the day. Spectacular skies that seemed to go on forever, the way the sky lit up in swirls of orange, pink and red.

Once he'd parked, they were walking from the back lot toward the house when movement behind one of the large storage buildings caught her eye. Two men, one of them a college-age kid, making her wonder if he was a brand-new recruit or the target Leigh had mentioned Fiona working with. She saw only a quick blur of movement, though it was enough to convince her something had gone wrong.

"Just a sec," she told Jake, pulling free. "I need to check something out." Without waiting for him to answer, she strode away, cursing the high heels.

Halfway up the grassy hill, she said the hell with it and yanked them off. Grateful for the mild Arizona weather, she dropped her shoes. Now barefoot, she broke into a run.

As soon as she rounded the corner, she saw the college kid, down on the ground huddled into a ball, arms up in a defensive posture to protect his face. The older AAG member, a stout, bald man with a mustache, kicked and pounded on the younger guy.

"Stop," Fiona ordered, her hands clenched.

Instead, the assailant smirked at her, one arm up in

the air, halfway to throwing another punch. "Make me," he said, sneering.

Aiming low, Fiona charged him, twisting at exactly the right moment and taking him down with a kick behind the knees. He lurched forward, bloodshot eyes wide with surprise, as she came back around with a second, well-placed blow, sending him face-planting in the dirt.

Slowly, he climbed to his feet, warily eyeing her.

Fiona rounded on him, hands up, glad for all those martial arts classes she'd taken as part of her FBI training. "Ready for round two?" she asked, her voice cool, even though she was vibrating with adrenaline.

Scrambling up to his feet, the bad guy shook his head.

"What's your name?" Fiona demanded. "I want to give it to Micheline so she can make sure you face appropriate punishment."

For the first time, stark fear shone in his face. "Please don't tell her. She'll put me in one of the cells. Let me just go pack my stuff and clear out of here."

"Cells?" Fiona cocked her head. "What cells?" she asked. Maybe, just maybe, she was about to learn something new. "I don't know what you're talking about."

But he'd already begun backing away, his large stomach shaking. "I can't," he stammered. He turned without another word and ran away, heading toward the same parking lot where Jake had left his truck.

Jake. She spun around to find him eyeing her as if she'd suddenly sprouted horns. Just then the kid groaned and staggered to his feet.

He had a bruised lip and a purpling under his left eye, which was swollen shut. Blood still ran from his nose, though he tried to wipe it away with the back of his hand.

Standing, he swayed slightly as he studied Fiona with his one good eye.

"Are you okay?" Fiona asked.

"I think…so." Flexing his arms, and then his legs, he eyed her. "I don't think anything is broken."

"Luckily. What on earth happened?" she demanded.

"Thank you for helping me," he managed, wincing as his fingers came into contact with a large gash on his cheek. "I came out here for a smoke, and he caught me." Smoking was definitely not allowed at AAG. "He took my e-cig away, and then he demanded I pay him one hundred dollars to keep quiet. Once I told him I didn't have that kind of cash on me, he just started whaling away on me."

"Come on." Fiona slipped her arm around the kid's slender shoulders. "Let's get you to the infirmary and see if they can patch you up."

Clearly forgotten, Jake trailed along behind Fiona and the battered kid, turning over what he'd just seen in his mind and trying to make sense of what he'd just seen. Quiet Fiona had fought the guy like a badass. Mulling this over, he waited outside in the hallway while Fiona talked to the person inside the area that apparently served as the AAG medical center.

When Fiona finally emerged alone, she seemed surprised to find Jake still waiting. "Oh," she murmured, her eyes widening. "I'm so sorry. I had to fill out a report while I was there, so Micheline can review it."

Micheline. Everything centered around the most avaricious, self-involved, evil woman he'd ever met. Sometimes he wished he could purge his veins of her blood.

Shaking his head, he focused once more on the slender woman standing in front of him.

"Do you have a moment to talk?" he asked, his tone clipped, though he struggled to keep from showing any emotion.

"Sure," she replied, her easy tone at odds with the quick flare of panic he caught in her eyes. "Let's go for a walk."

"Good idea." Away from the AAG center and any possible cameras or recording devices. No doubt she knew he planned to ask her what was going on and wanted to make sure no one else overheard.

She definitely wasn't what Micheline and the others believed her to be. He couldn't help but wonder what kind of explanation she'd give.

Side by side, not touching, not speaking, they strode out the front door. This time, instead of heading around back to that secluded little garden, she led the way down the driveway. By now, dusk had settled in. Soon it would be full dark.

"Well?" he finally demanded, when it seemed she didn't intend on speaking.

"Well what?"

"Who are you?" Stopping, he crossed his arms. "And don't say some random homeless woman who was found wandering the streets. I saw how you took that guy down earlier."

"Why can't I be both?" she asked, her tone reasonable. "You never asked about my past. How I became homeless, what the circumstances were leading up to my change in lifestyle. Isn't it obvious that at some point, I took some martial arts classes? Yes, and it was before

I became homeless. Thank you for not asking. All you ever wanted to focus on was the AAG."

Stunned, he swallowed. Because damned if she wasn't right. He'd been so blinded by the need to get her away from the cult that he hadn't taken the time to try and get to know her as a person. Of course, he'd only just met her earlier in the day. And he recognized her deflection as a way to avoid answering his question.

"I just got here," he protested. "And yes, of course I'm going to focus on what's right in front of me. I'm not planning on staying long. There'd be plenty of time to get to know you and your reasons once I got you away from this craziness."

"Why do you even care?" Her direct look challenged him. "As you said, we barely know each other. Maybe it just so happens that AAG is exactly what I've been searching for my entire life. The one place I fit in. Has that ever occurred to you?"

He blinked. Damn if she wasn't good at deflecting. He had no patience for games like this. All his life, he'd been a straight-shooting kind of guy. Micheline's opposite. Naturally, his mother would choose to surround herself with people she could manipulate. Sadly, as much as he hated to admit the possibility, Fiona felt she belonged here, no matter what he thought of her reasons.

Maybe she was right. What business of his was it whether she chose to stay with his mother? Yet every single time he glanced at her, his heart turned over in his chest. He'd never felt such a strong tug of attraction, such a powerful urge to spend time with someone. And yes, to get to know her better, in every way possible. Too bad he wouldn't have enough time to do that.

Since it seemed clear that continuing to press her

wasn't going to work, he decided to let it go. For now, maybe even forever. It depended on how long he actually stayed.

"Sorry." He grimaced. "It's been a long day. I woke up on my ranch this morning and…"

"Now you're here, right in the middle of a bunch of drama." She touched his arm, the light touch of her finger sending a shiver through him. "It's still early, though. We have a few seminars that run at night if you'd like to attend one of those."

So earnest, so sincere. Even though she had to know attending an AAG seminar ranked among the very last things he'd ever want to do.

"No, what I'd like is to see my mother," he said. "I just need a few minutes of her clearly precious time. I'm intending on going back home tomorrow."

Fiona eyed him, her face blank. "Let me check with Leigh," she began.

"Not necessary," he interrupted. "I'll just take myself to Micheline's office and see if I can catch her myself."

Full of righteous indignation that he hadn't had to work too hard to manufacture, he stormed off in the direction where he'd met his mother earlier.

The heavy wooden doors were closed this time. When he tried to open them, they wouldn't budge. Locked.

Rattling the handles one more time for good measure, he turned. "Frustrating."

"I'm sorry," Fiona said, her voice as calming as her serene gaze. "I haven't heard back from Leigh yet, but I know Micheline keeps an impossible schedule."

"This is ridiculous." He glanced at his watch. "She tracks me down after so many years of no contact, informs me she's dying—which I'm not sure I believe, by the way—so I drive all the way down here, and now she disappears. I might as well go home tonight."

A slight widening of Fiona's eyes was her only reaction. "Let me see if I can track down Leigh," she said, her voice still soothing. "Please. I'm not sure how well it will go for me if I lose you the very first night of your visit."

Masterful manipulation from Fiona, he thought. In fact, he nearly complimented her out loud. She intrigued him, this woman who fought like a ninja but made herself appear quiet and docile in order to remain under the radar. Unraveling her mysteries nearly made him want to stay a couple of days at least.

Nearly.

Except the one thing he could not stomach, thanks to his mother, was a liar. He avoided them like the plague. And the more time he spent with Fiona Smith, the more he realized she wasn't on the up and up. If he had any common sense, he'd go pack his suitcase right now and get the hell out of here. In fact, he'd go do that right now. The sooner he'd left this place in the dust, the better he'd feel.

Then he made the mistake of glancing at Fiona. She studied him, her gaze warm, her lips parted. Desire short-circuited his brain. "Don't do that," he rasped.

"Do what?" Picture of innocence.

"Look at me as if you want to eat me up." His body stirred—hell, more than stirred. Rock hard, in an instant.

She took a step closer to him. His mouth went dry. His heart thudded in his chest.

"Common sense be damned," she said before wrapping herself around him and pulling his head down for a kiss.

The instant she pressed her mouth against his, heat

flared, consuming him. Openmouthed, he lost himself in the taste of her, the lush curves of her body molded against his.

When she finally stepped back, they were both breathing hard.

"I think you ought to stick around awhile," she murmured, the heat in her eyes matching the one in his body. "It'll be…interesting, to say the least."

Chapter 4

The kiss had not gone as expected. Despite her initial intention to distract him, there had been nothing casual about it. Fiona had been warring with herself against the sensual lure of the man ever since she'd first laid eyes on him.

She'd acted completely on impulse, trusting her instincts. But what she'd thought would be merely a bit of a tease, a lighthearted flirtation, had erupted into an incredibly passionate kiss that had left her weak at the knees, her body aching in all the right places. Despite it being against every rule of undercover work, if Jake had asked right then and there, she would have been sorely tempted to tumble into his bed with him.

Luckily, he hadn't asked. Most likely he'd been as shocked by the raw force of that kiss as she had been. She had to wonder if that, coupled with when he learned about being switched at birth, would be enough to make him stick around a few more days.

Though part of her wanted to keep Jake here for purely selfish reasons, Fiona also sensed that his presence was somehow integral to whatever Micheline had planned. The FBI had set up a case file after receiving several complaints about the AAG swindling people out of their life savings. They'd learned of intricate financial schemes, fraudulent investments, and even potential money laundering. Then a former cult member had shown up claiming Micheline might be planning something big, something awful, hinting that it could end multiple lives. This had been the catalyst for the Bureau sending Fiona in undercover. She'd been tasked with not only obtaining proof of Micheline's swindling, but finding information about what exactly the AAG leader planned to do. If it was something that would harm innocent people, Fiona was to neutralize the threat.

After getting to know Micheline, Fiona would do whatever she could to gain the older woman's trust. Jake had unwittingly offered to help her out there by asking her to pretend to be a couple. If only he'd stay just a few more days. Right now, the AAG leader had proved to be both busy and evasive. Fiona had only managed to spend a few moments with her. She spent more time with Leigh than anyone else. Close, but not close enough.

And now Micheline couldn't seem to make time for the son she'd summoned home, even if only to reveal the truth about his parentage.

Honestly, though, Fiona couldn't blame Jake for considering leaving. She didn't understand what the hell kind of game Micheline was playing by avoiding him. As far as Fiona could tell, Jake had no idea he'd been switched with Ace Colton. Was that why Micheline didn't want to spend time alone with him? Was she planning on revealing the truth? Did she dread seeing his reaction?

This entire scenario puzzled Fiona. Jake had left home over two decades ago, and he and Micheline hadn't spoken the entire time. Not even once. Whatever had happened to send Jake running must have been awful, but why had Micheline made no effort to reach him until now? Did she intend to involve him in whatever big thing she had planned? And where did the Colton family come in?

Fiona sighed. While this wasn't her first undercover assignment, it definitely was the most complex. And getting more and more so with each passing day.

At least she thought she'd been able to convince Jake to hang around at least one more day. Not her finest moment, but even so, she hadn't been able to stop thinking about that kiss.

Which she needed to do pronto. She had to be sharp and focused in order to complete the job she'd come here to do. Unfortunately, the single kiss had only made her want more. So much more. She couldn't help but wonder if Jake felt the same way.

Just as she'd decided she might as well get ready to go to bed, her walkie-talkie chimed. Leigh was summoning her to her suite. Somehow, Fiona managed to keep from groaning out loud. She kept her voice cheery as she agreed to head that way.

Exhaustion warred with tension as Fiona trudged down the long, carpeted hallway toward Leigh's suite. Leigh had been given a deluxe suite, which included an anteroom she used as her office.

After a soft tap on the elaborate iron and wood door,

Fiona waited. A moment later, Leigh bade her to enter. When Fiona stepped inside, feet sinking in the plush carpet, Leigh remained seated behind a massive oak desk that had been polished to a high sheen.

"Micheline is very pleased with you." Beaming, Leigh wasted no time on pleasantries. "You saving Theodore Royce III has worked very much in our favor."

"Who?" Fiona blinked. Whatever she'd expected Leigh to say, it hadn't been this.

"The new recruit you kept from getting beat up." Leigh drummed her long, perfectly manicured, hot-pink nails on the desk in front of her. "And now I've been informed Ron Underhill tried to attack you. Rest assured, Micheline has made sure he has been dealt with."

Cell, Fiona remembered. Underhill had been worried about being taken to the cell.

"How?" Fiona asked. "What did she do to him?"

Leigh waved her question away. "That's not any of your concern. What matters is that Theodore is overwhelmingly grateful. He now trusts you completely." She smiled. "This process usually takes much longer. You've saved us quite a bit of time."

To do what? Uneasy now, Fiona waited to hear the rest of it.

Still smiling, Leigh continued. "Theo was visiting here today because he's that struggling freshman at Mustang Valley College I mentioned you helping earlier. He, like many of our members, is searching for something more. For the first time in his young life, his wealth hasn't bought him happiness. AAG has offered him assistance. We can help change all that."

"We can?" Fiona knew where this was going. The

thought made her queasy, but she managed to appear eager.

"Yes. It's what we do, as you know. Help him become his best him." She sighed, still smiling prettily, and brushed her hair away from her face. "Micheline is offering him entry into her new, specialized, individual courses. He will get a discounted rate of one thousand dollars for each of his first classes—how to judge worthy friends, how to choose a significant other, how to know if your parents are really not in your corner, and so on. Micheline will help him attain honest selfhood."

"Wow." This was all Fiona could manage to say. She wasn't sure exactly how many classes they'd get poor Theodore to take, but it sounded as if they planned to help relieve him of somewhere in the vicinity of ten thousand dollars.

Her comment made Leigh laugh. "Wow is right. What an opportunity for him." She winked. "Of course, those are only the first tier of courses. Once he's ready to move up a level, the price will also increase to five thousand dollars each."

Though Fiona nodded as if she was on board with the entire thing, inside she seethed. This kind of thing—AAG taking advantage of the young and uncertain or elderly and infirm—made her furious. Which of course, she couldn't let show.

"We'd like you to be the one to discuss this with him," Leigh continued, her voice smooth. "It should be a breeze, a shoo-in for your first networking task, since he already views you as his savior." Her smile faded, her gaze sharpening. "What exactly did you do to get Underhill off him?"

"Underhill? Was he that big bald guy?"

"Yes." Leigh shook her head. "He outweighs you by like a hundred pounds."

Praying there hadn't been security cameras, Fiona grimaced. "I'm not sure. It all happened so fast. He came at me and I twisted away. He got off balance." She shrugged, hoping she sounded modest and frightened. "It was awful. I was so lucky. Maybe he's seen me with you and knew Micheline was going to find out about what he'd done. Either way, he ran off." She took a deep, shaky breath.

No frown creased Leigh's perfect forehead to indicate she might suspect Fiona might be lying. Of course, around here, falsehoods were the flavor of the day.

"Anyway," Leigh finally continued. "We're going to set you up with a visit to Theo tomorrow. He's still in the infirmary, so you can stop by to visit and check on him. That's when you'll bring up the custom plan Micheline has developed for him." She rummaged through a small stack of papers, extracted one and passed it over to Fiona. "This is a list of all the classes we think would benefit him."

"Okay." Swallowing back nausea, Fiona accepted the paper. While this sort of thing was not in any way illegal, because Micheline gave people exactly what they paid for, it was unethical.

"Sit." Gesturing at the antique French chair across from the desk, Leigh gestured at an open wine bottle and two stemless glasses. "Would you like a glass of wine?"

Though she took a seat, Fiona politely declined. The last thing she needed would be to dull her wits around Leigh.

Leigh pouted at Fiona's refusal but poured herself a large glass. She took a deep sip and sighed. "Well, then, tell me how you and Jake are getting along. The last time I saw the two of you, you seemed very chummy."

"Chummy." Fiona pretended to consider the words, finally allowing herself a slow, sultry smile. "I guess you could say that."

"Good, good!" Leigh all but clapped. "Was it hot and heavy?"

Fiona nodded. "Honestly, I now believe in love at first sight." She looked down, swallowing hard, hoping she wasn't coming off as overly dramatic. "I think Jake does, too. I know it's sudden, but I'm pretty sure he feels the same way."

Watching her, Leigh took another deep drink of wine. "That's perfect. I'm absolutely thrilled and beyond happy for the both of you. Believe me, Micheline will be as well."

Which meant they hoped to use her connection to Jake as leverage. While she still had no idea what exactly Micheline might be planning, or even if it was a singular event, since the revelations had started leaking about Ace Colton, she imagine Micheline's jig was nearly up. That's why she couldn't shake the feeling that it would be very bad, truly awful. Catastrophic, even. A chill snaked up her spine. As long as she could get Leigh and Micheline to consider her as part of their inner circle, she stood a chance to stop the AAG.

Overexaggerating a yawn, which she covered with her hand, Fiona sighed. "I'm sorry, but I'm exhausted. It's been a crazy, long day. Though I'd love to stay and chat longer, if you don't mind, I'd like to take myself to my room and get ready for bed."

"Sure, go ahead and get some rest." Still smiling,

Leigh poured herself a generous second glass of red wine. "I'll talk to you in the morning."

As she walked back to her room, Fiona wondered if it was too late to stop by Jake's room and warn him. Her heart skipped a beat as she pictured him getting up from his bed, wearing only a pair of boxers low on his hips, his hair mussed and his sleepy eyes warming with heat at the sight of her.

Professional, she reminded herself. She needed to maintain her distance.

Though her steps slowed in the hall outside her room, with his right across the way, she forced herself to continue on inside her own space and close the door.

She caught sight of herself in the mirror, flushed and breathing fast. Turned on. "Not now, Evans," she cautioned herself, sotto voce. Continuing on into the bathroom, she washed the makeup off her face and brushed her teeth. She rummaged around in her dresser drawer, pulling out the old, soft T-shirt she often slept in.

Finally, she crawled between her sheets and clicked off the light.

The next morning, she got up early and meditated for her usual twenty minutes before showering. After drying her hair, she made a valid attempt to duplicate the makeup style that Leigh had used, but finally scrubbed it all off and redid her face in her usual, understated way.

In the cafeteria, she had her usual yogurt and fruit, along with a cup of strong coffee. She liked getting up this early, as it often turned out to be the only time she had to herself. Neither Leigh nor Micheline ever showed their face before eight. Fiona imagined they were still asleep at five thirty. She'd always been a morning person and, despite not having a concrete agenda, she liked to be ready for whatever tasks they might throw at her.

She poured herself a second cup of coffee and carried it outside to the front porch. Her favorite time of the day, no matter the season, was before sunrise, when the birds gradually came awake and the nighttime creatures went silent.

Peaceful. In a career like hers, she needed to steal small, steadying moments when she could. She took a sip of her coffee before heading over to one of the large rocking chairs.

About to sit, a sound, a blur of motion to her right had her swinging around, almost too late. A large shape launched itself at her, sending her coffee cup flying. It shattered on the wood porch.

At least her hands were free. She crouched, instinctively taking a defensive position. Large man, clumsy. Familiar, too. She launched herself forward. The top of her head caught her attacker in his large stomach, hard enough to knock the breath from him. The guy from yesterday, she realized. Ron Underhill.

Wheezing as he rasped for air, he stumbled, nearly going down. He grabbed the porch railing to pull himself up, still trying to get air. If she followed through right now, she could take him out quickly.

Instead, for some reason, she hesitated a bit too long. Long enough for him to catch a second wind. He pushed himself up, rounding on her, gulping in air. "Bitch," he snarled, still panting. "You're going to pay for what you cost me."

Damn, she wished she had her firearm. Since she didn't—couldn't, since packing heat would completely blow her cover—she'd have to take this guy down with her bare hands. Which might also blow her cover, though she had no choice.

Moving fairly fast for a guy with so much bulk, Underhill tried to rush her again. Too slow, though. Right before he reached her, she twisted, just enough to use her shoulder to knock him off balance. A swift kick took his legs out from under him, sending him crashing hard into the rail. He yelped in pain.

"Stay down," she ordered. "Don't make me hurt you."

"What the hell?" a voice said from the doorway. Jake, his voice as hard as his gaze. He stepped forward, eyeing her as if she'd donned a superhero costume. He might have been able to convince himself that what he saw her do yesterday had been a fluke, but twice would really be stretching it.

Several other men pushed their way out behind him, crowding around her, forming a protective circle between her and Underhill. At first, she thought they were protecting him from her, but then she realized they believed they were doing the opposite.

As if she needed their help. Since she needed to stay in character, undercover, she managed to arrange her face in what she hoped was a terrified expression. "Don't let him get away," she urged. "He attacked another new member yesterday, too."

Bart Akers pushed his way through the group. "Fiona?" he asked. "Are you all right?"

She simpered up at the brawny blond security man. "I'm better now that you're here."

Bart grabbed Underhill and hauled him to his feet as if he weighed nothing. "You're coming with me."

"Not to the cells," Underhill pleaded. "Let me go and

I promise I'll clear out of here. You have my word that you'll never see me again."

Ignoring him, Bart shoved his hands behind his back and secured them with a set of metal handcuffs. Randall Cook, the AAG center's handyman, asked if he could help. He and Bart were good friends, and they both worshipped Micheline and Leigh.

"We'll take care of him now," Bart said, dipping his chin at Fiona. "Are you sure he didn't hurt you?"

"Yes." She smiled sweetly, relieved none of them—with the possible exception of Jake—had seen her fight Underhill. Even then, she had no idea how much Jake might have seen. "You got here just in time."

She fought like a professional, with deadly, precise skill.

Watching silently as the security guard took the man away, Jake debated what exactly he'd say to Fiona. Who clearly wasn't at all what she seemed. They'd started to have a discussion about this yesterday, but he'd gotten nowhere. Damned if he'd let her snow him again.

"Whew," she said with a sigh, smiling up at him. "I'm sure glad Bart and the others got here in time."

"Are you?" Keeping his voice level, Jake eyed her. "You didn't appear to need any help. In fact, you looked like a pro to me."

She grinned, as if she didn't notice the tinge of betrayal in his tone. "Thanks," she replied. "Still, I'm glad help arrived before things got out of hand."

He shook his head, keeping his voice low and steady. "Either you level with me, or I'm out."

Clearly stunned, she eyed him. "I... I'm not sure what you mean."

"Cut the crap," he said. "You aren't who you pretend to be. Who are you and what are you doing in AAG?"

"I'm Fiona Smith," she replied. "And I've already told you my story."

Teeth clenched, he glared at her.

She glared right back.

Stalemate. Fine. "I'm done." Turning, he started to walk away.

"Wait." She caught at his arm. "I can't tell you."

"Can't? Or won't? I don't have time for this, Fiona. You know what? I've been worried because the last thing I wanted to do was be attracted to a woman who is in a cult, for Christ's sake. Not just any cult, but my mother's."

"Ouch." Wincing, she gazed deep into his eyes. "Are you really that attracted to me? We've known each other one day."

Ever honest, he gave her the truth. "I was. But not now. The one thing I refuse to deal with is a liar. Having Micheline for a mother drove that point home."

She winced again. "Please. I just need a little more time."

"For what?"

"To decide if I can trust you." Though her voice came out small, the fierceness of her expression had him wondering.

"Trust me?" Stunned, he looked away. "This coming from someone who puts their faith in a con woman. I don't understand, Fiona. Please, explain."

Something that looked an awful lot like desperation flashed across her expressive, beautiful face. "We all have our reasons for doing what we do. What's yours?"

Again, no explanation. Since he didn't appear to be getting anywhere by being direct, he decided to bite. "I don't know what you mean," he said. "My reason for what?"

"Right." She snorted. "I want to know why you're going along with pretending Micheline is actually your mother."

"Unfortunately, she *is* my mother," he said slowly, wondering if she'd completely lost her mind.

Something in her stunned expression told him the truth.

"She isn't?" He shook his head, as if by doing so he could clear it. "Micheline isn't my mother. Damn, what did that awful woman do now?"

Fiona looked as if he'd punched her in the gut. Shocked and worried and maybe even about to get sick.

"You didn't know," she whispered, looking around as if to make sure they weren't overheard. "Damn it, I'm so sorry. You really didn't know."

Because he felt like he needed to sit down, he did. Walked to the edge of the drive and sank down onto the manicured lawn.

"Micheline's really not my mother?"

She shook her head. "No."

"Seriously," he mused. "All these years…"

Fiona remained silent.

While he realized what she'd done by dropping this bombshell on him, as a distraction it sure as hell worked. For a moment. He wasn't even sure if he believed her.

"I'm not sure whether to feel relieved or what," he said. "But first, you sure as hell better tell me what you know. After that, I want the truth about you. All of it."

She sat down next to him, tucking her legs under her gracefully. "Micheline switched you at birth with another baby. No one really knows why."

Though his head had started to ache, he nodded encouragingly. "What other baby?" he asked, his voice a rasp.

"Ace Colton. You're really a Colton." She took a deep breath. "And Ace is actually Micheline's biological son."

"Ace Colton? Of Mustang Valley's founding family? *That* Ace Colton?"

"Yes." She took a deep breath. "Honestly, I didn't intend to shock you. I thought you knew."

"Not really." He shook his head. "Despite the way everyone in Mustang Valley reveres them, the Coltons are almost as self-serving as Micheline."

Fiona sighed. "Not really. Not even close."

Jake let himself digest this for a few seconds. Then, his natural skeptical nature kicked in. "And you know this how?"

"Apparently, Micheline marched into Colton Oil and confirmed it for them recently. The family tried to keep it under wraps, but some of the news—of a baby switch—leaked. No one knows yet what her motive for doing that was."

Again, he wondered where Fiona got her information. When he asked her, she simply sighed. "Word gets out. People talk."

"People? Are you telling me Micheline has someone working inside Colton Oil?"

"That I don't know for certain. But it's possible."

"Anything is possible," he drawled. "As to why she'd do something like that, Micheline has a reason for everything she does. I'm sure we'll all find out soon enough."

"Most likely we will," she agreed, the picture of innocence.

"Don't think I haven't noticed that you've been avoiding answering all of my questions about you. Finding this out is a hell of a big distraction, I'll admit." Grimacing, he shook his head. "But I'm still not planning on letting you off the hook."

She shrugged. "I don't blame you. But you have to understand, I can't always give you the information you're asking for."

"Why not?"

The sun had just begun to rise above the horizon, bathing them in a warm, orange glow. Despite the bright light, he couldn't read her expression as she stared at him.

"I just can't," she finally said. "As I said, I'm not sure how much I can trust you."

This earned a bitter chuckle from him. "Micheline's son who *isn't* her son? The one who, despite every awful thing I've seen her do, still came running back when she said she was dying of cancer." He shook his head, allowing the familiar bitterness to fill him. "That actually explains a lot. As a kid, I always wondered why she never seemed to love me." Even now, saying that out loud hurt. "I wonder what her end game is then. She's probably not even sick. Even before I left, I wondered how much of that was real."

"I agree," she murmured. "She seems remarkably healthy to me."

"I'm thinking it's all tied into whatever scam she's running now. It's always been about two things with her. Power and money."

Once more, she nodded.

Narrowing his gaze, he focused back on her. "You've dropped a hell of a bombshell on me with no warning."

"I'm sorry," she said, sounding sincere. "But I figured you'd want to know."

"It's a lot to process," he admitted. "And I will, just later. Now, enough about me. Who are you, really? I'm sure you'd hate for me to go to Micheline with my concerns."

Her eyes narrowed. "You wouldn't do that."

"Wouldn't I?" Bluffing, but she'd never know. Jake knew he excelled at bluffing. He made a hell of a poker player.

Her hard swallow told him he'd succeeded.

"Jake, I want to tell you the truth. Really, I do."

"But?" he prodded.

"But I can't take a chance of jeopardizing…everything."

He opened his mouth, intending to press again, but she held up her hand.

"I keep my ears open," she said, offering up a half-hearted shrug. "You'd be surprised at the kind of things you can learn when people find you invisible."

"Uh-huh." With his arms crossed and his expression skeptical, he let her know he wasn't buying it. One, two, another heartbeat while he waited for her to say more.

When she didn't, disappointment knifed through him. "That's all you got?" he asked. "The best you can do?"

He could have sworn he saw a twinge of guilt in her face, but she managed to smile. "That's it. I wish I had more."

He shook his head. "That's too bad. That tells me that you're more like Micheline than I realized."

The insult made her gasp. "In what way?" she asked.

"You're a liar, just like her. I can put up with a lot of things, but I refuse to deal with a liar."

Back stiff, he turned and walked away.

Once inside his room, he locked the door. He dug out

his laptop, powered it up and did a search for Ace Colton. Quite a bit turned up.

First, he pulled up the picture. Though they were both forty, the ousted CEO of Colton Oil looked nothing like Jake. But then, why would he? They weren't related. Instead, Jake realized he could actually see traces of Micheline in the other man's face. There, in the chin, maybe even the nose. While the other man's appearance seemed fashionably casual, he also exuded an aura of comfortable wealth. Because as a Colton, Ace would have been brought up wanting for nothing, especially love.

Except Ace Colton had been accused of trying to kill the man he'd believed to be his father. And, even worse, the fact that he wasn't actually a Colton had made the news. Ace had eventually been cleared and the actual attempted killer had been caught. Still, something like that had to leave scars.

Slightly queasy, Jake couldn't help but wonder what kind of life he might have had if Micheline hadn't taken it upon herself to switch babies. He couldn't help but want to know her reasoning.

He'd never know now. With four decades already under the bridge, he supposed the Colton family might be content to simply leave things the way they were. Though a simple DNA test would be able to prove or disapprove Micheline's story.

In that instant, Jake realized he wasn't going to be able to go home, not just yet. He wanted to meet Ace Colton. He assumed the other man would be just as curious about him, especially since Ace already knew about the baby switch.

Decision made, he grabbed his keys and left. To his surprise, no one intercepted him or tried to stop him.

He first drove to Colton Oil, but when he reached the parking lot, he realized Ace probably was too high up in the corporate ladder for Jake to simply walk in and expect a meeting. Still, he'd come this far. It couldn't hurt to try.

Once he'd killed the engine, he stared up at the building. If things had been different, he would have been comfortable in this place, known. Now, while he might have been a Colton by blood, since Ace had been ousted as CEO, they were both strangers here.

Inside the modern, industrial structure, which had been decorated in an upscale Western theme, he walked over to the huge reception desk and asked to see Ace Colton. He'd read in the local paper that Ace would be there today to meet with the board.

The young woman behind the counter looked him up and down before pushing her fashionable eyeglasses up. "I'm sorry, but he is no longer employed here."

"I understand. But I'm aware he's in the building and I really need to talk to him."

Expressionless, she studied him. "Do you have an appointment?" she asked politely.

"No," he drawled, leaning in confidentially. "But I have a feeling he'll be open to seeing me. Why don't you check, if you don't mind."

Though she sniffed, the corners of her pink-painted lips fought a smile. "Your name?"

"Jake Anderson."

She froze. Her eyes went wide. "Yes, of course," she said hurriedly. "I'll just let him know you're here."

Turning away, she quietly spoke a few words into the phone. When she hung up, she dipped her chin and pointed toward the elevator. "Second floor. He's expecting you."

"Thank you." As Jake started for the elevator, the doors opened. Ace Colton stepped out, a guardedly optimistic look on his handsome face. Jake froze, swallowing hard. He wasn't sure how to act, what to think. In fact, his first instinct was to back the hell away and claim this entire situation must have been a colossal mistake.

Ace, however, apparently had other plans. "You must be Jake," he said, shaking hands. "I heard you were in town and I wondered when we would meet."

Jake nodded, somewhat at a loss for words. "Is there somewhere we can go and talk?" he asked. "Somewhere private?"

"My thoughts exactly," Ace replied. "Since it's way too early to go to a bar, how about we grab some coffee at Java Jane's?"

"Sounds good." Though Jake had expected this meeting to be awkward, to say the least, Ace's relaxed, casual demeanor had a way of dissipating any tension.

"Do you mind if I drive?" Ace asked, jingling a set of keys.

"That depends," Jake responded. "Whether I have to cram myself into some kind of sports car or not. I have a really nice truck."

After a second, Ace laughed. "It's a Porsche. Does your truck have a lift kit?"

"Yep." Jake grinned back at him. "F-250. Custom everything. It's new. I special ordered it, and I'm pretty proud of that truck. This drive here was the first road trip." Plus, though he'd never admit it out loud, driving would help him regain some semblance of control in an admittedly crazy situation.

Ace pocketed his keys. "I'm in. Lead the way."

He whistled when he caught sight of Jake's pickup, the paint gleaming in the sun. "Nice."

He actually liked this guy, Jake thought. "Thanks."

They drove a couple of blocks. Ace pointed out the coffee shop on the right, and they parked. Neither man got out immediately.

"Are you as weirded out by all this as I am?" Jake asked.

"Yeah," Ace said. "I've got to tell you up front, I've never liked Micheline. But this, this takes the cake."

"That makes two of us," Jake replied, not bothering to keep the bitterness from his tone. "Let's go inside."

Side by side, the two men walked into the crowded coffee shop. "What'll you have?" Ace asked. "I'm buying."

"Just coffee," Jake answered. "Thanks." He looked around, impressed by the cleanliness and warmth of the place.

"Here you go," Ace said, handing him a coffee. "Now to find a place to sit."

Jake grimaced. "I've scanned the entire place. There are no empty seats."

"There's another room in the back. Follow me." Moving with the confidence of a local, Ace led the way through the crowd. They passed through a doorway into a smaller, less crowded room. "Perfect." Ace made a beeline for a couple of overstuffed armchairs near the window. "My favorite spot."

They sat. Jake studied Ace, making no effort to hide it. And Ace, in turn, studied him back.

"So *she* summoned you home to tell you the truth?" Ace finally asked.

"Micheline? No." Jake took a drink of his coffee. "She

still hasn't told me. She tracked me down to tell me she had cancer."

"Do you believe her? She said something about that when she stopped by Colton Oil."

"I'm not sure," Jake admitted. "I swear she seems desperate now, closer to being truly mentally ill than I've ever seen her. Of course, it's been twenty-three years since I left home. Obviously, she must have deteriorated in all that time."

"Twenty-three years? Wow." Ace whistled. "Your life must have been hell for you to take off at seventeen."

His life. The life that should have been Ace's. "I wouldn't wish it on you, man," Jake said. "None of this is your fault, or mine. I'm still reeling with the knowledge that I'm really not related to that b—" He broke off, realizing Micheline was actually Ace's biological mother. "She's crazy," he finally amended. "Truly delusional."

"Great, just great." Glum now, Ace gazed out the window with a contemplative expression. "That means it runs in the family."

Just as Jake was searching his mind for how to respond to that, Ace laughed. "This is so messed up." He eyed Jake. "You know you're going to have to take a DNA test. I did, and it confirmed what we already know."

"I figured. And I will. But you should know, I'm not after anything. I like my life. I've worked hard and own a small ranch north of here. If anything, I'd just like to get to know your family. *My* family, too, I guess."

Ace met his gaze. "That can be arranged. I'll just need a little time to get them used to the idea. Everyone is still in shock."

"I can understand that," Jake said. "I'm in the same state myself."

Clearing his throat, Ace nodded. "I'm sure you've read about me being framed for attempted murder. I was exonerated and the actual gunman was caught."

"I did." Jake wasn't sure what else to say. "That must have been tough."

"It was." Ace eyed him. "You do understand, once all the smoke clears, you'll most likely be able to assume a position on the Colton Oil board. You could even move to the Triple R if you want."

"I have my own ranch," Jake answered quickly. "But thank you. What about you? What will you do now?"

Ace grimaced. "I might start an energy consulting firm but that is still up in the air. I suppose at some point, Micheline is going to want to spend some time with me, too, and get to know me. Though she hasn't cared for forty years, so why would she care now?"

"Don't take it personally," Jake advised. "That's just the way she is. She cares about herself and only herself."

"But what about all those people who belong to AAG? Surely by now, at least some of them would have noticed she isn't what she seems."

"You'd think." Jake took another deep drink of his coffee. "But they see what they want to see. And Micheline is a very good actress. However, I'd still like to know why she switched us as infants."

"Me too." Ace sighed, also sipping his coffee. "Tell me about yourself," he urged. "I know we're not really related, but I feel like we could be brothers."

Though Jake preferred not to talk about himself, he complied. Ace Colton was surprisingly easy to talk to.

"I'm sure you've read about what happened to me," Ace said.

"When your—*our*—father was shot?"

"Yes." Ace nodded grimly. "I was framed for that. As if I'd ever hurt Payne. Luckily, they caught the guy who did it, a man who had a real grudge against my dad. But they suspected me because we all heard the news that I'm not really a Colton, at least by blood. That little bit of knowledge got me ousted from the board of Colton Oil and Dad and I got into an argument."

Jake winced. "Ouch. Though I know it's not my fault, I feel like I should apologize."

"No need." Ace waved him away. "My life is still good. I know my family—*our* family—still loves me, even if we don't share the same blood. I even recently learned I have an adult daughter from a long-ago relationship. Her name is Nova and she's pregnant. Which means I will soon be a grandfather."

"Wow. At our age?"

This made Ace laugh. "Yes. I'll be a young, hip grandpa." He leaned forward, his expression going serious. "Now tell me what it was like being raised by Micheline."

"Well…" Jake tried to think of a way to sound diplomatic. Then he decided the hell with it. Ace deserved to know the truth. "She's an awful woman," he said bluntly. "And always treated me like an afterthought or an unwanted pest. Which now makes sense. I ran away from home when I was seventeen and never looked back."

"Yet you returned now," Ace pointed out.

"She found me and made contact, claiming she has cancer." Jake shook his head. "Despite everything, she was my mother. Or so I thought. So I came back. Now, I'm glad I did. I always wanted a large family, with brothers and sisters."

"Well, you've definitely got that now."

"I do."

"I don't remember you from school," Ace pointed out. "Which seems weird."

Jake grimaced. "Micheline kept me home. She signed me up to be home schooled, but I mostly learned by myself. Luckily, I wanted to learn, so I was able to not only keep up with what everyone else was doing, but I graduated early."

"That's amazing."

Enjoying the camaraderie, Jake and Ace continued to share stories, talking and laughing until Ace's phone buzzed.

"My secretary is texting me," Ace explained. "I need to get back to the office. But I'd really like to get together again, soon." He handed Jake his phone. "Put your contact information in and I'll text you, so you can do the same."

After Jake dropped Ace off at the Colton Oil parking lot so he could retrieve his car, he couldn't stop smiling. Maybe something good would come out of this entire mess after all. He'd always wanted a brother. And family. The prospect of meeting them all was enough to make him decide to stick around Mustang Valley just a little longer.

Chapter 5

Considering Jake's words, aware he believed her to be as big of a fraud as Micheline, hurt more than it should have. Fiona wrestled with her conscience as she paced her small room. Being undercover did mean she had to play a role, and the most important thing here was her mission. Though she'd like nothing more than sharing the truth with him, in the end she couldn't risk Jake blowing her cover. There was too much at stake, including her professional reputation.

More importantly, if Micheline ever learned the feds were on to her, she might move up her timetable for whatever awful thing she had planned. They'd be caught unaware, and innocent lives could be lost. Fiona had no choice but to continue on playing the part of a fully indoctrinated cult member, no matter what the personal cost. Still, she ached for Jake. While she knew he would have eventually learned the truth, the fact that she'd been the one to unleash it on him, even accidentally, really bothered her.

Deep cover sometimes involved forgetting who you really were. So far, she hadn't achieved that level, and in this situation, she doubted she ever would. First, she wouldn't be here that long, and second, in a cult allowing oneself to actually be indoctrinated could be dangerous. Due to her intensive training, she honestly felt as if she was doing a good job of pretending. So good that Micheline and Leigh appeared to completely trust her. Everything she'd worked so hard to achieve appeared to be going forward exactly as she'd planned.

And then she'd met Jake. Talk about bad timing. One look from his blue eyes and she turned into a puddle of want and need. While she'd been attracted to other men, the way she felt about him was different. Stronger, more intense. As if she craved him with more than just her body.

The foolish, romantic notion made her scoff at herself. She'd never been a believer in sappy things like soul mates or love at first sight. This had to be simply an issue of overactive hormones or pheromones—something easily explained by science. Whatever the explanation, she couldn't stop thinking about him. Part of her hoped he would follow through on his threat to leave so she wouldn't constantly be tempted. The rest of her—*most* of her—wanted to throw herself into his arms and let passion take her where it may.

Not merely foolish. Dangerous. She'd need to be careful. Walking a fine line between her undercover persona and herself would be difficult, but not impossible. The knowledge that Jake hated liars shouldn't bother her, but it did. Far too much.

Jake already suspected something, though. Since she sensed the strong attraction went both ways, she figured he'd be easily distracted. Judging by the way they'd both reacted to the kiss, they'd both enjoy any distractions she decided to throw his way.

He probably wouldn't be a problem for too much longer, anyway. She knew he planned to go back home really soon, especially if his mother—who wasn't really his mother—continued to dodge him. Fiona couldn't blame him for wanting to put Mustang Valley in his rearview mirror. His entire childhood had turned out to be a lie. He'd built another life, his own life, far away from here. Once he'd gotten to know his new family and explored his options here in Mustang Valley, naturally, he'd want to get back to the familiar reality of his home, his ranch, even if just to put his affairs there in order. Unless Micheline found a way to stop him. Which Fiona wouldn't put past her.

After the incident with Underhill, Fiona had known better than to go look for Jake. After all, he'd made his feelings clear. She wished it didn't bother her so much—really, she barely knew the man, so it shouldn't—but it did. A lot.

Sighing, she twisted her hair into a neat ponytail and got dressed in her dressier day clothes. She wasn't sure what Leigh had scheduled for her, but she knew she was supposed to go to the infirmary and coerce a young man who'd just been beaten for no reason into signing up for a bunch of expensive classes.

For this odious task, she chose a different cheery yellow shift dress than the previous night's and tan heels.

Bright colors helped lift her spirits. While she hated the thought of doing what they wanted her to do, it helped if she separated her true self from the person she had to be here. Cultist rather than FBI agent.

Her heels clicked as she walked down the hallway on the way to the infirmary. Perched on the edge of one of the massive sofas in the lobby, Leigh nodded and gave her a thumbs-up sign as she passed.

Fiona managed to smile back.

When she reached the infirmary, she stopped by the front desk. "I'm here to see Theodore."

Barely acknowledging her, the middle-aged attendant gestured toward the back. "Room three."

Here went nothing. Taking a deep breath, Fiona went to the back.

Theodore looked up from his phone when she entered. "Hey," he said, pushing up his wire-rimmed glasses. "They promised me someone was coming to take me back to campus. Is that you?"

"Why not?" Secretly relieved, she gave him a genuine smile. "How are you feeling today?"

He shrugged, dragging his fingers through his curly hair. "Embarrassed. I came here thinking it would be different than college. But it's not. It all sucks. Just once, I'd…" Stopping, he shook his head, his brown eyes earnest. "Never mind. I should be thanking you for helping me instead of complaining."

"You're welcome," she said. "If you're ready to go, I can drive you back to campus. We can talk along the way."

Since he was already dressed, he hopped down off the bed. "Sounds good. Let's do it."

She walked him out, half expecting the woman at the

desk to stop them. Instead, she waved them past, still not looking up from whatever had her engrossed.

"It's a romance novel," Theodore confided, once they'd exited the room. "She reads them 24/7." He shrugged. "Whatever makes her happy."

This made her laugh. "You're a good guy, Theodore Royce the third."

Hearing her say his full name made him wince. "Just call me Theo. You're Fiona, right?"

"Right. Are you okay to walk to the back parking lot, or would you prefer I swing by here and pick you up?"

"I can walk," he hurriedly told her. "That guy didn't do anything to my legs. I have a couple of bruised ribs, though. You know, I still have no idea why he was even messing with me."

"Money," she replied. "He thinks you're rich, so he figured you could pay him."

"Rich doesn't mean stupid." He actually sounded indignant.

She took that as encouragement. Hopefully, he'd see through the sales pitch she was about to try to use on him.

They got into her vehicle, a government-issued sedan that, despite being painted maroon, still managed to look like an undercover police car. She waited until they'd pulled out of the long driveway before making her first attempt.

"I heard you might be interested in attending our self-enlightenment program," she began.

"Maybe." He shrugged. "I was, I mean. But now after what happened, I'm thinking there's nothing that can help me."

"Help you with what?" she asked, genuinely curious.

When he glanced at her, for a moment he let her see

his misery. "I'm not doing well in school. I don't mean academically, because I'm good there. I just can't seem to make friends or get dates." He swallowed hard. "I'm lonely."

Damned if she could actually try to indoctrinate this poor kid.

Theo didn't seem to notice her indecision. "Anyway, Leigh told me about the classes. They sound intriguing. And the price isn't too bad, either." He glanced at her, almost shyly. "I really want to learn how to become the best person I can be."

It's all a load of BS, she really wanted to tell him. Of course, she couldn't, so she simply pressed her lips together and tried to think of some kind of noncommittal response to give.

Luckily, it didn't appear one would be needed. Theo continued to talk, evidently relieved to unburden himself. "I like the idea of knowing how to choose friends," he mused. "So far, all I've met are people who just want to use me. And the idea of learning how to choose the right significant other—that blows my mind."

She nodded, keeping her gaze on the road, not trusting herself to speak.

They reached the campus, and Theo directed her to his dorm. When she pulled up in front and put the car in Park, she turned to look at him. "Maybe you should just focus on your studies," she suggested quietly. "You're a freshman. Give it time, and you might be surprised at how seamlessly you'll eventually fit in."

"But what if I don't?" His slender form radiated tension. "That's easy for someone like you to say. I bet when you were my age, you didn't have these kinds of problems."

His comment made her laugh. "You'd be surprised," she told him. "I was scared and shy and homesick. I mostly hid in my dorm room the first semester." Of course, that had been when she hadn't found her true calling: law enforcement. She'd started out taking business classes, until a chance lecture had piqued her interest. From there, she'd gotten her degree in criminal justice. Applying to Quantico had been a no-brainer next step.

Squeezing his shoulder, she hoped he took her words to heart. "I promise you, it gets easier. Just give it time."

"I'll try." Opening the door, he got out of the car. "And I'll think about trying one of the seminars."

"You do that." As she watched him walk away, relief flooded her. Along with anger at Micheline and her machinations. Freshman college students, new to living on campus and away from home, were particularly vulnerable. The idea that Micheline wanted to milk them for money infuriated Fiona. At least Theo had given her something to say when Leigh asked her how it had gone. He'd said he'd think about it. And using a version of the truth was always the best option when undercover.

When she arrived back at the compound, she sat in her parked car for a few minutes, watching the yard staff do their thing. Finally, she got out of her car and strolled inside.

Almost instantly, Leigh appeared, making Fiona wonder if the other woman had been watching for her.

"Well?" Leigh demanded. "How'd it go?"

"He said he's going to think about it."

Leigh pursed her bright pink lips together. "You'll give him a day. Then I want you to start pressuring him. At least get him to sign up for the first seminar. Most times, that's all it takes. One class to open their eyes to the boundless possibilities we can lay out in front of them."

It took an effort not to roll her eyes. "Okay. I'm guessing you have his phone number?"

"Of course," Leigh purred. "I'll text it to you. I want you to call him first thing in the morning."

Fiona nodded. "Will do." She eyed the other woman. Leigh always seemed to be posing for something, as if she carried her beauty queen title into every second of her existence.

"Jake went out today, too," Leigh said, flipping her blond curls over her shoulder. She looked around the room before pinning her sharp gaze on Fiona, clearly watching for a reaction.

Not sure how to respond, Fiona said nothing.

"I think he was looking for you before he left," Leigh continued.

This got Fiona's attention. "Was he? Did he specifically say that?"

"Well, no." Leigh giggled. "Not in so many words. But it was pretty obvious. He was wandering around the first floor as if he was looking for something or someone. I'm guessing that most likely was you."

"Or Micheline," Fiona put in. "She still needs to meet privately with him."

"How do you know she hasn't?" The unrelenting, fake cheerfulness in Leigh's voice had Fiona clenching her teeth.

"Has she?"

Leigh tittered. "No. She's really very busy."

"I'm sure Jake is, too. As a matter of fact, he mentioned something about leaving soon."

Just like that, her words managed to wipe the smile

off Leigh's face. "He can't," she said flatly. "Do whatever you have to, but make him stay."

"Why?"

Leigh blinked. "Are you questioning me? Seriously?"

"Yes." Crossing her arms, Fiona regarded the younger woman steadily. "I am. I need to understand why it's so important that Jake stay when it's clear Micheline doesn't find him a priority at all."

Just like that, all traces of friendliness disappeared from Leigh's face. "That is not for you to question, do you understand?" She waited a beat for Fiona to respond. When she didn't, Leigh repeated the question. "Do. You. Understand?"

The fury in Leigh's voice overrode Fiona's own innate stubbornness. Slowly, she nodded. She rearranged her expression, hoping she appeared abashed, even though inside she was seething.

"Good. Now." Leigh reached out and touched her shoulder, all friendly and confident again. "I want you to go look for Jake. Hang on him, bat those pretty brown eyes of yours, lay it on thick, do whatever you have to, but get him to stay." She paused to take a breath. "I'm counting on you. Micheline is counting on you. Heck, the entire AAG is counting on you."

That big? Deliberately, Fiona widened her eyes. "I'm honored," she whispered. "I'll do my best not to disappoint anyone."

"See that you don't," Leigh snapped. Then, softening her tone, she told Fiona how much Micheline valued her presence. "We all do," Leigh said, her earnest expression as intense as her tone. "We're committed to helping you become the best you."

"Of course," Fiona murmured, bowing her head. "And I promise that I won't let you down."

She couldn't help but catch Leigh's self-satisfied smirk as she turned away.

Head down, Fiona made it to her room. After closing the door, she debated taking a second shower, as if by doing so she could wash some of the icky feeling off her. She'd known coming in that she might be called upon to do things she considered unethical. She simply needed to do a better job of reconciling herself to being Micheline and Leigh's obedient little cultist.

The message had been clear—do whatever you have to do. They wanted her to seduce Jake. Hell, the thought sent a shiver of pure longing all the down her spine. One time, she thought wryly, where doing Micheline's bidding would actually be pleasurable.

Only Jake himself—knowing how betrayed he'd feel if he learned she'd used him—made following through on her orders difficult.

Enough, Fiona told herself sternly. She'd known this assignment wouldn't be easy. Time to pull on her big-girl panties and do what she had to do.

Oddly enough, as Jake drove back toward the compound, the first person he wanted to talk to was Fiona. A member of Micheline's evil little cult. Proof that he still was thinking with the wrong head.

Still, so much had changed in his life, and he had no one he could discuss it with.

Except Micheline, he reminded himself. Micheline knew. She'd always known. And for whatever reason, she'd let him grow up believing he was an only child and that she was his mother.

A family. He actually had a real family. For the sake of his own sanity, he couldn't allow himself to think about the missing years, the lost love. That would come later. Right now, he could only focus on the fact that he wasn't related in any way to that horrible, awful woman Micheline. He felt kind of sorry for Ace, who had to be bummed at the knowledge that he carried her tainted genes. Jake had spent years trying to shed the rot he'd worried he'd carried deep inside, at a cellular level. Now, the colossal relief of knowing he didn't nearly overwhelmed him.

Still stunned at the news, he suspected it would take a long while to shed the full weight of the false past he'd believed to be his.

Back at the AAG center, Jake strode through the lobby, keeping his gaze fixed straight ahead. He didn't want to talk to anyone, least of all Micheline or one of her minions. Including—despite the way his heart skipped a beat at the thought of her—the beautiful Fiona. Uninterrupted, he went straight to his room, where he closed and locked the door.

Another man had lived the life he should have had. And Jake, growing up among all the suffering that he had told himself had been character building, was in reality a Colton.

Even so, he wouldn't wish his childhood on anyone. Especially Ace. Once, he'd even thought he'd seen Michelle kill someone and dump the body, but he was young and it was dark and he could not be sure of what he saw. Ace would never know how lucky he was to have been spared that.

Sitting on the edge of his bed, Jake reflected on the unexpected ease of the meeting today. Ace had been a

hell of a nice guy. Odd how sometimes you met someone and felt that instant bond, as if they could be almost
a brother—definitely friends.

Of course, Jake had felt the same way about Fiona,
except stronger. That instant flash of connection. He
groaned out loud, hating the way his thoughts always
seemed to return to her. Even now, he still craved her.
A woman enthralled by a cult run by the evil woman
who'd raised him.

Thinking of all this made his head ache. So much
had changed in his life in the last twenty-four hours.
He needed to try and focus on that, instead of on something that could never be. No matter how much he might
want it.

He was a Colton. Ever since he could remember, he'd
heard stories about the powerful Colton family. They
were a large, close-knit family and involved in everything, from ranching to oil. Here in Mustang Valley, they
were spoken of with a kind of affectionate reverence.
Truthfully, on the outside looking in, Jake had always
assumed their success had to be due to the same kind
of machinations that Micheline employed. Just the short
time that he'd spent with Ace, hearing the other man's
obvious affection for the Colton family, had made Jake
begin to realize he might have been wrong.

And now he, too, was a Colton. Not that he planned
to hang around long.

A soft tap on his door startled him out of his reverie.
He immediately tensed, thinking maybe Micheline had
finally sought him out. Bracing himself, he turned the
knob and blinked. No Micheline, but the woman who
haunted his every waking moment. Fiona.

"Hi." Her uncertain smile cut straight to his heart. "I'm wondering if we could talk."

She wore another formfitting yellow dress and sexy high-heeled shoes. Forcing himself to think before he spoke, he swallowed hard. He knew better than to let her into his room.

"May I come in?" she asked.

He stepped aside and let her in.

"Thanks." She appeared restless, uncertain. She strode to his window, her long legs made even more shapely in her heels, and twitched aside the curtain to peer out.

Though she kept her back to him, he couldn't seem to tear his gaze away from her.

Finally, she turned. "I came here to apologize," she said, her voice as miserable as her expression. "I shouldn't have told you about being switched at birth that way. I honestly suspected—hoped—you already knew."

Surprised, he shook his head. "I had no idea. It came as a hell of a big shock to me."

"I see that now. Anyway, I know what you think of me, and I couldn't bear to have you hold this against me, too." She swallowed hard, drawing his gaze to her slender throat. "I'm sorry, Jake. Really sorry."

Though every instinct urged him to take her into his arms, he didn't. Even now, he suspected she might be playing him, acting on Micheline's orders or something.

His lack of reaction appeared to be what she'd expected. "Take care, Jake. It was good to meet you."

He let her get halfway to the door before reaching out. He didn't grab her—no matter how badly he wanted to haul her up against him and kiss her senseless. Instead, he touched her shoulder, a mere brushing of his hand as she passed.

But it was enough. Enough to make her stop short, turning to look at him.

"Let me help you, Fiona," he heard himself say. "You don't belong here, not with these people. I can set you up with the therapist I mentioned who specializes in deprogramming."

Her gaze searched his face. "Why?" she asked. "What do you get out of it? It's been my experience that no one does something for nothing."

"I want to help you, nothing more. I can let you stay on my ranch—your own room—if you need a place to stay." He let her see some of his inner turmoil in his expression. "I can't bear to see someone like you under Micheline's power."

"So that's it then. You want to get back at Micheline for what she did to you."

"No. Of course not." Considering, he amended his statement, adding in the truth. "Well, I would like to see her pay for what she's done. Not to me, but to others. A nice jail cell with a sentence of twenty to thirty years would do nicely, though."

After a startled look, Fiona laughed. Really laughed, the sound infectious and honest and going straight to his gut. "You really mean that, don't you?"

"I do. And I'm also serious about getting you help. You're too good for this place, Fiona."

He expected her to argue or protest, to make excuses or to flat out deny. He didn't expect her to wrap her arms around him and pull him in close for a kiss.

A kiss that seared his soul and stopped all rational thought. As their lips moved together, his heart pounded in his ears, and his body moved, too. Involuntarily pressing his huge arousal into her soft curves.

She let out a sound, a moan of desire, of need. Then, as he fought to gather up the willpower to pull away, she matched him movement for movement. Tongue, hands and that curvy, soft, sexy body that he so badly wanted to sink into.

Damn he wanted her, so badly the need for her made him shake. But still, he held himself back, unable to keep from wondering if this wasn't yet another soul-crushing trick ordered by Micheline.

Did it matter? Yes. Fiona had to be here of her own free will, not at the behest of AAG.

"Wait," he muttered, even as his body contradicted his words. Somehow, he managed to put enough space in between them to enable his head to clear. "I need to know. Did Micheline or Leigh ask you to come here and…"

She hesitated, just long enough to give him his answer.

"Sorry, but no." This time, he wrenched himself free. Despite his arousal, he moved to stand on the other side of the bed, using it as a physical barrier between them. "You're clearly not in your right mind. I won't take advantage of you like that."

Staring at him, she blinked. "I promise you, I'm in my right mind. No one is forcing me to be here."

"You still didn't answer my question. Were you asked to come here and…"

"Get you to stay by using whatever means necessary?" She sat down hard on the edge of the bed, dragging her hand through her long, thick, dark hair. "Yes. Leigh used those exact words with me a little while ago."

His heart sank. The rest of him still had not registered the stand-down order.

"But that's not why I'm here," she breathed, her eyes locked on his. "I'm here because I'm incredibly attracted to you. I want you, Jake Anderson. Nothing more than that."

Every part of him wished he could believe her. He cleared his throat, willing away his unrepentant arousal. "Leave with me," he told her, desperate to give her one more chance. "Let me take you away from here, get you some help. Then we might revisit this."

"I can't." Her sensual mouth twisted. "I can't leave. I have a very real reason for being here."

"Then tell me."

She shook her head and pushed to her feet. "Come with me," she said, holding out her hand. "Let's walk outside." She pointed to her ear, then gestured around the room as if to say she thought someone might be listening.

He wouldn't be surprised.

Looking down at himself, he sighed. "I'm going to need a minute before I can walk anywhere."

Though she nodded, the way she eyed him, as if she wanted to gobble him up, made losing his arousal even more impossible. Tearing his gaze away from her, he moved into the bathroom. He might need a cold shower, but hopefully it wouldn't come to that.

Briefly, he considered taking matters into his own hands, just to regain a measure of control. But because he really, really wanted to lose himself in Fiona, he settled for the quick cold shower.

When he finally emerged again, she still waited.

"I'm good," he said, aware she'd no doubt heard the shower.

"Then let's go." And she took his hand.

Of course, his body jolted again when she slipped her slender fingers into his hand. Ignoring it, he concentrated on putting one foot in front of the other, well aware that somewhere Micheline or one of her people would be watching.

Outside, he took deep gulps of the dry, fresh air.

They walked in silence, and Fiona didn't speak until they'd rounded a curve in the drive and put the house out of view. She stopped, tugging on his hand to make sure he did, too. Gazing down at her upturned face, for one heart-stopping moment he thought he might kiss her. But he remembered why they'd come out here, and didn't.

"I'm deciding to trust you," she said, her expression both vulnerable and earnest. "If you betray my trust, for whatever reason, know that you'll put numerous lives at risk, not least of all my own."

Not sure if she was being overly dramatic or her words were really honest, he simply nodded for her to continue.

She took a deep breath. "I'm really not sure I should do this," she mumbled. "But here goes. I'm an undercover FBI agent. I'm investigating the cult and Micheline."

It took a few heartbeats for her words to even register. Shock. Then, thinking of the way she'd fought, understanding.

"You're serious?" he finally asked.

"Yes. That's why I can't leave. And why I don't need to go see a deprogrammer. Micheline is planning something big, something awful, though we don't yet know what. In addition to that, we've received numerous complaints about her swindling money. Lots of money."

"You *are* serious," he repeated, shocked and stunned and overjoyed all at once. "That means you really aren't a brainwashed cultist."

"No, but I'm here to play one."

Just then he realized the chance she'd taken, trusting him. She'd risked her entire mission—maybe even her life—by trusting him. That was huge. Beyond huge.

He reached for her and she met him halfway.

As their lips met, he realized he'd just gained another reason to stay a bit longer. Now that he knew Fiona wasn't actually brainwashed, he could allow his burgeoning feelings full reign. And if Fiona planned to take Micheline and her cult down, he wanted to be here to see it.

Keeping the kiss short, he broke away. "Let's go back to my room."

"And finish what we started?" One brow arched, she smiled.

But it was the vulnerability still lingering in her dark eyes that undid him. "Yes," he said, grabbing her hand.

Chapter 6

Telling Jake made her feel as if a heavy weight had been lifted from her chest. She could breathe again, move again and let herself make love honestly again. Micheline and Leigh be damned.

I've jeopardized my mission, a little voice whispered inside her head. But no, she'd carefully considered. Jake had wanted to get her out, away from these people. There was no way in hell he was in with them. Especially after what Micheline had done to him.

They raced through the front door, through the lobby, earning more than a few curious stares. Instead of the elevator, they took the stairs, running up the steps hand in hand.

Once inside his room, he secured the door by putting the desk chair under the knob. When he turned, the raw need blazing from his face took her breath away.

"Come here, you," he said, holding out his arms.

Without hesitation, she went to him and wrapped herself around him.

"It's okay," he told her, nuzzling her neck. "I'm going to stay a little longer and help you."

She pulled him down to her, meeting his mouth with hers. Not only to silence him, but because she needed to kiss him as much as she needed to breathe.

This time, as they came together, tasting, touching, allowing the craving to blossom, she felt her eyes sting with the beginning of tears. "Please give me your word that you won't reveal what I've told you. I know you won't, but I just need to hear you say it."

"Don't," he told her, wiping a stray bit of moisture away with his finger. "I give you my word, you won't regret this."

That made her smile. "Put it off any longer and I might prove you wrong."

With a shout of laughter, he kissed her again, deepening the kiss until her head swam and her knees were weak.

"Too many clothes," she mumbled against his lips. "Off with them."

Again he chuckled. "Patience." He reached for her shirt. She batted his hand away.

"You first. I want to see you naked."

"Okay." Keeping his gaze locked on hers, he slowly unbuttoned his shirt. Once he'd removed that, he went for his belt.

"Let me," she demanded, tugging the buckle open. When she undid his jeans and went to pull down the zipper, his erection surged free.

"Careful," he rasped.

"Hot damn." Slowly pulling his boxers and jeans down past his hips, she couldn't take her eyes off him.

"Boots," he said, choking on the word. He dropped back onto the bed, groaning as she knelt in front of him, pretending to be going for his feet. Instead, she grazed her lips over the engorged head of him and then she took him into her mouth. All of him, deep. He tasted like man and salt and sex.

Moving slowly, she relished the power of her taking him that way. In and out, falling into a rhythm and feeling her own body throb.

"Enough." He pulled her up and off him, pushing her back against the mattress. "While that was…extremely pleasurable, I want to be inside you."

Grinning up at him, she reached for him. "I want that, too."

"Wait." He grabbed his jeans, located his wallet and removed a condom. Once he'd managed to pull it over his arousal, he went back to her and kissed her again. Deep and fierce, his hands coaxing her back to life, his erection huge against her belly.

Slowly, she opened her legs and guided him to her.

One push and he filled her. Completely. For a heartbeat or two, he held himself utterly still, letting her body adjust to his size. "You're so damn wet," he groaned.

"You're so damn hard," she shot back, thrilling to the way his body pulsed at her words.

She arched her back, anticipating his next stroke, and moved to meet him.

They moved together, fast and furious, a crashing crescendo of desire and need. So raw, so instinctively honest, so…good. When she felt the beginning starburst of release building, she cried out. Her body clenched around him, and she gripped him tight while she shuddered from the strength of her climax.

A moment later, one final push and he joined her.

They clung to each other, damp and sweaty, the sweet, musky scent of sex filling the air.

"Wow." Totally drained, she rested her head against his shoulder. "That was…"

"Good," he finished for her, kissing the top of her head. "Amazing. Unbelievable. Should I go on?"

Smiling, she shook her head. "You understand what they're going to think?" she murmured, turning her head so that her mouth was pressed against his ear. "That I seduced you in order to get you to stay. Did it work?"

His quick bark of laughter made her wiggle and raise her head to look at him.

"Yes," he responded, kissing the tip of her nose. "Though honestly, now that I've met Ace Colton, I was planning to stick around awhile anyway."

Stunned, she eyed him. "You met Ace? When?"

"Earlier today. After I learned about my true parentage, I drove myself over to Colton Oil. Even though Ace no longer is CEO, I'd read in the local paper that he would be there for some kind of meeting, so I went in and introduced myself. We hit it off. He's a hell of a nice guy."

Unannounced, uninvited, Jake had simply shown up and asked to meet the man with whom he'd been switched at birth. She had to admire his bravado.

"And he met with you?" she asked, just to be clear.

Jake tilted his head. "Yes. You sound surprised. Don't you think he had to be curious, too? Naturally, he'd want to meet the man whose life should have been his."

She let her gaze roam over his rugged, handsome face.

"You don't sound bitter. I don't know that I wouldn't be, if I were in the same position."

"Maybe a little," he admitted, lifting one bare shoulder. "But it's forty years in the past. There's nothing I or anyone else can do to change things. All we can do is move forward, one day at a time."

Admirable. She didn't know that she'd be able to be so sanguine if she were in his position.

He kissed her again, a quick press of his lips against her temple. "He's going to introduce me to the rest of his—of my—family," he said, his eyes drifting closed. "That should be interesting." He tightened his arms around her, pulling her in close.

Nestling into his embrace, she marveled at the myriad of complex emotions swirling around inside her. In the space of twenty-four hours, her entire situation had completely changed. On the one hand, as far as Micheline and Leigh were concerned, she'd been a good little cult member and done what they wanted by getting Jake to stay.

On the other, by revealing herself to Jake, she could have placed the entire undercover operation in jeopardy. Her gut twisted at the thought. But as she gazed at Jake's rugged profile, she just knew her trust wouldn't be misplaced. He wasn't a part of the AAG. Even before learning of his true parentage, he'd been destined for other things. He had his ranch, a life he'd built from the ground up. Soon, he'd have a new family to get to know. The machinations of Micheline Anderson and her merry little cult would figure very little in his world. Especially once he'd left here.

For Fiona as well. Once she'd completed this assignment, she'd go back to her job working out of the Phoenix office and her tidy little apartment downtown. Until her next assignment. Then this time she'd spent here in Mustang Valley would become nothing but a memory.

For now, she wanted to simply revel in the moment. She'd learned a long time ago to enjoy the happy moments when she could. Because in the crazy world she worked in, she knew they were few and far between.

She must have fallen asleep, because when she opened her eyes again, someone was trying to open Jake's door. Quietly, but clearly attempting to get the stuck door to open.

"Jake!" she whispered, nudging him with her elbow. He came awake instantly, and she held her finger to his lips to keep him silent.

Once more, the intruder rattled the door. The chair Jake had wedged under the knob held. Slowly, Jake sat up. "Who's there?" he asked, his voice stern.

"It's Micheline," a familiar voice answered back. "I think it's time we had a chat."

Talk about timing. Fiona's first instinct was to panic. How embarrassing! Her second had her burrowing deeper into the covers, thinking letting the cult leader find her here might not be a bad thing. After all, as far as Micheline was concerned, Fiona had simply done what she'd been told.

"Let her in," she murmured to Jake, keeping her chin up though her cheeks were hot.

One brow raised, he asked her if she was sure. When she nodded, he pushed himself off the bed, stepped into his jeans and, after zipping them, he answered the door.

"Micheline." He stepped aside, allowing her to see into his small room.

Fiona waved, just to make sure Micheline saw her.

"Oh." Micheline took a quick step back. Fiona had to stifle a smile.

"Sorry. I was busy." Jake dragged his hand through his hair. "Maybe you should have considered calling first."

"I didn't know you had company," Micheline responded, sounding a bit tense. Translation—her spies hadn't informed her that Jake was with Fiona. "But I had a cancellation, which meant a couple of hours opened up in my schedule. I thought we could get together and talk."

Jake glanced over his shoulder at Fiona before gesturing toward a chair. "Come on in. Have a seat. We can talk here."

Micheline didn't move. "Alone," she clarified. She cut her eyes to Fiona, pasting an utterly false beatific smile on her perfectly made-up face. "Fiona, honey. Would you please go on back to your own room?"

"Of course," Fiona replied, dipping her chin. "I'll need to get dressed first."

"What if I want her to stay?" Jake asked, crossing his arms. "Fiona and I have become very close. She can hear anything you want to say to me."

Interesting. Fiona watched Micheline, curious to see which way this would go. On the one hand, Fiona was supposed to do whatever the cult leader wanted. On the other, Micheline would want to placate her son. Especially if she ever revealed the truth of his birth to his face. She had no way of knowing Jake already knew.

Or did she? Fiona frowned, looking down to hide it. She'd long suspected the presence of cameras and/or recording devices, which was why she'd made Jake go outside to discuss her true identity. She generally tried to be super careful with what she said, but perhaps Jake had not.

"Fiona can stay," Jake repeated when Micheline didn't respond.

Micheline ignored him, walking over to stand at the side of the bed and peering down at Fiona. "Honey, my son and I need to have a private, personal conversation. Would you mind going back to your own room?"

Mindful of the role she had to play, Fiona nodded. "Of course." She wrapped the sheet around herself, got out of bed, grabbed her clothes and hurried to the bathroom to dress.

When she emerged a few seconds later, she flashed a shy smile at Micheline and hurried for the door.

Before she could exit, Jake grabbed her arm. "Wait."

She shot him a look, hoping it conveyed a *don't ruin this for me* statement. Evidently it did, for he let her go.

"Thank you, sweetheart," Micheline purred as Fiona slipped out the door.

Outside in the hall, Fiona paused to catch her breath. Part of her wanted to rush back in and stand with Jake. But if she wanted to continue to play the obedient little cult member, she couldn't. Whatever Micheline wanted, Jake would have to deal with it alone.

Bracing himself once the door closed behind Fiona, Jake turned back to face Micheline. He thought about making it easy on her and telling her he already knew, but why should he? Plus, she'd want to know where and when he'd found out, and how. Which would hurt Fiona and her mission.

Crossing his arms, he eyed the woman who'd raised him and said nothing.

"You don't have to look so angry," Micheline chided. "This is our chance to make up for lost time."

"Is it?"

"Yes." She reached out, clearly meaning to either hug him or squeeze his shoulder.

Neatly, he stepped away. If she touched him, he wasn't sure he could manage to conceal his revulsion.

Tilting her head, she considered him. "Why'd you leave all those years ago?" she asked quietly.

One of her tricks had always been to counter a question with another question instead of an answer, so he employed that now. "Did you even look for me? I was seventeen years old, out there on my own. Do you have any idea what kind of horrible things can happen to a boy that young?"

"Did they?" she asked. "I mean, did terrible things happen to you?"

Question after a question. He realized they could keep this up until the morning. "What do you want, Micheline?" he asked tiredly. "First you call me up and tell me you're dying, then you seem dedicated to avoiding me. Now all of a sudden, you've got something important to say. Why don't you just spit it out?"

Another woman might have decried the hardness in his voice or tearfully demanded to know what she'd done to deserve his apathy. Not Micheline. Either she already knew or she simply did not care. Jake would bet on the later. Or maybe even both.

"Fine," she sighed, her tone more annoyed than apologetic. "You're not really my son."

"What?" He snapped his head up, summoning back his first reaction when he'd learned the news. Shock and disbelief.

"It's true. We're not blood related. I switched you with another infant at the hospital when you were a day old."

Pretending shock seemed anticlimactic. Instead, he settled on rage. "Why?" he asked. "Why would you do such a thing?" Maybe now she'd give him some answers.

"I should have just given my baby up for adoption," she mused, still avoiding his question. "There was this other infant who wasn't doing so well. *You*."

Confused, he eyed her. "So you traded your healthy child? That doesn't even make sense." But then, knowing her, he realized it did. "You thought I was going to die, didn't you?" Horror filled him—fury, too.

Micheline, being Micheline, merely shrugged. She didn't even have the grace to try and appear ashamed. "To my surprise, you didn't. You thrived. The other baby started out sickly, but he did, too. *My* baby. I was able to keep tabs on him, because he became part of the most prominent family in Mustang Valley. My birth son is a Colton now. While you…" She let her gaze travel over him. "Clearly never felt any connection to me at all."

No remorse. No apologies. If anything, she seemed to be gloating. Horrible, awful woman.

When he'd been a child, he'd wondered what was wrong with him that his own mother couldn't seem to love him. As he'd grown and come to realize what kind of person Micheline actually was, he'd reckoned her lack of maternal instincts were a blessing in disguise. Despite that, he still carried scars from his younger years. This was one of the reasons he'd continually shied away from relationships: his fear of allowing any woman to hurt him the way his mother had.

"Do you even have cancer?" he asked abruptly. "Or was that sob story a ruse to get me to come home and see you?"

She narrowed her eyes. "How could you think such a thing?"

Again, not answering his question. "Because I know you. Do you or do you not have cancer?"

"I do," she finally replied, though she dropped her head to avoid meeting his eyes. "I'll be starting treatment soon."

"What treatment? Chemo? Radiation?"

"Yes. Both of those." She sighed heavily. "Instead of focusing on me, don't you want to know the name of the man who grew up with the life that should have been yours?"

Right for the jugular. She was a real piece of work, that Micheline. "You already told me. A Colton."

"There are a lot of Coltons all over the country," she countered.

"Sure." All he wanted now was to get her out of his room. "Who is it?"

"Ace Colton." Triumph rang in her voice. "He's one of the most valuable members of that powerful family."

Valuable. Odd choice of words. But sadly appropriate, since she always made sure Jake knew his existence held no value for her.

Be Your Best You. Her catchy little meaningless phrase flashed into his mind.

A flash of rage went through him, so strong he had to clench his hands into fists. He wanted to lash out, to tell her what he thought of her, and on top of that, how he felt about this, the ultimate betrayal.

Instead, he did none of those things. Partly because he suspected she wouldn't care and partly because he really wanted to know what she planned to do now.

Swallowing, he looked down at his feet, taking deep

breaths and stuffing his anger back deep inside. When
he felt he could speak normally, he raised his head to
find her watching him, her expression both gleeful and
yet somehow full of pseudo-concern. Even here, alone
with him, she still felt the need to continue to play a role.

"Why tell me this now?" he asked.

"I'm dying," she replied, injecting a note of pathos into
her tone. "And I'm trying to right the wrongs of my past."

Coming from anyone else, anyone but her, he might
have believed that. After all, that was exactly the kind
of thing a rational, caring human being might do in their
final months or years of life. But this was Micheline. He
might have been gone from her life for the last twenty-
three years, but he knew damn well she hadn't changed.
Not one bit.

"The truth, Micheline," he prompted, letting some of
his exhaustion show. "What's your angle?"

At that, she drew herself up. "I don't have an *angle*,
as you so charmingly put it. I run one of the largest self-
help organizations in Arizona. People look up to me, and
I help them. I *help* them, Jake. Not hurt them. Because of
me, thousands of people are becoming their best selves."

Ugh. If he heard that tired old phrase one more time.

"Are you afraid the baby-switch story will get out?"
he asked, watching her closely. "If your followers learned
what you did, maybe they wouldn't follow you."

That made her laugh. And laugh. So long and so hard
tears streamed down her cheeks. Finally, she got herself
together, grabbing a tissue off his dresser and dabbing
at her face. "Not likely," she managed.

Since he didn't have a response for that, he simply
jerked his chin in a reasonable facsimile of a nod. About
to tell her to get out, he closed his mouth when she spun

around on her expensive high-heeled shoes and strode to the door. "Take care, Jake." She fluttered her fingers. "I'm sure we'll talk again. I'm guessing you're sticking around awhile, since you and Fiona appear to have a thing going on."

"Maybe," he allowed. "But if I do decide to leave, I'll make sure and have one of your minions inform you."

"Minions!" She tittered, though her eyes remained hard. "How quaint. And really, you should give it a few more days. Things are just about to get really interesting around here. And you might be able to play a big part in it."

And then she left, shutting him in his room with a decisive click of the door.

He wanted to throw something, break something, toss back a shot or two of whiskey. Instead, he thought of Fiona, with her lush body and huge brown eyes. Though she too had lied to him, she'd had good reason. She had a mission, a task, and if there was anything he could do to help her accomplish it, he would. He wanted to dedicate his life to bringing Micheline down. Helping Fiona, who seemed as different from Micheline as night from day, would help expunge some of his bitterness and maybe even help him heal.

Things were about to get interesting around here, Micheline had said. Which meant Fiona was right—the cult leader had something planned, though he didn't know what, only that it appeared to involve him. And maybe even the Coltons.

Too drained to do anything but stay in his room, Jake tried to call Fiona, but she didn't pick up. He wondered if she'd been summoned by Micheline. Still, she was the last thing he thought of before he drifted off to sleep.

Ace Colton called right after breakfast the next morning. "The family would love to meet you," he said. "Payne was just released from the hospital. He's a bit weak, but he's eager to get to know you. Would you be available to come by the house for dinner tonight?"

"I'd love that," Jake replied.

"Perfect." Ace's voice turned serious. "I'll brief you a bit ahead of time. All the Coltons are trustworthy—the siblings, the triplet cousins—but Selina Barnes Colton, my father's ex-wife, is not to be trusted." Here he gave a small, self-conscious chuckle. "I guess I should have said *your* father's second wife. Selina is my ex-stepmother and is on the board of Colton Oil. She's a witch. At least Dad had the sense to divorce her. Genevieve is much nicer. Whatever you do, don't trust Selina. Just watch out for her, okay?"

"That I can do," Jake said. "I've read a little about all of them. As for Selina, I have some experience with women like that. I was raised by one."

"Ouch." Ace went silent for a moment and then continued on. "Anyway, even though it's going to be a huge family get-together, I don't want you to feel uncomfortable. I can try to get them to scale it back some. Payne got really excited and went overboard, despite barely being out of the hospital. Genevieve loves big parties. Though she's been invited, Selina is grinding her teeth."

"You know, I'd rather just meet your immediate family right now, if that's all right with you," Jake admitted. "It's already a lot to take in. Meeting the extended family right off the bat might be too much." Overwhelming, actually. Still in shock, he'd prefer to take this in small doses, a few people at a time.

"Thank goodness." Relief rang in Ace's voice. "At

least now I might stand a chance in hell of reasoning with Payne. Oh, and if you want to bring a date or a friend, that's fine, too."

Jake immediately thought of Fiona. Would she want to go, or was it too much, too soon? Though they'd made love, they barely knew each other. He guessed it would depend on whether or not a dinner with the Colton family fit into her mission. "I'll let you know," he said. "What time do you want me to be there?"

"How about seven?"

"Sounds good. I'll text you if I decide to bring someone."

"Ah, you've got to ask her first."

"Exactly." Smiling, Jake ended the call. He wouldn't exactly blame Fiona if she begged off going. Still, it didn't hurt to ask.

Chapter 7

As soon as she rose the next morning, Fiona showered and rushed through her makeup and getting dressed. At any minute, she expected either Leigh or Micheline to summon her and quiz her about her developing relationship with Jake. After all, the cult leader had walked in and found Fiona in Jake's bed.

When nothing happened, it almost felt anticlimactic. She guessed Micheline had seen enough to feel confident Jake would stay.

Fiona thought of Jake. Of the way his hands had felt on her skin, how his body had filled hers, how they'd fit together so well. While she wasn't usually prone to poetic, flowery thoughts about sexual mechanics, Jake had made her body sing.

Pleasantly sore, she wondered how he'd act around her now. Would things be strange? She hoped not. While

Micheline's dramatic entrance had made for an awkward ending to a wonderful night, she hoped Jake could get past all that. Privately, Fiona considered him the best part of this entire undercover assignment.

She pushed away her thoughts and made her way to the cafeteria for breakfast. Since only a small group of AAG members lived at the house full-time, the meals were set up buffet style. After grabbing a couple of spoonfuls of scrambled eggs, she took two slices of bacon and a muffin, filled her cup with coffee, and took a seat.

Jake appeared just as she took her first sip. He looked happy, she thought, watching as he went through the line and got his own breakfast. He made his way directly to her table.

"Mind if I join you?"

Her heart leaped at the sight of him, but she managed to keep her expression cool. "Have a seat."

Jake mustn't have been a morning person, either. She got it—most days she preferred not to have to speak to anyone until she'd downed a least one cup of coffee. They ate together in companionable silence, and it wasn't until they both finished their meal, when he offered to get her a refill, that she felt cheerful enough to initiate friendly conversation. "That'd be great, thanks."

"Cream and sugar?"

"No." She made a mock face. "Just black."

"Good choice."

When he returned a moment later, he placed both their coffees down on the table. "Do you want to hear what Micheline had to say last night?"

Immediately, she glanced around them, giving her head a tiny shake. "Not here," she mouthed.

"My bad," he mouthed back. "I forgot."

Curiosity won out. She pushed to her feet, taking another sip of her hot coffee. "Do you want to go for a walk? This is the best time of the day for that, as far as I'm concerned."

Taking the hint, he got up, too. "Sure."

Side by side, they took a leisurely stroll through the mostly empty lobby. Fiona made a show of gazing adoringly up at him.

Outside, he grinned. "You can stop with the adoring looks now."

"Who says I want to?" she quipped.

This made him laugh.

They continued on down the long, winding driveway. A small gravel path led to several of the maintenance sheds. Impulsively, Fiona took it.

"Where are we going?" Jake asked. "Are those storage buildings?"

"Yes, but we're not going that far." She looked around, taking care to make it casual. "I have no idea where they might have cameras hidden. I just want to make sure we don't have eyes on us."

"Paranoid much?" Jake teased. "Surely, Micheline doesn't have the entire grounds wired."

She shrugged. "Probably not. And I have to be paranoid. I can't take a chance on blowing my cover."

As they neared the largest maintenance shed, she spied a security camera mounted just under the roof. "Come here," she murmured, keeping her back to it. "Don't look, but I've spotted a camera. Give me a kiss so we can make it seem like we snuck off somewhere private to make out."

Again, that flash of a sexy grin. "Gladly."

He pulled her in close. The moment his mouth covered

hers, the lighthearted mood vanished. Passion, white-hot and fierce, flared instantly. For a moment, just that second in time, she allowed herself to give in to it, to him.

"Keep that up and we'll be doing a lot more than making out," he warned, the rasp in his voice matching the heat in his eyes.

"You're right." She took a deep breath, trying to steady herself. "I don't know why, but with you, I always get carried away."

Shaking his head, he yanked her close and kissed her again.

When he finally moved back, they were both shaking.

"Okay," she said, taking his hand and leading him back toward the driveway. "Tell me what Micheline had to say after I left your room last night."

Just like that, his smile vanished. Fiona actually felt awful for being the one to make it go away.

"Basically, she told me the truth. She switched me with another infant in the hospital. She even went so far as to tell me why."

Something in his voice… "Do I want to know?" she asked.

"Why not?" His mouth twisted. "She took me because one baby was sickly and the other wasn't and she wanted her child to be raised a Colton heir. ."

"Ouch." Wincing, she squeezed his hand. "She's a horrible person, but we already knew that. Still, that must have been hard to hear."

"It was. No matter that I know she's not related to me in any way by blood, despite being well aware of how awful and soulless she is, that still hurt. Made me wonder if all during my childhood, she might have been plotting to kill me and make it look like an accident."

Though she wouldn't have put it past Micheline, she kept that thought to herself. "Well, at least one good thing has come of this," she said instead. "You've got an entirely new family to get to know."

"True." He eyed her, his expression clearing. "Speaking of them, Ace invited me to dinner tonight. He said it would be okay to bring a plus-one. Would you like to go?"

"Me?" Her initial reaction was to refuse. First off, all they knew about her was that she was a member of AAG. Secondly, this was Jake's time, and why would the Colton family want an outsider to bear witness to what would surely be an emotional and touching reunion?

But then she realized maybe Jake might need her support.

And that trumped anything the Colton family might want.

"Yes, you." Leaning in close, Jake brushed a kiss on her cheek. "Up to you, no pressure. But I wouldn't mind having someone in my corner while I'm there. It's going to be awkward, no matter how you put it."

Just as she'd thought. He *needed* her. "I'd love to go," she responded. "It'll be fun."

He laughed again. "I wouldn't go that far. But it will be interesting, that's for sure. Meet me in the lobby around six thirty?"

"Perfect." Her phone chimed. She checked it and groaned. "That's Leigh. I'm being summoned. I'm guessing she'll want to go over my progress in convincing you to stay. I wish I knew why that's so important to Micheline. What part does she have planned for you to play?"

"I don't know," he replied. "If I can, I'll try to find out. In the meantime, I'm going into town to do some exploring. I'm guessing you won't be able to break free to go with me."

She tapped her phone. "It doesn't look like it. Enjoy your day and I'll see you tonight."

They walked back toward the house together, but instead of going inside, Jake veered off toward the parking lot and his truck. She stood in the drive and watched him go, waving once when he turned around to look back at her.

Inside the house, Fiona headed immediately toward Leigh's suite. To her surprise, no one answered when she knocked on the door. She tried the knob. It was locked. Now what?

She dug out her phone and texted Leigh. I'm here. Where are you?

Almost immediately, a text came back. I got called into a meeting. We'll have to reschedule later. There are a couple of good seminars starting up right now. Go learn.

Ugh. Attending another class ranked up there among things she'd avoid at all costs if possible. She responded with a smiley face emoji, aware that was vague enough that she couldn't be accused of lying later.

Now that she'd made it seem like she'd be occupied the next couple of hours, she could do some exploring. Ron Underhill, the man who'd been busted for attacking Theo, had mentioned something about cells. The stark terror in his expression meant they weren't a good place. Did Micheline have her own prison or holding cells somewhere on the property? Since Micheline acted like queen of her own little kingdom, Fiona wouldn't be surprised to learn the other woman meted out her own form of justice. Not just illegal, but if Fiona could obtain proof, it would be further grounds to not only arrest Micheline, but to shut the AAG down.

Though it was generally rare to find a house with a basement in Arizona, she had to wonder if Micheline had thought it worth the cost to have one. After all, if one were going to have prison cells, what better place to put them than underneath the house? Like dungeons in old castles.

Though she'd seen nothing to indicate this might be the case, the first thing she decided to look for was a door leading to a stairwell. She figured it wouldn't be any-where obvious or easy to get to, which ruled out the common areas. Maybe near the kitchen or the laundry area.

Generally, no one but the workers entered the kitchen, but when she pushed through the double doors, moving purposely as if she belonged there, no one stopped her. Which was good, because the best excuse she'd been able to come up with had been to say she'd gotten hungry and wanted to rustle up a snack.

After passing through the entire kitchen, which, with its gleaming stainless steel equipment, resembled some-thing found in a high-end restaurant, she emerged in a small hallway. Since she could now smell detergent and fabric softener, she guessed the laundry room would be down that way.

Why not? She might as well check it out since she'd come this far.

Sure enough, the next door on the left opened to a large laundry space, again more reminiscent of a hotel than a private home. Of course, the AAG center did house around twenty guests, plus maybe ten to fifteen staff members, though most of the workers made the drive in from town each day.

About to turn around and head back the direction from which she came, she realized the hallway didn't end after the laundry room, as she'd first supposed. A small hallway, an alcove really, sat on the right, just past it. And at the end of this, a door marked No Entrance.

Which meant it was probably kept locked.

Just in case, she tried the handle. To her surprise, it turned.

Glancing around her—she didn't even see any of the usual cameras she'd noticed everywhere—she opened the door and slipped inside.

Cement walls. And a concrete staircase, leading down. Still wishing she had her pistol, she began slowly descending the stairs, moving as quietly as possible.

Heart pounding, Fiona tried to imagine what she might find. A medieval-type torture chamber? A clean, gleaming modern prison? Or something in between?

At the bottom of the stairs, she encountered another door. Thick steel and windowless. This one was locked.

On the off chance that someone might have been careless, she stood on tiptoe and felt along the top of the door frame, hoping to find a key. No such luck.

Still, the mere fact that there was space under the house was worth looking in to. There had to be another entrance, she thought. Having only one way in and out would be unsafe, to say the least.

Turning, she retraced her steps. This time, when she went through the kitchen, she snagged a small bag of vegetable crisps from the pantry. One of the workers frowned at her but didn't comment.

She'd have to figure out another way to access the basement. Underhill's comments—and his very real terror—had made her curious to learn what other dark secrets Micheline might be hiding.

In downtown Mustang Valley, the well-decorated store windows and clean store fronts made Jake realize how much the locals loved this town. It also made him realize how seldom Micheline had let him leave. Even when he was a small child, she'd rarely taken him out in public. He'd actually believed that was normal until he'd learned from classmates about their celebrations.

Now that he knew Micheline had never really loved him, he had a better understanding of why his childhood had been so bleak. He knew now not to take it personally, but he wasn't sure how else to handle it.

Focus on the present, he reminded himself. He hoped and prayed the FBI could bring Micheline and the AAG down. And more than anything, he wanted to be there when it happened.

Once more, he pondered Micheline's actual plan. Was she trying to turn her cult into its own religion, make herself into the next prophet, sent by a higher being to tell her followers what to think and how to live their lives? Did she plan to delve deeper, beyond her Be the Best You seminars into something else?

He shook his head. Since he was sticking around here for a while—exactly how long, he hadn't yet decided— he hoped he could be there when Micheline was arrested and charged. She'd gotten away with so much over the years. Even before he'd left home, he'd been pretty sure he'd witnessed her hiding a body that one time.

Thoroughly exasperated with himself, he decided to put all thoughts of the woman who'd switched him at birth out of his mind. He needed to prepare himself mentally to meet the people with whom he should have been raised. The idea filled him with a crazy combination of anticipation and dread.

Ridiculous, if he thought about it. At forty years old, he'd overcome the handicaps of his past and knew he had an easygoing nature. Generally, he had no difficulties making friends. None of what had happened was his fault. In fact he, as well as the Colton family, was a victim in all this.

But would Payne Colton view it that way? From what Jake had read about him, the man wasn't someone who took well to being crossed. Surely, Payne wouldn't blame Jake for any of this.

Despite the mental pep talk he gave himself, he still felt nervous as he got ready to meet Ace's—*his*—family. He wasn't sure how they'd react to him now, with so many years gone by, especially after learning that all along, their true son had been living with a megalomaniac narcissist. *Their true son.*

He swallowed, the thought a bitter pill. Then he considered how Ace must feel, knowing his entire life had been one big lie. No matter what angle one came at the thing from, it all sucked.

A quiet tap on his door coaxed a reluctant smile. Fiona. Though they'd planned to meet in the lobby, she must have changed her mind and decided to come fetch him instead. He truly considered meeting her one of the best things about this visit.

Opening the door, he stared. She grinned at him, her long, dark hair swirling around her shoulders. She wore a silky white dress that clung to her figure and simple silver and turquoise jewelry.

"Well?" she asked, twirling slightly as she stepped inside his room. "Will this do?"

"You look amazing," he told her, leaning in for a quick kiss. "Let's go."

As usual, they made a show of strolling through the common area, hand in hand.

Once they were in his truck, she sighed. "This place is starting to get on my nerves. But you're not going to believe what I found. There's a basement under the main building."

She went on to describe a staircase with a door at the top and the bottom. "I couldn't get through, since the bottom door was locked."

"What do you think is on the other side?" he asked, backing out of the parking spot and driving down the long driveway.

"Well, when they dragged Underhill away, he started going on about cells, as in prison cells. I'm trying to see if perhaps Micheline has her own personal prison. Or torture chamber."

"I wouldn't put it past her." In fact, the more he considered, the more he believed Fiona was right. "I'll help you look for the other door," he said.

She eyed him. "It might be better if we look separately. There's much less chance of being discovered that way."

"Maybe," he allowed. "But it's also an easier explanation if we're caught. We can simply say we were looking for a private place to have a little fun."

This made her laugh, the sound light and feminine and making his heart squeeze. He needed to remember to be careful around this woman. The intensity of the feelings she aroused in him equaled how badly he could get hurt.

Following the directions on his phone GPS, Jake drove

through town and into the country, heading toward the mountains. On the way, they passed a huge wrought iron gate that barred entrance to a gated, clearly wealthy enclave. "I've never been in there," he murmured. "Until I began researching, I would have thought that would be the kind of place a Colton would live."

"Payne Colton is a rancher," Fiona said. "He and all of his family live at Rattlesnake Ridge Ranch. I've never been there, but I've seen lots of pictures. It's a gorgeous place, made to look like a luxurious guest ranch overlooking the Mustang Valley mountains."

"I'm aware, but how do you know all this?" he asked, curious.

She laughed. "Research. I had to do quite a bit of reading about Mustang Valley before I took this assignment."

They continued on, his GPS letting him know he still had about ten miles to go. The flat countryside seemed greener, maybe owing to the more fertile soil as they neared the high desert and the mountains.

Here there were what Jake thought of as ranchettes—wealthy people with luxurious homes and land who wanted to dabble in ranching or farming. He saw a smattering of horses, a few cattle, even a herd of goats, their glossy coats gleaming in the bright sunshine.

"This is beautiful," Fiona said, clearly impressed. "If I had money, I'd live someplace like this."

"Me, too," he replied absently. According to the GPS, they were nearly there.

She gave him a curious glance. "I thought you did. I swear you or someone told me you had your own ranch."

This made him laugh. "Oh, I do. But it's a real working ranch. Not all fancy like these."

"I'd love to see it someday," she said, surprising him.

Before he could figure out how to respond, the GPS announced they'd arrived at their destination. Ahead of them sat a home, surrounded by fenced fields. In the distance was an actual cattle ranch, with huge, fancy white barns, more fenced pastures and animals dotting the hillside. This place made his own small ranch look like nothing. He couldn't help but wonder what it must be like, running this kind of operation. He supposed he would have known, had not Micheline switched him and Ace.

"Wow." Jake slowed. "This is amazing. I wonder how much acreage they have."

"I believe I read thousands of acres," she said. "That's why there are no other houses after this one."

Gripping the wheel tightly, Jake turned into the long driveway. "Three stories and multiple wings." He shook his head. "This makes the AAG center look like a summer camp."

His comment made Fiona laugh. "Yes, it definitely does."

A huge gate marked the entrance to the ranch. Three *R*s were inset right in the center. "Rattlesnake Ridge Ranch," Fiona said. "I wonder if they really have a problem with rattlesnakes."

"That wouldn't work with livestock," Jake told her. "I'm sure they took care of getting rid of them."

"Maybe." Fiona shrugged. "But even if they wiped out the entire snake population one year, they couldn't ever completely eradicate them. Especially if they were so numerous the ranch was named after them."

"Annual rattlesnake roundup." Jake squinted into the sun. "That's what I'd do, anyway. And judging from the looks of some of those cattle, he's got some high-value herds here."

"Of course." Grinning, Fiona gestured at the expansive land, the stunning house, the quality fencing. "I mean, what do you expect for a Colton, right?"

He nodded. The Colton name had always been synonymous with luxury, the kind of lifestyle many in Mustang Valley wished they could emulate. Jake's research had revealed the family was not only wealthy, but kind. They participated in numerous charities and quietly helped many who were less fortunate. The more he learned about them, the more he realized they were to be admired.

Driving slowly, he finally pulled up close to the house. In addition to the driveway, there were separate garages with their own parking areas. He decided to park his truck there. They could walk up to the house.

They got out of the truck. As she walked to him, Fiona gazed around her. "Just think," she murmured, squeezing his shoulder. "If things had been different, you would have grown up here."

He grimaced, refusing to acknowledge the ache her words caused inside him. Not just the ranch or the riches or even the Colton name, but the idea of family, people who would stand by your side no matter what. Something he'd never had and never believed he would. "Probably so. I can't imagine. I've never seen a ranch like this."

"I wonder if this is why you became a rancher. Maybe it runs in your blood."

"That's a very real possibility." He didn't let on that that, too, hurt him. He'd never known the truth of his past, his heritage, his family. Now at long last, he might finally get some glimpses of understanding of some of the factors that had contributed to making him the man he was today.

Side by side, they walked up to the front door, and

he pressed the doorbell, wondering if there would be servants.

Ace himself answered the door, grinning. "Welcome," he said, clapping Jake on the back.

"This is Fiona Evans," Jake said. "Fiona, Ace Colton."

She held out her hand, but Ace pulled her in for a hug instead. Eyes wide, she made a face at Jake over Ace's shoulder, making him smile and breaking up some of the tension coiled inside him.

"Come on in," Ace invited.

When they stepped into the foyer, a delicious smell drifted their way. Mexican food, Jake thought. His favorite.

As they walked inside, Fiona's heels clicking on the wood-look tile floors, he caught sight of several people gathered in the kitchen. His heart jumped into his throat.

Some of his unease must have shown on his face.

"Relax," Ace murmured. "It's all good. Just my dad and my brothers and sisters, along with their significant others." He gave a self-conscious laugh. "Correction, *your* brothers and sisters. I managed to get them all to come to dinner on short notice. Please understand, my father—*your* father—just got out of the hospital." He glanced toward the kitchen. "He's still a bit weak, though don't let him know I said that. He prides himself on being strong."

"I remember hearing about that," Fiona interjected. "He was shot, wasn't he? I'm so glad to hear he's on the mend."

Jake glanced at Ace. Payne had been shot and in a coma at the very same hospital where Jake and Ace had been switched at birth. Ace had actually been accused of shooting him after it was discovered he wasn't Payne's son. As Ace had told him, the real killer had been caught, but Ace had lost his job as CEO of Colton Oil since the company's bylaws stated the company's CEO had to be a biological Colton.

Enduring all of that must have been hell. Jake couldn't help but admire Ace for making his way through it so well.

"Are you ready?" Ace asked. "They're all eager to meet you."

"Likewise," Jake replied, pretending his stomach wasn't clenched into knots. As if she knew, Fiona slipped her arm through his, offering her physical support.

Then the introductions started. An older man with silver hair moved slowly over, leaning on a cane. "Damn bandages," he muttered. He stepped forward, his gaze intense as he shook Jake's hand. This must be his father, Payne, with his latest wife, Genevieve, standing slightly behind him, her expression both concerned and friendly.

His *father*. Jake had never figured he'd even know his father's name, never mind meet him. Wary, a bit uncertain, Jake eyed the older man, not sure what to say or how to act.

Before Jake and Payne could even exchange words, the older man enveloped Jake in a gruff, partial hug. "Sorry, I'm still a bit sore," Payne said. "We've known about your existence a good while now, though we had no idea who you'd turn out to be. You don't know how good it is to finally meet you."

"Same here," Jake replied.

Ace clapped both men on the back. "First we all got an anonymous email, letting us know I was switched with another infant in the hospital. Next, some guy named Jace Smith claimed to be the Colton baby that was switched."

Ace shook his head. "This must have infuriated Micheline, because she eventually waltzed into our office and announced she'd been the one to do it and she alone knew who was the missing Colton heir."

Spoken without a single note of rancor or bitterness. Again, Jake couldn't help but admire the man.

"I'm almost glad I was in a coma for most of this," Payne said. When he raised his head to look into Jake's face, Payne's eyes gleamed with unshed tears. "She's a piece of work, that Micheline. I wish you could have met Tessa," he said, his voice breaking. "Your mother. You look so much like her. She died from lung cancer years ago, when all three of her children were young. She was kind, loved animals and had a big heart. She was an amateur photographer, always with the camera. Pretty damn good at it, too. She would have been thrilled to meet you."

Rummaging in his pocket, he pulled out a wallet and extracted a creased photograph. "This was her, holding who we thought was Ace in the hospital. She had no idea any of this ever happened."

Accepting the snapshot, Jake's breath caught in his chest. His mother had been beautiful, with long, dirty-blond hair and a kind, expressive face. *Tessa.* The woman who'd carried him, birthed him and lost him, had never known her baby had been switched. And now she never would. Jake couldn't believe she was dead. Ace must have forgotten to mention that. Jake nodded, struggling to find the right words. To his surprise, tears stung the backs of his eyes, too. "She's lovely," he managed, passing the photograph back. "I would have loved to meet her."

"I would have liked that as well," the old rancher said. Turning slowly, he eyed Ace and beckoned him over.

"You're both my sons, no matter what. Please understand that."

Ace smiled. "Thanks, Dad." He raised his head and sniffed the air. "That food smells insanely good. When are we going to eat?"

"Let Jake meet the others first," Payne chided, seemingly oblivious to the way his current wife continued to glare at his back. "Come on, Jake. Let me introduce you and your lovely friend to the rest of the family."

Grabbing Fiona's hand, Jake followed his father. He met his full sister Ainsley, an attorney for Colton Oil, and her fiancé, fellow lawyer Santiago Morales. Next his brother Grayson, a first responder who kept his arm around his date, Savannah. Then his younger half sister, Marlowe, a pretty blonde who said she was the current CEO of Colton Oil, her fiancé, Bowie, and their baby son, Reed. Her twin Callum, a muscular man who said he worked as a bodyguard, appeared with his live-in love, Hazel, and her daughter, Evie. Hazel was a chef and had prepared their dinner this evening. Ace's daughter Nova, visibly pregnant, smiled shyly while her beau, Nikolas, shook Jake's hand. Rafe Colton, Payne's adopted son, was there with his fiancée, Detective Kerry Wilder, and so were Marlowe's and Callum's brother, Asher, and his love, Willow, with their baby daughters. Jake also met a petite, slender woman with reddish-blond hair named Sierra Madden, Ace's girlfriend. Triplet cousins Spencer, Bella, and Jarvis Colton—along with their respective partners, Katrina, Holden, and Mia, plus Mia's son, Silas—were also in attendance.

Selina, Payne's second wife, had apparently declined to attend, as Jake saw no sign of her.

By the time the introductions had finished, Jake felt

better. He'd give himself a fifty-fifty shot at remembering the names, but everyone seemed kind and easygoing.

"Time for dinner," Genevieve announced, her soft voice matching her large, kind eyes. They all traipsed after her to a large formal dining room. Inside, an amazing Western-style, cedarwood table had been set with plates of every color. The decor seemed like a mix between Western and a Mexican fiesta. Elegant, yet homey. He liked it a lot.

"Fiestaware," Fiona breathed. "My favorite."

"There are place cards on the table," Genevieve continued, her formal tone softening some as she looked at the twins. "I know Hazel has prepared an amazing meal for us tonight."

With much scraping of chairs, they all sat down to eat. Looking around at his new family, a sense of peace settled in Jake's heart. These, he thought, were his people. Someday he might be able to sit at this table and feel as if he belonged here. Tonight would be the start of something good.

Chapter 8

"You know what? I don't want to go back to the AAG center," Fiona murmured, her head resting comfortably on Jake's broad shoulder, after dinner. "That was some seriously good company. And the food…" She rolled her eyes, even though he couldn't see. "Wow. Just wow."

"Better buckle up," he advised, smoothing her hair away from her face. The husky note in his voice heated her blood. "You know as well as I do that we both have to go back."

He was right. After all, they couldn't sit in the Colton ranch and make out like a couple of horny kids in the front seat of his truck. With great reluctance, she slid back into the passenger side and fastened the seat belt. "Did you enjoy yourself?" she asked.

"Yeah, I haven't tasted carne asada that good outside of a pricey restaurant," he replied.

She glanced up at him. He stared straight ahead, his concentration on the road as he drove, but there'd been a hint of remoteness in his voice. As if he'd shut down to avoid dealing with what surely had to be a tangled web of emotions.

Her phone pinged, indicating a text. Can you talk? Holden texted.

"I need to make a call," she told Jake. "Work related. It'll just take a second." Then, instead of texting Holden back, she punched in the number to call him.

"What's up?" she asked.

"Not much," he answered, his tone cheerful. "I wanted to check in with you and see if you've learned anything new."

"I might. That depends." She told him about the basement and the possibility of cells or a jail of some sort under the house. "I'm working on trying to gain access," she said. "They also had me working on some poor college freshman, trying to get him to sign up for seminars at a grand a pop. They prey on people who are desperate enough to try anything."

"True. Unfortunately, as long as their victims receive what they were promised for their money, it's not a crime."

"I know. But there's more, though I don't have concrete evidence yet. Our intel is correct. Micheline is planning something big, though I haven't been able to learn yet what it might be. I'm trying really hard to gain the welcome coordinator's confidence."

"Leigh?"

"Yep. And they've assigned me to get close to the son in order to get him to stick around." She shot a quick glance at Jake, who continued to watch the road, though she knew he was listening.

"What's he like?" Holden asked.

"Jake? Oh, he's all right," she replied, grinning. "He's easy on the eyes, so that helps."

"Well, that's good, I suppose. As long as he's not another one of those crazy cult members." Holden sounded amused. "Keep me posted if anything changes."

She promised she would and ended the call. "My colleague," she explained. "I try to keep him updated periodically, but I can only do it when I'm not at the center."

"Makes sense." He eyed her thoughtfully. "Is it hard to play your role?"

"Sometimes," she admitted. "Especially when I have to do something that's abhorrent to me, like try and fleece a young college student. But I know it's for the greater good in the end. Once we get enough information to arrest and convict Micheline, I'll be proud of myself for doing my job so well."

"I'll be looking forward to that day, too."

A thought occurred to her. Crazy, maybe. But she could use all the help she could get.

"Maybe you should play along, too," she said, not sure how he'd receive this idea.

As she'd expected, Jake shot her an incredulous look. "Play along how?"

"Well, clearly Micheline needs you for some part of her plan. What if you were a willing participant?" When he started to speak, she held up her hand. "Hear me out. As you know, Micheline is all about two things. Money and power. If you can convince her that you crave those as well, she might be willing to let you in on her little plan."

"The woman switched me with another baby at birth."
The flat note in his voice and the tight set of his jaw spoke
volumes. "Why would she care what I want?"

The more she considered, the more she liked the idea.
"If it benefits her, she'll care a lot."

"No." Just that. Nothing more.

"I understand." She shrugged. "I'll admit that I'm disappointed, too, but I get it. Sort of."

As she'd suspected it might, her response earned her
another sharp, sideways glance.

"It'd make your skin crawl," she continued. "I know it
does mine. Everything that woman stands for is the opposite of my own beliefs."

"But if in the end, what you do helps keep her from
hurting other people, it's worth it," Jake finished for her.
"No need to pile it on any thicker. I get it. I'll do it. Or at
least try. What do you suggest?"

Now it was her turn to eye him. "Tell her you want
to meet with her. Refuse to take no for an answer. Then,
when you do, tell her you want something in return for
all the grief she's caused you. Play it by ear. I guarantee
she'll relate."

"Oh, she'll relate," he said, his voice grim. "Greed is
one of her highest motivators."

Fiona nodded. "Remember, don't do anything that will
put you in any sort of danger. But if you can get her to
think you're completely on board, and she might stand to
gain financially, then you might be able to learn something important."

"Why not?" he said. "It'll keep me from getting bored,
plus I'll feel as if I'm actually contributing toward Micheline's downfall."

He spoke without rancor, his tone matter-of-fact. She

wondered what all he'd seen in his seventeen years with a woman who'd never wanted him and certainly hadn't loved him. She considered it a small miracle that Jake had grown up relatively unscathed.

"Did someone help you?" she asked. "After you left home? Seventeen is awfully young for a kid to be on his own. Did you even have any money?"

"Actually, I did. Micheline had me homeschooled, so I didn't have any friends my own age. I started working at Burger Barn when I was sixteen. Micheline didn't know. By then, she was already busy starting up her foundation." He grimaced. "The people I worked with—other teens mostly—were my first real friends. Despite the temptation to party with them, I saved every penny I made. Because I already had a plan. I also managed to keep it hidden from Micheline. If she'd found it, she wouldn't have had any qualms about taking every cent."

"That doesn't surprise me," Fiona remarked.

"Yeah. And I did have help. I used some of my money to buy an old motorcycle. I headed north, figuring I'd keep going until I found a place that felt right."

He went quiet for a moment, clearly lost in his thoughts. "I was driving through this small ranching town when I saw someone toss a kitten from a car window. I pulled over, and the little thing was still alive, though injured. I picked it up and drove to the veterinary clinic I'd just passed." He shook his head. "They were amazing. The vet, an older man named John Letcalf, rushed the kitten into emergency surgery to repair a broken jaw. They let me hang out in the waiting room and gave me a drink and some chips. I think they knew…"

Watching him, her heart swelled. He'd been through so much.

After a moment, he continued. "In the end, Dr. Letcalf fixed the kitten and promised to find it a home. And he offered me a job and a place to stay." His voice had gone rough. "If not for him and his wife, I don't know what would have happened to me."

Fascinated, she nodded. "So you worked at the vet clinic?"

"No. Actually, he and his wife lived on a ranch. He hired me on as a ranch hand. It was a big enough place that the hands had their own bunkhouse. I learned everything I know today about cattle ranching from that job. Believe me, it wasn't anything near as fancy as the Coltons' operation, but was a profitable, working cattle ranch."

"Is that the same one you own now?" she asked.

"No. Dr. Letcalf's wife got dementia. He retired, sold the veterinary clinic to two of his partners. His son took over the ranch. He let me stay on, but I knew it would be only temporary. When one of the neighboring ranches went up for sale, I bought it. It's much smaller—only a couple hundred acres—but works for me."

"I'm impressed." She smiled at him. "Let me guess. You saved up every penny you made working for Dr. Letcalf."

He nodded. "You would be correct. I wasn't able to pay cash for the place, but I had more than enough for a hefty down payment. Still, Dr. Letcalf had to cosign for me. I had no credit history at all."

Unable to resist, she reached over and touched his arm. "Still, you overcame tremendous odds and made something of yourself."

"Thanks." He glanced at her, making her wish it

wasn't too dark to read his expression. "What about you? What's your story?"

"I grew up in Phoenix. My father was a police officer and my mother a teacher. I was an only child. I had a basic, boring, wholesome childhood." She swallowed hard. "It was great, actually. Until the day my dad was killed by a drunk driver. Life changed in an instant."

"I'm sorry," he said.

She nodded. "Thanks. After that happened, I focused my entire life's purpose on becoming a cop. When I got to college, I took criminal justice classes. The FBI recruited me right after graduation, and here I am."

"That's impressive, too," he told her.

"Maybe. I always wished my dad were alive to see what I've done with my life."

"I'm sure he knows. What about your mother?"

"Oh, she's proud, though she can't really relate. She retired from teaching and keeps busy with a bunch of volunteer work. She still lives in the same house I grew up in, though she's remarried."

They turned down the long drive leading to the AAG Center.

"I wonder how she came up with this idea," Fiona mused of the AAG. "Even her catchphrase is kind of general, as if she couldn't think of anything better."

"She was working toward something like this even when I was a young child," Jake said. "Because she truthfully believes everyone else is an idiot, she always used short, catchy sound bites." He shrugged. "It seems to have worked out for her."

"Yeah." Fiona shuddered. "But try sitting through seminar after seminar, hearing *Be Your Best You* over and over. Now, whenever someone says it, I fight the urge to be sick."

He laughed. "Well, we're here. You'd better get ready to put your game face on."

"I'm ready," she said, though she was reluctant to get out of the car. "What about you? Are you sure you're up for this?"

Slowly, he nodded. "I like that you're giving me the option of saying no. But I really want to help, even if every time I have to be nice to that woman, I want to vomit. It helps to know you can relate."

"Oh, can I ever." She got out of the truck, waiting for him to join her. Together, they walked back toward the house. When he took her hand, interlacing his fingers with hers, warmth blossomed inside her. Right before they reached the front porch, she turned to face him. "Good luck with Micheline."

"Thanks. I might even go look for her tonight."

As it turned out, Jake didn't have to go through all of the trouble of badgering Micheline for a meeting. She appeared at his door moments after he got in himself. *Good.* After meeting his family and seeing the ranch, he now understood what all she'd taken from him. At least Payne had survived. Jake felt bad enough that he'd lost the opportunity to meet his late mother. He was grateful he'd have the chance to get to know his father.

Now, he braced himself for the confrontation about to come. At least she knocked this time.

"Micheline?" He didn't have to pretend to be surprised. "What are you doing here?"

"I've been waiting for you to come back," she said.

"A little birdie told me you paid a visit to the Rattlesnake Ridge Ranch."

Which meant she must have already spoken to Fiona across the hall. "I did," he replied. "I can't believe that all of that could have been mine. My little ranch is nothing compared to that spread." He glared at her, keeping his expression hard. "You owe it to me to help me figure out a way to get part of that place. They view me as an outsider and likely always will. Since you switched me with Ace forty years ago, it's on you to make sure I'm not cheated out of what's rightfully mine."

Mouth slightly agape, she stared at him. "How do you suggest I do that?"

Instead of answering, he crossed his arms.

She crossed the room, going to his small window and pushing aside the curtains. "I may have an idea or two," she said thoughtfully. "But as I'm sure you've already guessed, I'll want a cut."

"A cut?" This was the tricky part. "Why would I give you anything? You're the one who basically ruined my life."

"If you want my help, you've got to be willing to pay," she snapped. Then, softening her tone, she continued. "Look, I'm pretty sure there's a way we can work together, but it's got to be mutually beneficial."

Boom. Slowly, he nodded, though he kept his jaw tight. "I'm listening."

She began to pace back and forth, making the short distance in a few strides, as if standing at the front of one of her packed lecture halls. "You have something of value now, Jake. Yourself. You're one of them, a Colton. They don't want to lose you again. We just need to figure out a way to make them understand they owe you.

All those years when they were raising someone else's child…" She stopped, gazing off into the distance, her eyes slightly unfocused.

It took an effort, but Jake managed to refrain from shaking his head. An act. He'd seen her play this one before. Maybe her persona had become so ingrained in her, she couldn't help but carry on with her role-playing. She probably no longer remembered how to be honest or human. "You know some guy tried to pass himself off as the baby who was switched."

"I heard. Payne Colton mentioned him. Jace Smith."

"Yeah. He thought he could pull his own con. Little did he know that I was Luella Smith."

"That's your real name?" He couldn't help but gape.

"Micheline Anderson is who I am." She shrugged, the movement both elegant and weirdly frenetic. "He went away finally. I'm sure the Coltons must have asked for a DNA test."

"I've been waiting for them to ask me to take one," he said.

"Go ahead and take it. I guarantee it will confirm you are a Colton. I should know."

"I will. The sooner I can prove my identity beyond a shadow of a doubt, the quicker I can get what I deserve."

Too much? Conscious of holding his breath, he forced himself to exhale. Meanwhile, Micheline watched him with narrowed eyes and flat expression.

"Let me think about it," she finally said. "Once I devise a workable plan, I'll let you know."

Which meant she hadn't fallen for it. She didn't believe him. Maybe she knew him better than he gave her credit for.

He dipped his chin. About to tell her it sounded good,

he reconsidered. "I thought you already had some sort of plan," he said.

Her blank stare didn't fool him. "Why would you think that?"

"I don't. Maybe because you so badly wanted me to stick around for a while. I knew there had to be a reason."

She blinked, a rapid fluttering of her false eyelashes. One of her tells, which meant she was about to straight up lie.

"Don't." One hand forestalled her. "I've had enough of your BS. Just give it to me straight."

"Fine. How would you like to become not only CEO of Colton Oil, but a multimillionaire?"

Though these were all things he could get on his own, he decided to play along to see where she might be going with this. "I'm listening."

"Let me work on it." Confident again, she reached out and touched his arm. It took every ounce of self-control he possessed not to flinch away from her.

"Make it worth my while," he said. "And I promise I'll make sure it's worth yours."

With a smile and a brusque nod, she spun on her heels and left his room, closing the door firmly behind her.

After she'd gone, he debated taking a long, hot shower. Even pretending to go along with her made him feel unclean, like no amount of soap or water could wash the stain away.

Instead, he found himself crossing the hall to stand outside Fiona's room. He tapped lightly, in case she'd fallen asleep. A second later, she opened the door with the wild hair and wide-eyed yet sleepy look that he found sexy as hell. She still wore the outfit she'd put on to have dinner at the Coltons and hadn't yet washed her makeup off.

"Did I wake you?" he murmured.

"No," she lied. "I might have just closed my eyes for a minute or two." Stepping aside, she gestured at him. "Come on in."

He did. Once she'd closed the door, he took in her room, a carbon copy of his but in reverse. Odd how a few items here and there could make her space so feminine. She'd clearly made an attempt to decorate, which for some reason surprised him.

"It's not much, but I tried to make it feel like home," she said, correctly interpreting his thoughts. "I mean, why not? I knew I was going to be living here, after all."

"Micheline just left," he began.

Fiona quickly shook her head, one finger against her lips to quiet him. She moved forward, wrapping herself around him. "Not here, not now," she murmured, so quietly he had to strain to hear it. And then she kissed him.

Instantly aroused, he let himself drown in her, the contradictions of her athletic yet soft body, her sensual nature and the air of innocence she managed to maintain despite no doubt having seen things that would give grown men nightmares.

She was wild yet restrained, beautiful and smart and the most interesting woman he'd ever met.

Still kissing, they helped each other get rid of the clothing that stood between their skin. Naked, eager, they rushed to press their bodies together once more.

Later, much later, he held her in his arms as she dozed, wondering how the hell he was ever going to be able to let her go.

Waking in the early morning, Jake gathered his clothing and crept back to his room. Good thing he did, because no sooner had he gotten out of the shower than Micheline knocked on his door.

He couldn't help but remember how he couldn't even get her to talk to him when he'd first arrived.

"Here." She shoved a cardboard cup of coffee at him as she breezed past. "Drink up. I want you awake when we hammer out the details."

Details. At any second, he expected her to whip out a contract for him to sign.

Taking a sip of his coffee, he eyed Micheline fidgeting near the doorway. The coffee—whatever it was—tasted rich and expensive. It certainly wasn't what they served in the lunchroom or the lobby. "What is this?" he asked, making sure his appreciation showed in his voice. "It's amazing."

"I have it flown in from Jamaica," she said, drinking deeply of her own mug. "My own personal blend."

Noting the way her hands shook, he wondered if she was on something. Or perhaps, *off* her meds. He had no idea what she might be taking or for what. One thing was for sure—he didn't believe she was doing anything for her supposed cancer.

Finally, she stopped moving long enough to perch on the single chair. "I've thought about several possible scenarios," she began. He couldn't help but notice the way her pupils seemed enlarged. Definitely drugs, he thought. Though what kind?

He took another drink of the rich coffee, allowing himself to savor it. "Go on," he replied, his tone neutral. He realized how little Micheline truly knew about him. Did she really think he'd go to such lengths to avoid the work of getting to know his family?

"You could sue the Coltons," she announced. "They owe you for all the years of lost benefits. I bet they would have paid for you to go to college. And your rinky-dink little cattle ranch—they probably would have bought you a much nicer one. You should take them to court and make them pony up. I bet they feel so guilty, they won't even fight you."

Was she high? Because that was the craziest bunch of nonsense he'd ever heard her utter.

Remembering Fiona's advice, he swallowed back an incredulous response. Instead, he pretended to consider Micheline's words.

"I'm not sure that would work," he finally allowed. "I'd become their enemy. I want power and influence, as well as money. That can only be gotten if I'm part of them, not against them."

She narrowed her eyes at him before sipping again on her drink. "That takes time, which is the one thing I don't have an overabundance of. I need to get my hands on a lot of cash fast."

"Why?"

The disgusted look she shot him made him want to smile, though he managed not to.

"Because I don't have long to live," she snapped. "Are you honestly that stupid?"

He locked his jaw, breathing deeply, summoning up enough self-control so he didn't snarl something equally rude back at her. Old habits apparently died hard. Instead, he arranged his features into what he hoped would be a suitably abashed expression. "Sorry. I guess I just don't like to even imagine the possibility of you being gone."

Instantly gratified, Micheline preened. "I *knew* you hid your attachment to me," she gloated. "I never could understand how you made yourself stay away so long. You must have missed me terribly."

Talk about wanting to gag. He managed to make himself nod.

"You may be right," she admitted, jingling multiple bracelets on one of her arms in a repetitive motion that set his teeth on edge. "I'll need to think on it. Now that we're working together, if any good plans occur to you, be sure and discuss them with me immediately."

"Of course I will."

"Good." She pushed to her feet, finally stopping the noise. "I'll be working mostly out of here the next week. Let Leigh know if you need to see me."

"Will do." He held back his sigh of relief until she was actually gone.

At the doorway, she spun around so fast, she staggered. For one awful second, he thought she might go down. Instinctively, he moved to catch her, but she managed to grab on to the door frame and catch herself right before he reached her. Her coffee, however, slipped from her grasp and spilled all over the floor.

"Are you all right?"

She lifted her head and met his gaze, her lips pulling back from her teeth in what he supposed she thought was a smile. "I'm fine." With that final lie, she shook her head and pointed to the spilled coffee. "Make sure you clean that up."

Once she'd gone, he grabbed one of the extra bath towels and mopped up the mess. Luckily, the AAG center provided maid service, so he knew someone would change the towel out later that day.

Wow. Eyeing his own coffee cup, he carried it over to the sink and poured the rest of it out. Quite simply, he'd lost his taste for Micheline's expensive coffee. In fact, he wasn't even sure he could eat breakfast.

One thing was for sure—he now had a newfound respect for Fiona and her ability to do her job and somehow manage to maintain her sanity.

He decided he'd go across the hall and see if Fiona needed some help waking up.

Just the thought had his body instantly hard.

The soft tap on his door startled him. Had Micheline come back? He swore under his breath and went to the door.

Fiona stood there, barefoot, wearing a T-shirt and tiny shorts, her eyes huge. "Mornin'," she said, her husky voice stirring up all kinds of trouble inside him. "May I come in?"

Instantly, he stepped aside. Barely had the door clicked shut behind him than they were wrapped up in each other's arms.

They shed what little clothing they had on quickly, still kissing. Skin to skin, they fell together onto his bed. One thrust and he buried himself deep inside her. Instantly, she convulsed, her body caressing his. So warm, so tight, enough to drive him mad.

Somehow, he managed to hang on to his rapidly shredding self-control. Once her shudders had subsided, he began to move. Slowly at first, but as momentum built, he abandoned all attempt at restraint.

Each time they came together, it was fireworks and trumpets: crazy stuff he'd never really believed in. They fit perfectly, and though they hadn't known each other very long, lovemaking felt instinctive. Somehow, he felt he knew just what to do and how to do it to take her to the edge of the cliff and beyond. And as for her…just one touch, one look, one kiss and she sent him over the moon.

After, sated and content, they lay in each other's arms. He propped himself up on one elbow and looked at her.

"What?" she asked, peering up at him through drowsy eyes.

"You're beautiful," he mused. "And special." Taking a deep breath, he decided he might as well go for it. "I'm falling in love with you."

She froze. Then, refusing to look at him, she slowly edged herself out of his arms. "Don't," she said.

Whatever reaction he'd expected, it hadn't been this. "Don't what?"

"Don't ruin this." Still, she wouldn't look at him. He felt the awful weight of her words settle in heavy in the pit of his stomach.

When she finally turned to meet his gaze, her expression stern and full of resolve, he knew what she was going to say before she even opened her mouth.

"We're good together, true. And I like you, Jake Anderson. I like you a lot." She reached out her hand to touch him. He jerked away.

"Don't be like that," she urged, her voice soft. "We're good together. I know it as well as you do. But I need to focus on my life here, becoming my best me. You know what I mean. Until I do that, I won't be able to—"

"I get it." He cut her off. Ever conscious of the probability of someone listening. Two could play that game. "What if Micheline *herself* wants you to be involved with me?"

Her eyes widened. "She does." She sounded confident. Certain. "At least that's what Leigh told me. I'm not sure what her motivation is, though. I'm sure it's something nefarious."

"We'll see about that," he muttered, more for the benefit of anyone listening than anything else.

"Jake. You don't mean that."

"You're right," he responded immediately. "But there's one thing you should know about me. I don't give up easily. I know beyond a shadow of a doubt that we can have something special."

She nodded, her expression sad. "It's just bad timing," she began.

Since his chest already hurt, he knew he didn't want to hear anymore. Not right now. Not for a good while. Hell, maybe not ever.

A horrible revelation hit him. Was Fiona using him to help her make the case against his mother? Again, he didn't have to wonder if she could actually be this deceitful. Micheline had long ago set the bar for that.

He needed to shut down the emotions swirling through him, and quickly. If he'd truly been such a fool, he'd deal with it later, when he could go off somewhere and lick his wounds.

Grabbing up his clothes, he dressed hurriedly, without looking at her. "Take care, Fiona." He crossed to the door without a backward glance, opening it and stepping aside so she could pass. "I'll be seeing you around, I'm sure."

Chapter 9

She'd done the right thing, turning Jake down, Fiona thought. Even though right now, it didn't feel like it. She truly believed this, beyond any shadow of a doubt. But then why did her heart feel as if it was breaking? Why did the backs of her eyes sting and her throat feel like it had closed up?

The vulnerable look in Jake's eyes, the hope turning to pain, killed her. He'd eyed her steadily, as if he knew the truth no matter how much she might deny it. But how could he, when she didn't even know it herself? The only thing Fiona knew for certain was her job. Over the years, she'd built a reputation as someone reliable, someone who didn't make mistakes. She'd already made a huge one by revealing her mission to Jake. She couldn't compound that by making another one.

Rule number seven of the undercover handbook: don't

get seriously romantically involved with someone. Male agents had casual flings all the time. She'd definitely heard the stories.

Since Micheline herself had, for whatever reason, wanted Fiona to get close to Jake, everything had seemed to naturally fall into place. A little fun, some mind-blowing sex and no one got hurt. Except now apparently, Jake had.

When she'd allowed herself to give in to the insane attraction she felt toward Jake, she'd never expected this. The absolute certainty that he could definitely be the one. Even worse, she wasn't sure she could trust the feeling. How much of it was due to the role she played while undercover here at the AAG center? If she'd met him during her regular, normal life, working from the FBI field office, and they'd gone on the usual dates at trendy gastropubs or bars, would things have ignited so quickly between them?

She didn't know. For that reason alone—okay, that was only one of the reasons—she had no choice but to focus on the mission. When all of this was finally over, the case wrapped up in a neat little bow, maybe then she'd have the luxury of finding out if what she and Jake had might be real.

Leigh buzzed her a few minutes later, summoning her to her suite. Instantly alert, Fiona told her she was on her way, glad to have something to focus on besides the mess she'd made of things with Jake.

When she got to Leigh's hallway, she realized Leigh stood in the doorway, waiting for her. The other woman practically buzzed with excitement.

"Come in, come in," Leigh urged. "There's a lot going

on today, but Micheline asked me to speak to you specifically."

Fiona followed her inside. "About what?" she asked,
wondering if she'd be called on the carpet for her rebuff
of Jake. While she knew they listened in on her, if Leigh
brought this up now, it would be tantamount to admitting
her room and Jake's had been bugged.

"Take a seat." Leigh gestured toward a pair of antique
chairs near her fireplace. Idly, Fiona wondered how many
of the rooms in this place actually had fireplaces. Not
too many, she'd bet.

Fiona sat.

Instead of sitting next to her, Leigh bounced around
the room. In place of her usual fashionable high heels,
Fiona noticed Leigh was barefoot. And so hyped up, she
couldn't stay still.

Drugs? Fiona wouldn't have thought Miss Mustang
Valley was the type, but who knew. If Micheline had ordered her to take something, no doubt Leigh would have
obeyed. Though why?

Increasingly alarmed, Fiona repeated her question.
"What's going on, Leigh?"

"I've just been enlightened," Leigh exclaimed. "And
it's like a giant lightbulb just turned on. I can see much
more clearly now, and everything is so beautiful."

"Did you take something?" Maybe not pills. Maybe
she'd eaten peyote or smoked mushrooms in some sort
of bizarre ceremony Micheline had organized.

"Of course not." Rather than indignant, Leigh appeared distracted. "I'm hyper because I've got a lot on
my mind."

Fiona nodded, pretending she understood. Better to
say nothing and simply wait Leigh out.

"Micheline sometimes gives me private lessons," Leigh finally said. "She and I were talking about a new philosophy she came up with. It was sent to her in a dream."

With difficulty, Fiona kept from rolling her eyes. "What is it?" she breathed instead, leaning forward and hoping she looked intensely interested.

"What if—" Leigh's earnest expression seemed at odds with her giant dangling feather earrings swinging furiously every time she took a breath. As usual, the beauty queen had dressed more like a fashionable coed than a competent employee, minus the shoes. "—to be our best selves, we must die and be reborn?"

Religion? Or something else, something darker? Every instinct on alert, Fiona slowly nodded. "I'm listening," she said. "That seems intriguing. What exactly do you mean?"

"I know that sounds like a religious teaching," Leigh continued. "But when they say 'born again,' they mean it figuratively. I'm speaking literally."

Still not sure where the other woman was going with this, Fiona eyed her. "When you say…"

"Yes. Death." Excitement flashed in Leigh's eyes. "What if we must die so we can be reborn as our absolute best selves?"

Horrified, Fiona decided to treat this statement as if she thought Leigh might be joking. "You first," she said. "I happen to like being alive."

"Think of it," Leigh continued, clearly deciding to pretend she hadn't heard Fiona. "A covenant, between all of the AAG and Micheline. All of us, crossing over at once. Imagine the news coverage. And then, imagine the shock when we're all reborn."

Like the Jim Jones thing at Jonestown. Mass suicide. It took every bit of acting skill Fiona possessed not to reveal her complete and utter horror. Then, her FBI training kicked in.

Details. She needed more details.

"Sounds like you already have a plan," she managed, the tremble in her voice coming naturally. "How long would we have to prepare?"

"No plan." Though Leigh demurred, Fiona didn't believe her.

"Are you sure?" Fiona pressed. "I mean, if we're going to do something like that, I'd like to know as far in advance as possible."

Though Leigh hesitated, she finally grinned. "It's still in the planning stages," she allowed. "A lot depends on money. Micheline is trying to work out those details."

"Now I'm really confused. What does money have to do with any of this?"

"Think, Fiona," Leigh chastised. "We have quite a few wealthy members whose families might pay handsomely to keep their loved ones alive."

"Like a ransom?" *Think* indeed. "What good would money be, though, if Micheline was dead?"

"Dead?" Shuddering dramatically, Leigh shook her head. "Micheline has no intention of dying and being reborn. Why should she? She has no need. As our leader, she's already the best version of herself she can be."

Fiona shouldn't have been surprised, but… Seriously. How did Micheline get her followers to believe this nonsense? "What about you, Leigh?" Fiona asked softly. "Are you already your best self?"

With a sly smile, Leigh used one hand to push back her hair. "What do you think? Not only am I Micheline's right-hand woman, but Miss Mustang Valley. How much better could a person get?"

Typical. Let the others do the crazy stuff. Those in charge, or close to the leaders, got off with a free pass.

Despite the flash of anger that shot through her with Leigh's statement, Fiona nodded. "Okay, humor me. I'm really trying to understand. What does that mean? Only Micheline's top people get to avoid the whole 'let's get reborn' thing?"

Some of her bitterness must have shown in her voice. Leigh cocked her head. "Worried, are you? I don't know, but if I were you, I'd be busting my tail to prove myself an invaluable member of the AAG. Maybe then you, too, could avoid that fate."

That fate. Almost as if Leigh knew exactly what Micheline would be asking her followers to do. Almost as if she were an accessory to murder. She wondered how someone like Leigh would fare in prison. Not too well, she suspected.

"Anyway, keep this between us for now," Leigh ordered. "We're not ready to roll it out yet. Micheline still has a lot of planning to do."

Though Fiona wanted to ask what would happen if any of the members, such as herself, declined the whole die-and-be-reborn experience, she didn't want to blow her cover. The devout groupie she'd been playing would probably do whatever Micheline asked.

"Thank you for telling me," Fiona enthused. "I'm so honored."

"You should be." Leigh beamed at her. "How are things going with Jake?"

"Hmm." Noncommittal, Fiona grimaced. "He's wanting to go too fast," she said. "I need to focus on my studies."

"He's falling for you? Perfect!" Clapping her hands, Leigh jumped up and down. "Micheline will be so excited!"

"Why?"

"Why not? Come on now, Fiona. Show a little enthusiasm. You are rocking this assignment." She peered at Fiona, considering. "You know, this might just be enough to distract Micheline from your failure with Theodore. He never returned any of our calls about scheduling some seminars."

Good. Even though Fiona hung her head as if ashamed, inwardly she rejoiced.

"You must do better," Leigh chided. "That assignment was handpicked for you by Micheline herself. If you don't watch it, she'll be sending you out to campus to troll for your own students."

Fiona nearly snapped her head up at that. She definitely didn't need to get sent somewhere outside the AAG center. That would defeat the entire purpose of her undercover assignment.

"I'll try harder with Jake," she responded meekly. And she would. Jake had agreed to work with her. He would simply have to figure out a way to separate emotion from the job. Especially since Leigh had hinted at mass suicide.

"See that you do." Smiling again, Leigh looked Fiona up and down. "Maybe you need to dress a little bit sexier, you know?"

Startled, Fiona shook her head. "I don't have—"

"Oh, that's right," Leigh interrupted. "You only had the clothes on your back when we rescued you and took you in." The subtle reminder wasn't lost on Fiona, who managed to nod and look embarrassed.

"No problem," Leigh continued on cheerfully. "I'll

have some things sent over. You must keep Jake Andrews interested enough to stick around. Micheline really needs him to be here at least ten more days."

A time frame. Though inwardly she perked up, Fiona took care not to reveal anything of her interest. "Ten days, huh? I'll figure out something."

"See that you do." Turning to her computer, Leigh clicked her mouse and began to read whatever she had on the screen, clearly dismissing Fiona.

Jake saw Fiona coming across the lobby, and his entire body tensed. Judging by her purposeful stride and the intent look on her beautiful face as she headed his way, she wanted to talk to him. He braced himself against the hopeless rush of attraction and waited.

"Do you have a minute?" she asked, her curt tone pitched low. "For a walk outside?"

He shrugged, deliberately casual. "Sure. Why not?"

When she slipped her small hand into his, he couldn't prevent his instinctive initial reaction—shock. But then he tightened his fingers around hers.

Neither spoke until they were several hundred feet down the driveway. "What's going on?" he asked finally.

"I just got out of a meeting with Leigh." She shook her head. "I'm to do whatever it takes to keep you around here at least ten more days."

As she'd probably known he would, he picked up on the time frame immediately. "Ten days? What's going on in ten days?"

"I don't know for sure," she said slowly. "But judging from what Leigh was hinting at, it's not going to be good."

He waited while she eyed him, clearly trying to decide what to say.

"Mass suicide." Her voice hardened. "But with a catch. From what I understand, she's planning to ask for payment from their families in order to save some of the wealthier members' lives. How she plans to explain this to her followers, I have no idea. It's crazy."

Jaw tight, Jake grimaced. His stomach turned at the thought of the depths to which the woman he'd once believed to be his mother was capable of sinking. "No surprise there. The lure of money has always been her motivator. All the rest of it comes secondary. Micheline is one of those people who doesn't care what she has to do to pad her pockets. Even murder, apparently."

"But this will be too blatant. She'll face charges. A full bank account won't do her any good in prison. And the feds will probably freeze her bank accounts." She shook her head. "If she's looking for notoriety, this will get her that. But the risk of getting caught is really high. I'd think it outweighs whatever monetary gain she'd stand to get."

"Unless she has a plan," Jake said, unable to keep from wanting to hold her. "And believe me, Micheline *always* has a backup plan."

"I've got to find out what it is." Rubbing her temples, Fiona sighed. "Jake, I know we had…words earlier. But you did agree to help me, and right now I need your help. I was basically told to turn up the heat with you. Leigh is even going to send me over some more revealing clothes to wear."

His heart skipped a beat at the thought of what she might wear. "We can work together," he said, keeping his voice level.

"Can we?" Her gaze found his. "We'll have to act as if we're really into each other."

"Act?"

This teasing question earned a smile from her.

"We've got that covered," he continued. "We'll continue on as before. And I promise I won't bring up anything about—"

"Feelings," she said, slightly breathless. "Not now, not yet, okay?"

Yet. That single word made him happier than he should have been. Proof once a fool, always a fool. "Sounds good." Still deliberately casual.

"Thank you." Her frown showed him her thoughts had already turned elsewhere. "If I'm going to find out exactly what Micheline has planned, I'm going to have to push. Try to get closer. The only way she'll trust me enough to—"

"Stop." Unable to help himself, Jake brushed a kiss across her lips. "I know you'll do whatever you have to do in order to stop her. But know this. Micheline trusts no one but herself. Not even that perky coordinator of hers."

"Leigh."

"Right, Leigh." He kissed her again, lingering this time. "Leigh might think she knows everything that's going on, but I guarantee she doesn't. Micheline will probably leave her twisting in the wind, holding the bag."

Swallowing hard, she nodded. "Kiss me again," she demanded. "In case someone is watching."

Wisely, he swallowed back a chuckle at her justification and covered her mouth with his.

For a moment, just a brief heartbeat or two, nothing else existed but the two of them.

When they finally broke apart, they were both breathing heavily. "You are a hell of a distraction," she told him.

"You needed to break your focus. You were on the verge of—"

"Panicking?" Interrupting, she shook her head. "Maybe. Maybe not." Professional Fiona had returned. "The more I hear about this, the messier it gets. I like clean cases, all wrapped up in tidy bows. Of course, the vast majority of them aren't anywhere close to being like that."

"And I can promise you this one will never be." He let his gaze roam over her, allowing himself to reveal his very masculine appreciation for her sensual femininity. She blushed, which fascinated him, and cleared her throat.

"How much longer are you staying?" she asked, not even bothering to try and pretend her question was casual. He liked that about her.

He laughed. "Oh, I'm not going anywhere until this is over. No way could I go back to the ranch without seeing how this all ends. I've got people in place running things for me. Plus, I'm really enjoying getting to know the Coltons. They're really good people."

"They seemed like they were," she agreed. "Much better than the family you formerly believed was your own."

"True." Cocking his head, he eyed her. "What are your plans for the rest of the day?"

"I'm going to do some exploring. I need to find out what's in the basement."

"Now?"

"Why not?" She shrugged. "The longer we wait, the closer we get to whatever horrific event Micheline is planning. I just need enough evidence for an arrest. Failing that, at least enough to obtain a search warrant."

"I'd think you already would have enough evidence," he commented. "Especially with her asking you to fleece a college student."

"I wish. While that was unethical, at least in my opinion, it wasn't illegal. She offered him a service—self-improvement classes and counseling sessions—for payment. No, I need more than that."

He could prove nothing about his "mother" without evidence, he realized, and even if he could, he'd only been speculating as to the end result. While Micheline might have acted in an unsavory manner, he had no idea if she'd committed any actual crimes. Gut instinct said yes, but hunches didn't stand up in court.

Fiona bumped him with her shoulder. "Earth to Jake. What's going on in that mind of yours?"

He shook his head. "I get what you mean about needing evidence. I'm just trying to come up with the best way to obtain it."

"I just wish I'd managed to get deeper into Micheline's inner circle," Fiona commented. "But Leigh tends to act as a very effective deterrent. No doubt that's why Micheline keeps her around."

"Micheline has a certain type she goes for," he said. "Underneath all that outward self-confidence, I'm willing to bet Leigh is a very insecure person. Maybe even has mommy issues, which is a role Micheline is happy to fill for her."

"Interesting analysis." She gave him a considering look. "And actually very good. You're probably right. Let's go back."

Still hand in hand, they strolled toward the entrance and into the lobby.

"One of Micheline's goons is headed our way. Her security detail, Bart."

"Ugh." She made a face. "Something about that guy gives me the creeps."

"I'm sure that's the reason Micheline hired him."

Bart continued sauntering toward them, smiling a smug smile, as if he enjoyed knowing how people reacted to him. When he reached Fiona, he stopped, raking his gaze up and down her.

Fiona's jaw tightened, but she didn't react. Jake knew she wanted to, though. Only the fact that she played a role undercover prevented her.

"What's up?" she asked, her voice cold.

"Just doing my rounds. I thought you were supposed to be in Happiness 101," he said, referring to the popular seminar going on right now in the auditorium.

"I've already done that one," she replied, her bright smile so false it made Jake's teeth ache. "I'm actually about to go do self-reflection and then journaling."

Bart yawned, not bothering to hide his bored expression. "Sounds like fun. Keep after it." And he sauntered away.

"He's up to something," Fiona declared. "Not sure what. If I wasn't afraid of getting caught, I'd follow him."

The idea of what a man like Bart might do to a woman like Fiona if he had her alone and up against a wall made Jake cold.

While he knew better than to suggest she take a pass on that one, he also knew he should distract her. "I want to kiss you so damn bad," he said, telling the truth.

Lifting her chin, she challenged him with her gaze. "What's stopping you?" she asked.

So he kissed her, right there in the lobby of the AAG center, for all the other guests—and cameras—to see.

Drowning, Fiona thought. From the instant Jake's lips touched hers, everything else disappeared. For a few seconds, she kissed him back, allowing herself to get lost in the taste of him, in the feel of his hard body pressed against hers.

But then, as all good things must, she knew it had to come to an end. She had a job to do, after all.

"Whoa," she teased, stepping back and hoping the entire lobby couldn't see how hard she was breathing. "Potent stuff. But I really need to stay on track and get back to work. I want to try and find the cells."

Blue eyes dark, he nodded. "Then let's look," he said. "Do you want to split up or search together?"

This—the ability to go with the flow and make a move when required—was one of the things she loved about him. Wait—*loved*? Surely not. She hadn't known him long enough.

But yet…

Shying away from any deep thoughts about her emotions, she reminded herself to focus on the job. Her mission mattered the most right now. She could sort out her feelings about Jake later, just like they'd agreed.

"Let's split up," she said. "I still think if we do it that way, there's less likelihood of us getting caught."

"Maybe. But I'd rather we stick together. That way if trouble comes, we face it side by side. We have each other's backs."

"Too obvious," she argued. Before she could say another word, her walkie-talkie buzzed. She glanced at it, saw Leigh was once again summoning her and sighed. "I'm really getting tired of this thing. I've got to meet up with Leigh again. Go ahead and start searching without me if you want. I'll touch base with you later."

"Sounds good." He leaned in and kissed her cheek, surprising her. She had to actively fight the urge to turn her head so that her lips met his.

"Please be careful," she said instead, already moving away.

On the way to Leigh's suite, she wondered if the continued summons made the younger woman feel more powerful. She didn't remember Leigh doing this so much before—usually they'd run into each other somewhere around the center. Maybe that meant Fiona had been shifted to a position of greater trust.

After tapping on Leigh's door, she stepped inside.

"There you are!" Leigh smiled at her. "Close the door and come in."

Fiona took her time complying. Finally, she turned and faced Leigh, who remained seated behind her massive desk. "What's going on?"

"We have another plan," Leigh announced, her voice high-pitched with excitement. "Micheline wanted me to discuss it with you."

Instead of playing her usual role—which was to mimic Leigh's enthusiasm, Fiona crossed her arms and shook her head. "Why doesn't Micheline discuss it with me herself?"

As expected, Fiona's comment had Leigh narrowing her eyes. "Listen to you, Miss High and Mighty," Leigh snarled. "I think you are getting way too big for your britches. Why would you even think Micheline would need to discuss anything with you personally?"

Fiona blinked. While she'd expected a put-down, she hadn't anticipated this level of vitriol. Despite that, she stuck to her guns. She could always quickly back down if things escalated too fast. "If what she wants me to do is important enough, I'd think she'd want to tell me herself."

"I'm her messenger." Mouth tight, Leigh spoke angrily. "I can't believe you of all people are acting like this. After all we've done for you."

How much to push? Fiona debated. She wanted to get on an inside track with Micheline, but she really couldn't take the risk of alienating Leigh.

"I'm really not trying to cause trouble," Fiona responded, her tone conciliatory. "I just feel like these days Micheline is distancing herself from me—from us. When I first got here, I saw her a lot more. She coached me personally. Now, if she has anything to say to me, she has you do it. I miss her."

Leigh's hard expression softened. She even got up and came around her desk to place her hand lightly on Fiona's shoulder. "I get it, really I do. But Micheline is really busy. She's even been communicating with me via email lately. I haven't even seen much of her, and I'm her trusted employee."

Interesting. Email. "When was the last time you actually saw her in person?" Fiona asked.

"Don't worry about it." One flip of her hand dismissed Fiona's question as Leigh went back behind her desk and took a seat in her leather office chair. "Micheline has another job for you. When she finishes firming up the details, she'll need it carried out right away."

Leigh took a deep breath, pausing as if for dramatic effect. "You should know, this plan involves the Coltons."

Instantly alert, Fiona nodded. "What about them?"

"First, I need to ask you a possibly delicate question. Is there any chance you could be pregnant with Jake's child?"

Floored, Fiona simply stared. "Um, I don't know. I guess." Though she took her birth control pills religiously and Jake had used condoms, she supposed there was always a very small, remote chance. Unlikely, but still...

"Perfect." Beaming, Leigh fiddled with a stack of gold bracelets. "Micheline might need you to pretend to be pregnant."

"What?" Fiona felt sick again. Was there no end to the horrible things Micheline would ask her to do? "Would I have to tell Jake that, too?"

"Of course. Even better if you can convince him to play along for a cut."

"A cut of what?" Fiona asked, though she suspected she already knew. Heaven help her if Micheline wanted to try to sell the Coltons a mythical baby.

"Money. Duh." Leigh rolled her eyes. "Micheline hasn't unveiled the rest of her plan to me yet, but trust me when I say there will be lots of cash involved."

"Doesn't that ever bother you?" Fiona asked. "All the emphasis on money? The purpose of the AAG is supposed to be helping people figure out how to be the best versions of themselves. I don't understand why Micheline is so fixated on—" She almost said *extorting people for cash*, but stopped herself just in time.

"It takes lots of money to keep this place running," Leigh snapped. "Everything Micheline does is for the greater good. Everything."

Leigh's fervent defense of a con woman seemed par for the course. Fiona figured Leigh didn't even realize she was in a cult. Oddly enough, most of the people she encountered here shared the same lack of awareness. She found this both strange and unnerving, a testament to Micheline's powers of persuasion.

"Anyway," Leigh continued. "For now I need you to simply convince Jake that you're carrying his baby. We won't do anything else until Micheline decides for sure what course of action to take."

No sure what else to do, Fiona nodded her agreement. This assignment just kept getting weirder and weirder—and more and more dangerous.

Chapter 10

Watching Fiona walk away, Jake hoped he didn't wear his heart on his sleeve. She was beautiful, his Fiona. *His?* When had he started thinking of her that way? He didn't know—didn't actually care. Despite her declaration that she couldn't do a serious relationship right now, he knew there would come a day when all the obstacles were gone. He understood that the way he felt about her was the sort of thing that only came along once in a lifetime. The trick would be to make her realize that, too.

After all this was over.

The intrigue, the drama, the danger that seemed to swirl around Micheline like a storm over the desert. He couldn't wait to see her arrested, brought down. And hopefully before she hurt anyone else in the process.

Remembering what Fiona had said about the door to the basement, he deliberately wandered over toward the kitchen, figuring he could claim hunger and the urge to find a snack as an excuse. But before he even made it halfway across the lobby, the beefy guy who acted as Micheline's bodyguard intercepted him.

"Micheline would like a word," Bart said, his tone and aggressive stance indicating the subject wasn't up for debate.

Following the guy, Jake wondered why Micheline just didn't simply have a meeting with everyone at the same time—him and Fiona and Leigh. Instead, she apparently had Leigh meeting with Fiona separately. He had to wonder why. Maybe she had some plan to pit them against each other. But of course, only if it benefited her.

As he walked into her office, she greeted him with a huge smile. "I hear congratulations are in order," she cooed.

Since he had no idea what she might be referring to, he simply waited.

"I'm surprised you're not more excited," she continued.

Clearly, she was going to make him ask. "About what?"

"Becoming a father!" The gleam in her eyes chilled him to the bone. "How thrilling!"

Becoming a…what? Still trying to process her words, he didn't immediately respond. Just stood staring at her, as if waiting for her to laugh and say, "Just kidding."

Except she didn't.

Her smile faded. "Oh dear. You didn't know."

He hid the rough flash of anger. Though he was 99 percent sure Micheline was acting out another one of her scams, he decided to play along. "You mean Fiona? She can't be pregnant. She'd tell me if she was."

Micheline's smug expression had him gritting his teeth. "She's afraid. That's why she hasn't said anything to you. She's meeting with Leigh right now to discuss her options."

Sure she was. More likely getting her script from Leigh as to how they wanted her to play along. Games. Micheline always had several balls in the air at once.

He needed to become better at playing this game. Still, it had only been a few days since he and Fiona had slept together. There's no way she or anyone else could know whether she was pregnant yet.

"It had to be someone else," he said, proceeding to outline his reasoning. Micheline watched him closely, the gleam in her eyes letting him know she had expected this reaction. How could she not have, with the statistical impossibility of the scenario she'd mentioned?

"Most likely." Micheline shrugged. "Does that matter to you? Are you going to dump this poor, homeless woman and let her fend for herself?"

"Maybe." He crossed his arms, aware he'd be more believable if he stuck to his guns.

"Very well." The malice in Micheline's smile chilled his blood. "I'm guessing you're more like me than either of us realized."

A statement which she damn well knew would virtually guarantee to make him do the opposite.

"Damn." Walking over to the couch, he allowed himself to drop down and sit. Covering his face with both hands, he thought furiously, trying to figure out how he should react. "You know I'd never abandon her. But why wouldn't she come to me first?" he asked, his voice breaking. "She knows how I feel about her."

"And how is that?" Micheline's tone sounded cool and disinterested, even though he knew damn well she wasn't.

Hell, he didn't know how Fiona did this. He already felt queasy, and now he was actually going to bare his soul to one of the most narcissistic women on the planet. "I'm falling in love with her."

"You are?" Yep, that was pure glee. She didn't even bother to keep that particular emotion in check. "Then I know you'll want to do the right thing for her."

Slowly, he raised his head. "Which is?" Was she going to insist he marry Fiona?

"Help her find the baby the best home."

Though he should have known better, disappointment flooded him. For all of three seconds. "Oh? You don't want me to marry Fiona and promise to support our baby?"

The incredulous look she gave him let him know how far off base she believed he'd gone. "Of course not. Your child could have all the luxuries in life that you missed out on."

Though warning bells—hell, *sirens*—were blaring inside his head, he kept his face expressionless. "Do go on."

"He or she should be brought up among the wealthy, the cultured. People of his own blood."

He stared at her, hard. Hoping at least a hint of his revulsion leaked through in his glare. "You want to give my child to the Coltons." A statement rather than a question.

She laughed. Micheline actually laughed, causing him to grind his teeth and clench his jaw as well as his fists. "Not *give*," she said, shaking her head. "More like *sell*."

Sell. What the actual… He could only imagine what Leigh and Fiona were now discussing. A fake pregnancy, along with a completely illegal and unethical and just plain despicable act: selling a baby that didn't even exist to *his* family!

Worse, he knew Fiona would want him to pretend to go along with it. But he suspected Micheline would know something was up if he did. She understood him at least that well.

"Why would you do that?" he asked, hoping he sounded reasonable. "The Coltons are my actual family. Any child born from my blood is already theirs. Why would you think they'd be willing to pay *you* anything?"

If she noticed the emphasis he put on the word *you*, she didn't react. "Because if they don't pay, I'll make sure the child will disappear."

Horrified, he didn't even try to hide it. "You'd kill my baby?" he demanded.

She held up both hands. "I didn't say that. The decision will ultimately be up to Fiona. She might decide to give the baby up for adoption."

Fictional, he reminded himself. There actually wasn't a baby. Yet. Maybe never.

"Or keep it," he growled. "Fiona would make a damn good mother. Jeez, Micheline. You never change."

His disparaging comment didn't appear to faze her. "I am consistent," she agreed proudly. "Plus, you need to understand where Fiona is in her life. She's only been here less than a month. We picked her up homeless, living in the streets. She has become part of our family here at AAG."

About to storm out, he remembered—just barely—that he had a role to play, so he restrained himself. "I want to talk to Fiona first," he said. "Since this is our child, the decision really should be between the two of us first."

Her smug smile told him she believed she had Fiona in her back pocket. "Of course. Take your time. I'll check in with you tomorrow."

As soon as he left her office, he went in search of Fiona. He saw her in the lobby, helping one of the elderly AAG members get settled with a book.

"Do you have a moment?" he asked, keeping his tone polite. "To take a short walk outside?"

Gaze searching his face, she nodded. "Are you comfortable?" she asked the old woman, pulling up the light blanket and tucking it in around her waist.

"Fine, dear. You go for a walk with your nice young man."

Fiona blushed but she didn't correct her. "Let's go," she told Jake. "I can't stay long. I've got a few more tasks I need to handle here at the center."

Though he could barely contain his impatience, he managed to wait until they were out the door, down the porch steps and halfway down the driveway.

"Is there something you forgot to tell me?" he asked, his voice harsh. "I met with Micheline just now. She said you were talking to Leigh."

"About the pretend baby?" Though she spoke without inflection, pain and anger flashed in her eyes. "And Micheline's strange scheme to sell him or her to the Coltons?"

"Exactly!" He expelled his breath in a sigh, hoping to release some of his tangled-up emotions. "This is a new low, even for someone like her."

"I agree." Her calm voice acted like a balm upon his rage. "Of all the things I've had to do while here, this is the absolute worst."

"Because who would do that? Who would actually

sell their own child?" He realized part of the reason this bothered him so much was due to his own circumstances. Micheline had switched him with another baby and actually hoped he would die.

"You do know the baby isn't real, right?" Fiona asked, touching his arm. "I'm not actually pregnant."

He blinked. "I know."

"Do you? Because you sound uncertain."

Considering, he finally nodded. "Probably because Micheline talked like you really were. In fact, I'm pretty sure her henchwoman Leigh probably told you to lie to me and say you really are pregnant."

"She did at first, but then she kind of left it open. She even mentioned offering you a cut of whatever they rake in."

He didn't bother to hide the disgust that filled him. "More proof that Micheline never really knew me. Because if she had even the slightest clue who I am, she'd know I'd never abandon my child the way she did me."

"Come here," she said. "Right now." And she tugged him into her arms, holding him tight.

Just like that, all the frustration and impotent rage drained away.

"You can do this," she continued, her arms still wrapped around him. "*We* can do this. Just think of the end result."

Micheline behind bars. "You're right," he said, raising his head. "I guess I let emotion get the better of me. She's such a—"

Fiona kissed him then, midsentence, midbreath. Kissed him as if she were dying and he might be her last hope for survival.

After a moment, he relaxed enough to kiss her back.

This woman, he thought, even as he drowned in sensation. The scent of her, the feel of her, the taste of her filled him with both yearning and the certainty that she was the one. Even if she didn't know it yet.

With Micheline plotting and scheming, Fiona had a suspicion that events might occur along an accelerated timetable. Which meant if she was going to locate these cells or whatever might really be in the basement, she needed to do it quickly. She hadn't seen Underhill either, so either he'd been dismissed or Micheline had locked him up.

If the inner door remained locked, then she had to locate the key. She decided to stake out the laundry room. Eventually, someone had to go into the basement. She'd watch from there and see. Most likely, whoever had basement duty would have been given the key for their shift, but she also wouldn't have been surprised to see they stashed it somewhere close to keep things simple. After all, they'd probably figure no one would want to break *in* to the basement, only out.

Luckily, even though the center had maids who picked up the laundry every week, Fiona had enough clothes to pretend to be doing her own laundry. While she felt quite certain this would be frowned upon, at least she'd have a credible excuse if anyone caught her. She bundled them up and stuffed them in a large tote, hoping this would help keep them hidden from view, and trudged downstairs, through the lobby and past the kitchen to the laundry room.

She'd finished her first load and moved it to the dryer when she heard male voices coming down the hall. Two of them, and it sounded like they were arguing. She moved to the dryer closest to the doorway and bent over to shuffle around her clothes inside it, hoping that way she'd be mostly hidden.

"It's your turn to sleep down there," one of the men said. "I had that duty all of last week, and I did it."

"I really don't want to," the other guy replied. "After the lights go out, it's creepy as hell."

"Then leave them on."

"I tried that. It's still creepy down there."

"Tough." A rattle of metal, like a full key chain.

Fiona took a chance and raised up enough to peer around the doorway. Both men had their backs to her now. One big man, with close-shaven hair and broad shoulders. The other held a large key chain and appeared to be trying to extract one of the keys from it.

"I need to give you this," he said. "It's impossible to get off this thing."

"Keep it. Harley told me a couple of weeks ago where he kept a spare key hidden."

"Out here?" Man Number One sounded outraged. "Why would he do something so stupid? Those brainy types never have any common sense."

"No, not out here," Number Two replied. "In the laundry room. No one would think to look there."

Fiona's heart stopped. Damn it. She glanced around. No place to hide. If they came in here to retrieve the key, she was busted.

On the other hand, she'd know where the key had been stashed.

Holding her breath, she braced herself for the two men to appear. Luckily, she had her laundry, so she continued to slowly place one wet clothing item at a time into the dryer.

"Here it is!" the first guy announced, all triumphant. "I got it off the chain. The key is your responsibility now."

A moment later, she heard the solid metal door open. Once the men went through, it clanked shut behind them. And then she heard the sound of the dead bolt clicking into place as they locked it.

Damn. It had been left unlocked last time. She could only hope the key fit both locks. It must, since they'd discussed one key rather than two.

Getting to her feet, Fiona looked around. Somewhere inside this laundry room, a spare key had been hidden. All she needed to do was find it.

Aware that at least one of the guards, if not both, would eventually return, presumably after completing their check on things, she started searching. First, she checked all the obvious places—inside the linen cabinet, on the shelf near the detergent and fabric softener, and behind the bins used to pick up the dirty towels. No sign of a key.

Think. It had to be someplace easily accessible but still well hidden. If the guard was too lazy to carry a key around with him, he wouldn't want to expend a lot of effort to get it.

The folding table. She checked underneath. Sure enough, someone had glued a small plastic pouch near the front corner. Inside, she found a metal key.

Triumphant, she slid it into her pocket and went to check the dryer. Since her stuff was still wet, she left it there for now and strolled on out and back to her room. She'd come back and retrieve it later.

The key. She had the freaking key. Inside her room, she closed the door. Keeping it in her pocket—because she still wasn't sure if there might be a camera here or there—she debated not only where to hide it, but whether to show it to Jake.

While she appreciated his help, the FBI wasn't in the practice of endangering innocent citizens. Going down into the basement could be considered hazardous, therefore she didn't think she should involve him. Best to go it alone.

Now to figure out when. Clearly, the place was well guarded at night, since the two men had talked about having to sleep there.

It would have to be during the day. From what she'd seen, the guards left periodically, whether to have a meal or just take a break. She'd need to time everything perfectly, so she'd need to learn when the guards left. Patience, she reminded herself. She'd keep an eye on the hallway and make notes whenever she saw guards leaving or arriving.

Satisfied with her plan, even if it was going to take a few days, she decided to focus on Leigh and, by proxy, Micheline.

Micheline's latest scheme—inventing a fake baby and then trying to sell it to the Colton family—seemed sloppy. Especially for someone usually so meticulous with details. She seemed to be all over the place, at least judging by what Leigh passed on. Schemes of a mass suicide, extorting money from the Coltons, milking impressionable college students: all indicated Micheline was ramping up her attempts to increase her fortune.

Why? What had changed? All along, the AAG had continued to churn away, staying just under the radar of law enforcement. They were widely perceived as charlatans and well-known for bilking people out of their life savings, but due to not only the lack of complaints, but

the fact that people received services such as seminars
and self-help classes, as well as books, no actual charges
had ever been filed.

In fact, until the Mustang Valley Police Department
had received several calls from worried relatives believing their family members' had not only lost their savings
in her schemes but that their lives might be in danger, law
enforcement had considered their hands to be tied. And
then, when an informant had mentioned money laundering, the FBI had gotten involved.

Now this—rumors of something big, something dangerous about to occur had Fiona feeling the pressure.
Though undercover stings often were long, drawn out
affairs, she knew she couldn't let anyone die if there was
a way to prevent it.

She went for a long walk by herself and called Holden
while she was out. Once she'd outlined Micheline's latest scheme, he whistled. "Are you sleeping with him?"

Though she flushed with embarrassment, she kept her
voice steady. "I am. It's a long story."

"Ok." To his credit, Holden didn't judge. "Though selling a baby is definitely a crime, considering what other
misdeeds we think she's committing, or about to commit, that's small potatoes, though."

"True," she agreed. "I don't even know if she'll actually follow through. But it's the first time I've actually
witnessed her doing something that could constitute an
actual crime. Yet."

"Just wait and watch," he said. "And be careful."

"Always. I did figure out a way to get into the locked
basement. I've just got to get the timing right. Who knows
what I'll find down there? Since she has the place heavily
guarded, it might be something interesting."

"Heavily?" Holden sounded skeptical. "As far as I know, she only has two men working security detail out there."

"Really? The way they talked, there are at least three. Who are they?"

"I'll text you pictures," Holden replied. "One of them is Randall Cook. He's thirty-nine, tall, thin, a bit of a sad sack. Brown hair, brown eyes. He's been at the center for four years, working as a handyman. Worships Micheline and Leigh."

"Who's the other?"

"Just a sec." Holden clearly riffled through some papers. "Micheline's bodyguard, Bart Akers. Big and brawny with a blond crew cut."

"I've seen him around," she said. "Met him even."

"He and Randall Cook are good friends. If Micheline has anyone guarding whatever is in the basement, those two would do it."

"What about the third guy?" she asked. "They mentioned him hiding a key."

"No idea. The only other male in Micheline's inner circle is in custody. Harley Watts. He's a tech geek, and he does a lot of dark-web work for Micheline. He sent the initial email about Ace not being a biological Colton to the Colton Oil board. So far, he's not talking." He snorted. "He appears to think Micheline hung the sun and the moon."

"There's more than a few like that out here," Fiona responded. "I honestly don't get it. Nothing I've seen in Micheline's character should inspire that kind of blind loyalty. Even her teachings are pretty lame."

This comment made Holden chuckle. "Yeah, but clearly not everyone feels that way."

"Well, if there are only two guards, that will make this much easier to manage," she mused.

"Maybe so. But again, take no chances."

"I gotcha."

"And don't involve Jake Anderson in that. It's too dangerous," he advised.

"I wasn't planning on involving him. It's bad enough that Micheline lied and told him I was pregnant with his child."

"She's reaching for straws. But why the sudden, desperate need for money?" he asked.

"That's what I'd like to know." She thought for a minute. "Though I'm sure you've already done this, can you have someone check out her financial records again? Look for any huge payments she might have made. Or any large purchases."

"Will do. And keep me posted if you happen to learn anything more about this possible mass suicide she's planning."

Fiona agreed. If she had concrete evidence of something that horrendous, Micheline could be charged with attempted murder. The trick would be to stop her before anyone got hurt.

After hanging up, she turned around and went back inside.

Staking herself in the lobby initially seemed simple. She had no official scheduled duties, other than the multitude of seminars she was supposed to attend. While she still tried to show up periodically for one or two, for the most part she skipped out on them. The constant repetition gave her a headache.

But that afternoon, every time she got into position so she could see if anyone emerged from the hallway near the kitchen, either Leigh called her with a task or some-one in the lobby needed her help.

Finally, she got a rare Micheline sighting. Even bet-ter, the cult leader was accompanied by her bodyguard, the big goon who'd been one of the two men going into the basement.

"What's up?" Jake said behind her, startling her. "Watching Her Highness move among her subjects?"

The analogy made her smile. "Yep."

"Is it me, or does she seem a bit off?" Jake com-mented. "Look at how jerky her movements are. And her eyes seem a bit...wild."

Without being too obvious, Fiona watched Mi-cheline. From this distance, she couldn't hear what the other woman was saying, but Jake did have a point. If she'd been anyone else, Fiona might have thought she was drunk or on something. And who knew, she might very well be. That would definitely explain the sudden, desperate need for cash. Or even worse, Leigh's strange statement about death and rebirth. She shuddered at the thought.

"Maybe it's her illness," Jake said, just a hint of sar-casm in his voice. "Though I really don't think she's actu-ally sick. That's the problem with people who constantly cry wolf. It's hard to know when to believe them."

Ever mindful of potential cameras or listening devices, Fiona made a sympathetic face. "Cancer is hard. So is the treatment. If she's started chemo..."

Though Jake made a face, he didn't comment. Instead, he jerked his head in Micheline's general direction. "She's headed this way," he said.

"Great," Fiona mouthed, before plastering what she

hoped was a worshipful smile on her face. "Micheline," she gushed. "It's so great to see you!"

Micheline nodded, as if acknowledging the compliment. "Leigh mentioned you were feeling a bit…left out. Since I wanted you to understand how much I value you, I decided to put aside some of my very valuable time and chat with you. How are you feeling?"

"Fine," Fiona began, and then realized Micheline was asking because of the imaginary pregnancy. "I haven't had a chance to get down to the medical center and pick up the prenatal vitamins yet, but I'll do it today."

"Good, good." Now Micheline turned and faced Jake. "And you. Now that you've had a little bit of time to reflect on this, have you come to any decision about your involvement with this baby?"

Fiona could see Jake trying to figure out something diplomatic to say. "He and I are still discussing this," she interjected. "Jake wants to get married and move away to live on his ranch. I'm trying to convince him that our child deserves so much more."

Spoken like a true, brainwashed believer. It took everything Fiona had not to gag on the words. While she knew in reality she was definitely not pregnant, the idea of handing over a baby to strangers for money was abhorrent. And even if Micheline was successful in extorting the Coltons, Fiona didn't think it likely that she'd get a whole lot of cash.

"I want to talk about the new thing you're working on," Fiona said boldly. "I'm interested in learning about what's involved with being born again."

Micheline looked from Fiona to Jake and then back again. Her mouth worked, but no sound came out. Judging by her confused expression and frown, she had no idea what Fiona meant.

"Like in church?" Jake asked, clearly hoping to prod the conversation along.

Instead of answering, Micheline just smiled. "Stay tuned for details," she said, and then moved away, her bodyguard moving right behind her.

If he was here, that meant the other guy must be down in the basement. If the place was kept guarded at all times, which Fiona now doubted. Micheline simply didn't have the staff for that. Which was good as far as giving her more time to explore the area once she figured out the guards' schedule.

"That was weird," Jake mused. "She really seemed disconnected and unfocused."

"I'm sure it's just because she has a lot going on," Fiona offered, ever conscious of her role. "It's a heavy responsibility being the spiritual leader for so many people."

"Not to mention being overly involved in decisions for an unborn child that may or may not actually be born."

Fiona winced. "Don't talk about our baby like that," she said, putting her hands protectively over her still-flat stomach. "Come on, Jake. I know all of this is a shock, but you must know Micheline has our best interests at heart." She cut her eyes over to the lamp on the decorative table near them. She'd long ago spotted the tiny surveillance camera mounted there.

Giving a small nod, Jake grimaced. "I need some time alone to think." He shook his head and walked away, leaving her alone in the lobby once again.

Chapter 11

Though he'd assumed Fiona would come after him, Jake wasn't too surprised when she did not. This situation could go from bad to worse, and she needed to be on top of her game in order to deal with it. Honestly, he couldn't blame her.

He wasn't usually a gut instinct kind of guy, but he couldn't shake the feeling that something major was about to go down. Whether it was Micheline's bizarre attempt to ransom off Fiona's imaginary baby or something else, he had no way of knowing. Plans had been set in motion, the FBI had Fiona undercover and hopefully by the time the smoke cleared, the woman who'd raised him was going to go down.

For that, he could definitely manage to pretend to be something he wasn't. He'd never be as good at it as Fiona, but she'd probably had training and years of practice.

Despite being constantly aware Fiona had to play her role, he had to admit doing it himself creeped him out. But then he'd always prided himself on being an up-front, straight-shooting kind of guy. He didn't like games, he'd never aspired to become an actor and playing along with Fiona was the first time he'd ever done anything like this. He hoped he never had to again.

He caught sight of Micheline's bodyguard, Bart Akers, talking earnestly to the center's handyman, Randall Cook. Despite the difference in their appearances—Bart clearly worked out and exuded confidence, while Randall appeared to slouch his way through life—the two men appeared to be good friends. Jake studied Randall carefully. Though Jake had seen the thin, mopey guy lurking around, he'd never actually had a conversation with him. Whatever Randall and Bart were discussing must have been important, judging by Bart's frequent, emphatic hand gestures and Randall's defensive posturing.

Finally, the handyman walked away, head down and shoulders bent. Bart stormed off in the opposite direction. Jake made a split-second decision to follow Randall, just for the hell of it. Since Randall appeared lost in his own thoughts, Jake doubted he'd even notice.

To Jake's surprise, Randall headed toward the huge kitchen area. Where Fiona had mentioned the door that went to the basement was located. Interesting. Maybe Randall was headed there right now. Jake wondered what would happen if he followed him. If and when the handyman noticed him, Jake could come up with some spur-of-the-moment story explaining his presence. He figured since Randall knew Jake was important to Micheline, he'd be safe.

Randall wove through the equipment, neither looking

at nor acknowledging any of the other employees. Walking confidently, Jake followed. Randall never looked over his shoulder or indicated any awareness of being followed. Several of the kitchen workers glanced up as they passed, but no one commented. Proof that they were used to Randall coming and going. Jake assumed that meant that they simply believed he was with Randall, who remained oblivious.

Worked for him.

Out of the kitchen finally, and into a short, narrow hallway. They passed a laundry area with several industrial-size washers and dryers. Randall stopped at a metal door and dug in his pocket for a key ring. He then proceeded to curse under his breath as he tried various keys until he finally located one that worked.

After opening the door, he slipped inside, letting it slam shut behind him. Jake rushed forward and grabbed the knob, bracing himself for the sound of a dead bolt being engaged.

It didn't happen. Either Randall didn't plan on being inside too long, or it never occurred to him that someone might want to follow him. Either way, Jake decided it was too good of an opportunity to miss. He couldn't wait to see Fiona's face when he told her.

Cautiously, Jake opened the door. Once inside, he carefully closed it, taking care to make as little sound as possible. He found himself in a well-lit staircase, with metal steps and a handrail. This seemed awfully institutionalized for a private residence, but who knew what Micheline actually used the basement for.

Basement. Who in Arizona even had a basement?

Moving down the metal stairs as quietly as possible, he wasn't surprised to find a second door at the bottom.

This was the one Fiona had gotten to as well, only to find it locked. However, judging by Randall's attitude, Jake figured this time it wouldn't be. Turning the handle, he found he was right.

Now came the hard part. Since he had no idea what the layout might be on the other side of that door, he couldn't judge how exposed he'd be once he stepped through. He'd have to do some fast talking if discovered, that's for sure.

He took a deep breath, pulled the door open and stepped inside. And found himself blinking at the bright fluorescent lighting.

At first glance, he might have thought he was inside a large animal shelter. Rows of tall cages, roughly eight by six feet, lined one wide hallway. The sharp ammoniacal tang of urine mingled with disinfectant stung his nose.

What the...?

He took a step. The first few cages were empty. But then he caught sight of the occupant in the next one and froze. A man, beaten and bloody, barely conscious, lay on the concrete floor. His clothes were ragged and filthy, stained with blood and dirt and bodily waste.

Stunned, Jake stood in front of the cell, trying to make sense of what he saw. A moan came from the next cage up, drawing his attention. The occupant there—female—peered up at him with sunken eyes, her long hair tangled and dirty, her body all bony angles, as if she'd been starved for weeks.

Beyond her, he caught sight of yet another person—prisoner? As he went to head that way, pain exploded in the back of his head, and he went down.

When Jake opened his eyes again with a pounding headache, it took a moment for him to realize where he'd ended up. He lay on a cold, cement floor and there were metal bars. A locked cell.

Hell. Micheline's basement.

Gingerly, he felt the back of his head, unsurprised to find a large and painful lump. Obviously, Randall or someone had come up behind him and clubbed him hard enough to knock him out. And now they'd locked him up in a cell, just like all the other poor souls he'd spotted earlier.

It would be okay, he told himself. Micheline would put a stop to this. She needed him for her little scheme with the Coltons.

"Hey," he called out, pushing himself up to his elbows and wincing at the blinding pain in his head. "Where are you? Show yourself."

But no one—not Randall or Bart or anyone else—appeared. None of the other prisoners even responded, as if they'd grown used to hearing unanswered pleas for help.

For the first time, a small prickle of dread went through him. How often did Micheline's hired men make their rounds? Judging by the condition of the others, not on a regular basis. Jake remembered Fiona saying something about Randall spending the night down here. That could be good or bad, depending on how one looked at it.

Fiona. He started to groan out loud, but even that small sound made his aching head throb. They'd had a disagreement. She might not be looking for him at all for hours, maybe days.

His only hope was Micheline, of all people. Even the thought made his head hurt worse.

When her walkie-talkie buzzed, Fiona gritted her teeth and considered tossing the thing into the nearest arrangement of silk flowers. Leigh again, of course. Summoning Fiona once more. Almost as if she might be testing Fiona to see how much she could take before breaking.

Obediently, Fiona trudged to Leigh's suite. Knocked on the door, waited for Leigh to tell her to come in and then went inside.

This time, instead of waiting behind her desk, Leigh stood just a few feet from the door.

"About time you got here," she said crossly. "I'm swamped, and I don't have time to wait for you."

Instead of responding that she'd come as soon as she'd been called, Fiona apologized.

"Here." Leigh handed her a stack of leaflets. "I've got a job for you. There's going to be a Gathering."

"A what?" Juggling the papers, Fiona barely managed to keep from dropping them.

"A Gathering." Leigh high-fived the air. "It's a big deal. Micheline is inviting all of her fans and followers. We've been working nonstop making sure the mailers go out. We're also doing mass emails, but these are for the older folks who might not have access to computers."

Intuition tingling, Fiona looked down at one of the fliers and started to read. She looked up at Leigh, hiding her alarm. "Is this…" She licked her lips, her heart racing. "Is this going to be the born-again ceremony? The big one?"

"It just might be." Leigh practically sang the words, though her heavily made-up eyes were still cold and calculating. "I'm so excited!"

Fiona pretended to share in Leigh's fake joy. Meanwhile, her insides were jumping. She had to find out the actual plan and then not only come up with a way to stop it, but surefire proof that Micheline was the instigator.

Once she had, she could call Holden and have a team brought in to carry out the arrests.

Leigh would be going down, too. The beauty queen might be naive, but so far she'd done nothing but go along with her boss's unethical, moneymaking schemes. And since she'd appeared to sanction the mass murder—as long as she herself didn't have to die—Leigh would also be charged.

But there was more, and like the excellent FBI agent she knew she was, Fiona wanted to find it. The existence of some sort of basement cells, where people were being held prisoner without rights to a trial or hearing, would clinch it. She had to figure out a time and get herself down there.

"What are you waiting for?" Leigh sniped. "Is there something else you need?"

"What do you want me to do with these?" Fiona asked, holding up the leaflets.

"Take them to campus and put them up, pass them out, whatever you have to do in order to get more people to come. College kids love the idea of stuff like this."

Feeling queasy again, Fiona nodded. "Will do."

"Get going," Leigh ordered, shooing her away with one hand. "We're short on time."

Fiona clutched the papers to her chest and hurried toward the door. Only when she'd gotten in the front seat of her car and locked the doors did she take the time to thoroughly read one.

This Friday. The date jumped out at her. All of this would be going down in less than a week. Which meant Micheline would have to try and sell off the mythical unborn baby before her followers committed mass suicide.

It was going to be a busy week. Fiona started the car

and drove to a local office supply store. There, one could rent the use of a paper shredder. Fiona paid her money and began rapidly shredding the documents. She kept back three copies, but she didn't want to take a chance on any of these getting in the hands of a single student.

Once she'd finished, she drove over to campus, parked and got out. Just in case Micheline had installed a GPS tracker on her car.

She spent a good half an hour walking around after stopping in the campus bookstore and picking up some fliers advertising a concert by a local band. These she tacked up on bulletin boards and telephone poles. If anyone had followed her to make sure she'd completed her task, unless they stopped and looked at the posters, it would appear she had.

Then she drove quickly back to the AAG center. Maybe if she could get in unnoticed, now would be the perfect time to check out the basement.

First, she needed to make sure both Bart and his friend Randall were elsewhere in the center. Walking with purpose, she strode through the common area as if she had an urgent task, looking for them.

She found them in the dining hall, sitting together and chowing down on hamburgers. Which meant there wouldn't be a time better than right now.

Heart pounding, she rushed through the kitchen, out the back door and down the hallway by the laundry room. The first door was locked, but her key fit. After gaining entrance, she made sure to lock it after her, just in case.

Clattering down the metal steps, she reached for her weapon, which of course she didn't have. Habit. But she sure did wish she'd found a way to arm herself, at least while down here. Bottom line—she didn't feel safe. She could fight and she could run, but she had no recourse against a man with a weapon. And she'd seen the side piece Bart carried in a shoulder holster. As for Randall, she doubted he even knew how to use a pistol.

The second door was also locked. No surprise there. Once again, her key worked. She took a deep breath and yanked it open, stepping inside. Out of reflex, she carefully locked it behind her and pocketed her key.

Then and only then did she turn and allow herself to process what she saw before her.

During her time in the FBI, she'd paid many a visit to jails and prisons. This place, with its row of metal cells and strong urine smell, appeared to be an attempt to recreate that, though on a much smaller scale. There was only one long row.

Underhill had begged not to be taken to the cells. Now she knew exactly what he'd meant.

The first two cells were clean and empty. In the third, a huddled pile of clothes looked eerily familiar. She hoped—oh, how she hoped—there wasn't a person underneath.

As she moved closer, her heart in her throat, she realized exactly who she saw lying in a mess of blood on the concrete floor. Jake.

She must have gasped or made some other sound of disbelief, because he raised his head. His face—his handsome face—was now so swollen he was barely recognizable. Swollen, bruised, his split lip combined with blood—so much blood—made him look like something out of a nightmare.

"Jake." Her heart broke. How the hell had he gotten in here? And why? "Who did this to you?"

But he'd lost consciousness and slumped back to the floor. And of course, his cell door was locked.

She tried her key, even though she guessed it wouldn't work. It wasn't even the right size.

"Jake," she whispered. "I'm going to go get you some help."

A moan from the next cell had her squinting. She took a hesitant step toward the sound, stopping short when she realized Underhill was the next prisoner. He'd been beaten, too, though not as badly nor as recently as Jake. Beyond him, in yet another cell, she saw what appeared to be an extremely emaciated woman.

Micheline, she thought, battling back a flash of fury. Micheline had done all this. Maybe not personally, but no one in the AAG center acted without her orders.

She pulled out her cell phone, intending to call Holden. No signal. Of course. But she could still use the camera. Photographic evidence would go a long way. She snapped pictures of everything—the setup, the cells and the prisoners themselves. Twice she tried to text them, but with no signal, they wouldn't go through.

Jake still hadn't moved, though she thought she could see his chest rise and fall as he breathed. "Please stay alive," she murmured and spun around to go.

Hands shaking, she unlocked the first door, barely remembering to lock it again before rushing up the stairs. She fumbled with the key and dropped it. Telling herself to breathe, to stay calm, she bent over and picked it up. As she straightened, the dead bolt turned and someone on the other side shoved the door open, right into her. Unprepared, she stumbled backward and grabbed for the handrail, barely stopping herself from falling down the stairs.

Bart came slamming through the door, expression

hard. The instant he saw Fiona, he pulled his pistol. "Keep your hands where I can see them," he ordered.

The irony of the situation wasn't lost on her. But she was too worried about Jake to care a whole hell of a lot what Bart thought. "Go get Micheline," she demanded. "Or Leigh. Or both of them. Right now."

His upper lip curled in a sneer. "I don't take orders from you. And with you sneaking around in places where you don't belong, you don't have a lot of bargaining power."

"I don't care." With a pistol pointed at her, she didn't want to make any sudden moves. Especially since she didn't know what kind of training Bart might have had.

"Does Micheline know Jake is in here?" she asked, softening her tone somewhat. "He's been badly beaten. He needs to get immediate medical care."

"You don't say," Bart drawled. "I'll get right on that." He gestured with his gun. "Now you, move back down the stairs. Keep your hands where I can see them at all times."

Would he shoot her? For the first time, she wondered if Bart and Randall were running their own little shop of horrors down here without Micheline's blessing.

Somehow, knowing what she did about Micheline, she doubted that. "You can't hurt me," she said, infusing her voice with way more confidence than she felt. "Micheline needs me too much to lose me."

"Does she now?" Judging from his snide smirk, he doubted that.

"Call her and see." Fiona decided to brazen this out. "Call her right now. I've had just about enough of this. Jake is hurt and—"

Moving so swiftly she didn't have time to react, he

shoved her hard, sending her tumbling down the metal stairs. It happened so fast, a split second in which one moment she'd been whole and the next, her entire body screamed with pain.

She'd broken her ankle, she thought, though since she could still move her legs, she hadn't broken her neck. Though she could have. Or her back. Bart had pushed her, knowing full well she'd be badly hurt, maybe even paralyzed, and he hadn't cared.

Calling on her own inner strength, she grabbed the handrail at the bottom of the stairs and hauled herself to her feet. Excruciating pain sliced through her when she tried to put her weight on her right ankle, which meant definitely broken.

"You tried to kill me." She didn't have to feign disbelief. "What the actual hell?"

"No," he drawled, coming about halfway down, his weapon still aimed at her. "If I wanted to kill you, I would just shoot. But…" He took another step, bringing him closer. "I know Micheline will likely want you alive, just like your boyfriend. Though she won't give a rat's ass what kind of condition either of you are in."

"But she will," she informed him. "She needs the baby I'm carrying to leverage what influence she has."

"Baby?" Momentarily fazed, he eyed her. "Right."

"I'm serious," she protested.

He ignored her. One more step, then another, until only a matter of feet separated them. He waved the gun in a way that made her consider snatching it away from him. If she'd been able to stand on both her feet, she might have tried. As it was, all she could do was glare at him and hope he didn't pistol-whip her.

"She won't care if I have some…" He licked his lips, pupils darkening. "Fun."

Horrified, she realized what he meant. He planned to rape her. "Not in this lifetime," she snarled, catching him by surprise. "I promise I will fight you," she said, letting him see the steely resolve in her eyes. "And you might be bigger than me and stronger than me, but I will hurt you. In more ways than one." She bared her teeth in a savage smile. "In fact, you're probably going to end up having to kill me before I'll let you lay one hand on me."

He took an inadvertent step back before he caught himself. "Move," he ordered. "There's a cell down there calling your name."

By now the pain had become so intense perspiration broke out on her forehead. She could barely hobble on one leg.

"The cell," he repeated. "Now."

Since she didn't have a choice, she did as he said. Once she'd made it inside, he slammed the door shut and locked her in. "Slide me your phone," he said.

"No." She stuck out her chin. "There's no service here anyway."

"Slide. Me. Your. Phone." He gestured toward Jake. "If you don't, I'll make sure and hurt your boyfriend even more than he already is."

Judging by the anticipation in his face, he actually hoped she'd refuse. Disgusted, she reached into her pocket, pulled out her phone and slid it across the floor to the edge of the bars.

"Thank you." Pocketing it, he smiled. "Enjoy your stay," he said, mocking her. And then he turned and clomped back up the stairs, slamming and locking the door. Now alone, she sank down to the floor and removed her shoe. Her ankle had swollen and turned black and blue. Examining the rest of her aching body, she took a quick inventory. She had various other cuts, scrapes and bruises, all caused by her fall, but as far as she could tell nothing else appeared to be broken.

On the other side of her, separated by a low metal partition, Jake moaned. Her stomach twisted, even as her own throbbing pain made her nauseous. Bart had pushed her down the stairs, but who knew what he or Randall had done to Jake.

Her only hope—oh, the bitter irony—was that Bart would contact Leigh or Micheline and they would order her to be freed, along with Jake. Jake needed medical treatment immediately. Her broken ankle wasn't life-threatening. Whatever they'd done to Jake might be.

Hours passed, how many she had no idea. She'd relied on her phone for checking the time, so didn't even own a watch. The throbbing in her ankle seemed to intensify by the minute, and no matter how she shifted her position, she couldn't seem to lessen the pain. No more sounds came from Jake's cell, which worried her. She even tried calling his name several times, but he never responded.

Damn. If anything had happened to him, she'd bear full responsibility. She should have urged him to get out, to go back to his ranch, to stay safe. But she'd let the attraction blazing between them distract her. Now, she hoped neither of them had to pay the consequences of her foolishness.

Foolishness. Was it, though? They hadn't known each other very long, but she couldn't imagine going through another day without him in it. He had to be all right. He had to be. She refused to accept any other outcome.

Finally, she managed to doze, though the slightest

movement brought stabbing pain and she'd wake, perspiring and disoriented. Though she'd seen others locked up here, the absolute silence wore on her as heavily as some kind of sensory deprivation torture. She, who'd never been the slightest bit claustrophobic, began to feel acutely aware of the size of her small cell.

She understood what they—the AAG, Micheline or just Bart and Randall—had going here. A prison of sorts, where offenders were locked up without legal representation or access to a fair trial. Inhuman and cruel treatment, including beatings and starvation, denying medical care and who knew what else.

There was no telling how much time had passed when Fiona heard the clunk-click sound of the dead bolt unlocking. She tried to push herself to her feet, but her swollen ankle screamed in protest, so she abandoned that idea. She couldn't even manage to get to her knees.

Bart came through the door, followed by Micheline. Fiona's intense relief at seeing Micheline faded at the furious expression on the older woman's face. Micheline moved forwarded, holding something in her hand, brandishing it like a weapon. As she stopped outside Fiona's cell, Fiona realized Micheline held her cell phone, the one Bart had taken from her right before locking her up.

At least, Fiona thought, the phone was a burner. She kept nothing stored on it, with the exception of Holden's number.

"You little idiot," Micheline spat. "What the hell were you doing snooping around down here?"

Fiona said the first thing that came to mind. "I was looking for Jake. We had a fight, and he was upset. I wanted to make it up to him."

"Jake?" Micheline turned and looked at Bart, who

nodded. "Why didn't you mention that Jake was here, too?"

He shrugged, his expression mulish. "I honestly didn't think about it."

"Or you didn't want her to know what kind of shape he's in," Fiona interjected. "He's pretty beat-up, Micheline. He needs medical attention right away."

Micheline rounded on Bart. "You idiot. What did you do to him? Right now, Jake is a valuable commodity. You'd better not have messed that up."

"I didn't do anything to him," Bart replied, his tone sulky. "Randall caught him snooping around down here and hit him a few times with a baseball bat."

Fiona gasped. "No wonder he looks so bad."

"Show me," Micheline demanded.

Bart led her a few steps down the row, stopping in front of Jake's cell.

She cursed. "Get him up to the medical area immediately."

"But…" If Bart even briefly considered arguing, he clearly changed his mind. "Yes, ma'am. Right away." He used his walkie-talkie to call someone—probably Randall—and then nodded. "I'll get him moved out immediately."

A moment later, the door opened, and Randall hurried through. He kept his head down, refusing to make eye contact with anyone. Judging by the extreme submissiveness of his posture, Fiona wondered how it could be possible for him to beat anyone. But then again, some of the most horrible crimes had been committed by the least likely individuals.

"You two." Micheline pointed. "Get Jake up to the medical area right now. See that he gets treatment. And

Randall, don't you ever beat one of my guests without checking with me first, understood?"

Randall mumbled something that sounded like agreement and nodded. Then Bart unlocked Jake's cell, and he and Randall hefted Jake up between them, half carrying, half dragging him along.

"No way is he going to make it up those stairs," Fiona called out, worried out of her mind. Even her own pain faded into the background as she tried not to imagine the damage to Jake's already broken body if the two men tried to drag him up metal stairs. Even worse if they failed or dropped him.

Bart shot her a poisonous look, but when Micheline agreed with Fiona, his expression changed.

"Get a stretcher and a couple more men to help you," Micheline directed. "He's already in bad shape. The last thing I need you to do is kill him. He's important to one of my plans."

Of course, Fiona thought grimly. Micheline didn't care about Jake, despite having raised him since birth. She only wanted him whole so she could still use him to try and bilk the Coltons for money. And Fiona had to put a stop to that, somehow. No matter what.

Chapter 12

Previously in his life, Jake had been kicked by a horse, gored by a bull, and crashed a motorcycle, but he'd never hurt like this. Since he'd lost consciousness after the first blow, his assailant must have simply kept on beating him, just for the hell of it.

Judging by the way he felt, the weapon of choice had been either a crowbar or a baseball bat or along those lines. He had a pretty good idea that more than one bone had been broken, and judging by how much it hurt to breathe, two or three ribs. Or more. He couldn't tell. His entire body felt like one giant throbbing mess of pain.

He jolted awake when someone—two men—lifted him under his arms and tried to drag him out of his cell. Silently screaming, he mercifully blacked out and knew nothing else until he woke up in some kind of hospital bed.

Which meant at least they'd let him out of the cell.

But taking him to a hospital? Risky on Micheline's part. One of his eyes was too swollen to open, but he used the other one to try and figure out his location.

Not a hospital, he realized. He wasn't hooked up to any machines, for one thing. And the room didn't have that sterile feel of most hospitals.

Then where? Dimly, he thought he remembered Fiona saying something about a medical area at the AAG center. Of course—Micheline wouldn't take a chance on him telling anyone what had happened to him.

But did they have the resources to patch him up? He knew he needed an ER, a skilled physician and some medicine. At least the pain seemed to have subsided, which meant most likely he'd been given some sort of drugs. He felt…good, actually. Yep, definitely drugs.

Lifting one arm, he realized someone had bandaged his chest. Which would definitely help with his ribs.

He wanted Fiona. Would they tell her where to find him? And if they did, would she even visit? The thought made him frown. He could swear he'd heard her voice, down there in the basement. Had he hallucinated it, driven crazy by pain and wishing for the one person who might be able to make him feel better?

Once again, he must have drifted off. When he opened his eyes again, his mouth felt dry and his stomach empty. Moving his head slowly, he looked for a nurse or an attendant, hating the way the entire world seemed to move drunkenly along with him. Vertigo, which meant strong medicine.

An older woman with a bright smile appeared in his line of vision. She adjusted his bed, raising him into a half sitting, half reclining position, and handed him a paper cup with ice water in it.

"Drink slowly," she advised. "Give your body a chance to get used to fluids."

Accepting the cup, he took a sip, resisting the urge to down the entire thing. Since his mouth was so dry, he took a few ice chips and let them melt on his tongue.

For one absurd moment, he caught himself wishing he had a living mother. But since he didn't, he figured it must be whatever drugs they'd given him that made him entertain such crazy thoughts.

Carefully, he set the cup back down on the metal tray and closed his eyes.

He must have drifted off to sleep. The next thing he knew, someone brought in a plastic food tray and placed it near his cup. "Soft foods only," the smiling attendant told him. After she'd left, he glanced around the room, only to see he was alone.

"Fiona," he croaked, as if by saying her name he could somehow summon her.

When she didn't appear, he shook his head at his own foolishness, then winced as the room spun and dipped alarmingly.

Once he felt steady again, he opened his eyes and gingerly reached for the covered plate. Inside he found a bowl of lukewarm chicken soup and a container of green Jell-O. Slightly nauseated, he went ahead and tried a spoonful of soup.

It tasted delicious. Surprised, he tried another. Before he knew it, he'd finished the entire bowl.

After he ate, he dozed. He knew there was something important he needed to do, but he couldn't seem to muster up the knowledge of what it might be. Instead, he let himself sleep. He figured he'd probably remember once he'd gotten some rest.

Fiona. Jake came awake with a start. His entire body hurt. Even breathing made him shiver with pain. Which meant the drugs had worn off. But at least his mind wasn't befuddled.

Fiona was in some sort of trouble. He tried to think, to remember if she'd been with him when he'd descended into the basement to find Micheline's prison.

No. She hadn't. But then why did he remember hearing her voice? He thought back, wincing as he recalled Bart and Randall trying to pick him up, thinking he could somehow walk up the stairs. And then Fiona had insisted he wouldn't be able to, so Micheline had asked them to get a stretcher.

Fiona had been there. How? And why? He doubted Micheline had brought Fiona down there to show off her prison. Plus Leigh would have been there, and he didn't remember hearing Leigh's voice.

Which meant…what? Had Fiona been taken prisoner, too? Had they—Randall or Bart—beaten her, too? Fury heated his blood. So help him, if either of those fools had touched one hair on her head, he'd make them regret it.

He had to go check on her. Glancing around, he saw he'd been hooked to a single IV, though the hanging bag had gone dry. His painkillers, no doubt. There didn't appear to be any kind of machines monitoring him. Taking a deep breath, which brought on so much pain he broke out in a sweat, he tried to push himself up on his elbows.

Not happening. Not today, his broken body screamed.

Still, he persisted. Damned if he'd lie here and rest while Fiona suffered. He had to get to her or, even better, figure out a way to bring in reinforcements.

There had to be someone in the FBI he could call. But first, he had to get out of this bed and find a phone.

Finally, after several excruciating attempts, he managed to sit up enough that he could press the button to electronically adjust the bed. Now, with back support, he could sit, and hopefully the pain levels would subside enough for him to try to get up from the bed.

A quick glance under the sheet made him realize he wore no clothes, not even his underwear. He didn't see them anywhere in the room, either. Guessing they'd been bloody due to his beating, he imagined his captors had tossed them in the trash somewhere or incinerated them.

There had to be something he could wear. Even a hospital gown would be better than wrapping a bedsheet around himself and trying to walk down the hall. Though he would if he had to. Once he made it back to his room, he could grab a change of clothes and check on Fiona.

His phone. He could simply call her, and once she answered, he'd let her know where to find him. If only he had his phone.

Evidently, they'd taken that, too. Glad he'd password protected the thing, he took a fierce kind of pleasure knowing they wouldn't be able to use it. Unless they pressed his thumbprint on it while he was unconscious, which was entirely possible.

"Looks like you're going to live."

Jake looked up. The same attendant from earlier stood in the doorway, eyeing him.

"It appears so," Jake replied. "What's the prognosis?"

"Since they wouldn't take you to the hospital for X-rays, I can't be entirely certain, but I think you have a couple of bruised or broken ribs. It looks like whoever beat you kept the blows centered there. You're lucky, because they could easily have taken out a kneecap or an elbow. You've got a lot of bruises and cuts, but as far as I can tell without X-rays, nothing else seems to be broken."

Jake nodded, wincing at the pain this caused. "My head?" he asked. "No fracture? They clubbed me in the back of my skull to knock me out. It still hurts like hell."

Coming closer, the woman smiled. "You have a pretty big gash there, so I'm guessing that's the source of your pain. And your nose doesn't appear to be broken, surprisingly. Initially, I even thought one of your cheekbones was fractured, but it's not."

The lackadaisical approach to medicine floored him. Something of his thoughts must have shown on his face, because she frowned. "Look, I'm just an RN. I'm supposed to be treating colds and strep throat and the occasional infected cut. Not something like this." She waved her hand at him. "I demanded you be transported by ambulance to the ER. You looked terrible and I wasn't sure you'd make it. They wouldn't let me call 911, so I did the best I could."

"They?" he asked. "Meaning Micheline."

Slowly, she nodded. "And Leigh. I've seen far too much of this kind of thing lately. Now that I know you're stable, I'm quitting. I can't work for people like this."

If they let her leave, he thought, though he didn't say it out loud. He wouldn't be surprised if she didn't end up in a cell down in the basement, too.

"You called?" Bart's voice, startling both of them.

Suddenly, the nurse wouldn't meet Jake's gaze. "Yes. He's well enough to be transported back to his cell."

"What?" Jake tried to push away from the pillow, but the blinding pain knocked him back instead.

"I'm sorry," the nurse said before lifting a needle and giving him a shot in the arm. Everything went black after that.

* * *

After Jake had been taken away on a stretcher, Micheline turned to face Fiona.

"I don't know what I'm going to do with you," she said, her gaze cold. "You got yourself into this mess. Maybe I should see how you plan to get yourself out of it."

Dammit. Micheline couldn't abandon her now. Not when everything seemed so close to coming to a head. Fiona decided she might as well throw caution to the wind. She'd beg if she had to. "I only took your advice," she said, well aware of how much Micheline liked having her ego stroked. "I decided to let Jake think I wanted to marry him. I followed him, and when I saw him come down here, I got curious."

Expression impassive, Micheline shook her head. "Have you never heard the cliché expression about curiosity killing the cat?"

"Please, help me. I think my ankle is broken." Fiona lifted her leg so the older woman could see her swollen limb. "I'm sorry I came down here, and I swear it won't happen again. Would you please have someone take me for medical attention?"

Instead of answering, Micheline made a show of studying Fiona's phone. "This is an odd choice for a cell phone," she mused. "A disposable one, the kind people who aren't on the straight and narrow path might use."

"Or people with limited funds," Fiona pointed out, shifting slightly and then wincing from the pain. "As you know, I've been homeless. That phone was all I could afford, and even then it was a stretch. I prepay my minutes and rarely text." Luckily, she routinely deleted both her call history and text messages. Nothing would show if Micheline did a cursory search of the phone. A fact Micheline probably already knew. She wasn't the type to leave anything to chance.

"I'm not really tech savvy," Micheline continued. "But luckily, I have someone in my employ who is. He was able to go into your phone and retrieve deleted text messages and contacts. Plus he showed me all the pictures you took of my little holding area down here."

Fiona blinked. She knew better than to say anything. It was entirely possible Micheline could be lying, hoping to draw Fiona out.

"Are you working with the FBI?" Micheline asked. "Because I see quite a few texts and calls with Holden St. Clair, who as I'm sure you are aware, happens to be an FBI agent who spends quite a bit of time here in Mustang Valley. He also is dating Bella Colton."

Heart racing, Fiona didn't respond. Her cover was well and truly blown. Not only that, but she had a broken ankle and had been locked up in a basement cell. No one knew she was here, not even Jake, who'd been so badly beaten, he probably didn't even know his own name.

"As you might remember," Micheline continued, "the AAG will become internationally famous as of this Friday, when all my followers will ingest the substance that will kill them, so that they may be born again." A slight smile played over the older woman's face as she took in Fiona's shock and dismay. "I've decided to have you go first. I'll livestream it to social media so that everyone— including your friend Jake—can watch you die."

"But what about the Coltons and my baby?" Fiona asked, her hand cradling her nonexistent bump protectively.

"That plan was too flawed. I've decided to simply ransom Jake to them." Her smile looked more like a baring of teeth. "He's the real Ace Colton, after all. Their flesh and blood. I'll just make sure they understand that you have convinced him to die so he can be born again. I have someone inside the Colton organization handling this for me right now. If they want him to live, they'll need to deposit ten million dollars in an offshore account. I'll also require a private plane and pilot."

Which meant that Micheline didn't need Fiona anymore. Then the rest of what she'd said sank in. "Why say that I'm the one who convinced Jake to die?" Fiona asked, wincing as she shifted her weight and made her ankle throb even worse. "Why involve me in that plan at all?"

Micheline laughed, the trilling sound grating on Fiona's nerves. "I want them to hate you," she said. "That way, no matter how this shakes out, they won't attempt to save you."

How this shakes out. Picking up on that, Fiona decided she might as well go ahead and ask. "You aren't planning to stick around and see for yourself, are you?"

"Of course not. I'll be long gone, to some sun-kissed beach and my ten million dollars, plus whatever else I can rake in from other families desperate to save their loved ones. My name will go down in history while I enjoy my new, carefree life." Micheline's smug tone had Fiona clenching her teeth.

"You honestly don't care how many people you kill?"

Micheline shrugged. "Honey, if they're that stupid, I'm doing the world a favor." She checked her watch. "I'll leave you to your cell and your pain. Remember, if it gets too bad, we can end it all a little bit early."

With that, Micheline spun on her stylish heels and marched away. Fiona heard her climbing the metal stairs and opening and closing the door.

"She's gone," a familiar voice said. Underhill. "Welcome to the cells. By the time you've been here awhile, starving and with your broken bones untreated, you'll probably beg her to let you drink the poison."

"Is that what you plan to do?" Fiona shot back. "Do you really want to go out that way, Underhill? Death by poison can be very painful."

Silence. Clearly, his goading didn't extend to thinking that far ahead.

Her ankle's throbbing made Fiona nauseated. She tried various positions on the concrete floor. While getting comfortable would be impossible, she'd settle for whatever caused the least amount of pain. Then and only then did she allow herself to close her eyes and try to rest.

Sometime later—she had no idea how long—the sound of the door opening at the top of the stairs caused her to jerk upright. The sudden movement brought a stab of agony, but she pushed through it. Alert, she listened. She knew she had to come up with some sort of plan of action in case Micheline or Leigh showed up and tried to get her to ingest some sort of toxin.

Two voices, both male. Bart and Randall. She'd need all her strength if Bart tried to hurt her again. She couldn't allow her pain to distract her.

They'd been the ones who'd taken Jake away on the stretcher. Did that mean they were bringing him back? Surely not. If anyone had ever needed to go to the hospital, Jake had.

Much cussing ensued as the men slowly made their way down the stairs. Fiona managed to prop herself up into a sitting position so she could see. Sure enough, one of the men appeared, moving slowly since he carried one half of the stretcher.

Finally, they made their way to the bottom of the stairs. Jake lay, still unconscious, on the stretcher.

At least he appeared to have been cleaned up. Worried sick, Fiona watched as they carried him back to the empty cell he'd occupied before. Setting the stretcher down, one man unceremoniously rolled Jake out and onto the floor.

"Is he alive?" Fiona asked, drawing the attention of both Bart and Randall.

"He is," Bart answered, his smirk and leer making her skin crawl. "He'll probably be around long after you're gone. He's way more valuable to Micheline than you'd ever be."

Randall laughed at this, pushing his glasses up his nose. The other two men simply stood there, expressions bored, waiting until they were given the okay to leave.

"Come on," Bart finally said, when she didn't give him the reaction he'd evidently been waiting for. "We're done here. Let's go."

They clomped back up the stairs and left, locking the door behind them.

Damn. Scooting across the concrete floor, she tried to peer around the dividing wall separating her cell from Jake's. But she couldn't.

"Jake," she said, raising her voice. "Wake up."

"We're all awake now, lady," Underhill complained. "Would you mind keeping it down? I'm trying to get some sleep back here."

"Wouldn't you rather get out?" she countered.

"Hell yes, but how do you think you're going to manage that? Even if you could get out of the cell, there are two locked doors between this basement and the main house. If by some miracle you were able to make it through those, there are cameras everywhere between there and freedom. They'd grab you before you made it anywhere near an outside door."

Wisely, she didn't share the fact that she possessed a key to the double doors. "You'd be surprised at what I can do," she said instead.

Underhill laughed and didn't reply. The other prisoner, the poor woman in the last cell, didn't make a sound at all.

As the hours passed, Fiona would have thought the pain from her broken ankle would have subsided. Instead, it seemed to intensify. She'd never broken a bone before, and how badly it hurt came as a shock.

Finally, she drifted into a kind of uncomfortable doze. But every movement, no matter how small, brought a sharp reminder of her now swollen and black-and-blue ankle. She'd had to take off her shoe earlier, and now even her sock felt too tight.

When the door at the bottom of the stairs opened, she pushed herself up onto her elbows, muffling a groan at the pain. No way did she plan on letting Bart catch her unprepared.

Instead of one of Micheline's male henchmen, Leigh came through the door, striding directly to Fiona's cell. She stood a few feet back from the bars, as if she thought Fiona might reach through and grab her.

Fiona spoke first. "Please tell me you're here to get me medical help."

Instead of answering, Leigh just stared, frowning. The look of distaste on her perfect features made Fiona's skin crawl.

Not knowing how to react, Fiona settled for refusing to break eye contact. Simply staring back, she wondered how long this would go on.

Finally, Leigh shook her head. "I have just one question," Leigh said, her cold tone dripping disdain. "Why? Why would you do this to us? After all we did to help you? We took you in, set you on the path to becoming a better you, and you betray our trust? *Why?*" Her voice rose with the final sentence.

So much drama. With a Herculean effort, Fiona managed not to let her face reveal any expression. "Leigh, are you aware you're part of a cult?"

Leigh's face contorted. "AAG is *not* a cult. I wish everyone would stop saying that. We do so much good, helping people—"

"Find their best selves," Fiona finished for her. "I know, believe me. Cut the nonsense, Leigh. You need to strip the blinders off your eyes and sit down and take a long, hard look at what you're a part of. If Micheline goes through with this little born-again gathering she's planning, you'll be an accessory to multiple murders. Do you honestly think she's going to stick around to see the results of the horror she's unleashed? Do you?"

Something—Fiona wasn't sure what—flitted across Leigh's expression. Realization, maybe? Fiona could only hope.

But immediately, the stubborn, intractable look came back. "Everything Micheline does is for the good of the AAG."

This time, Fiona refused to let a comment like that slide past. "Is it now? Do you truly believe asking your followers to commit a mass suicide is a good thing? Bilking confused and lonely college kids out of their money with a bunch of false promises, is that a good thing? Tell me, Leigh. Honestly. Tell me some real and true good things the AAG has done."

Leigh opened her mouth to speak. And closed it. When

she finally did offer up her thoughts, her tone carried way less confidence. "What about our seminars? We help people feel good about themselves. We give hope, often to those for whom there is no hope left."

"Reciting from the leaflet?" Fiona asked dryly, moving just enough to set off more throbbing in her ankle. She sucked in a breath, trying like hell to ignore the pain, but perspiration broke out on her forehead just the same.

"What do you want, Fiona?" Leigh dropped all pretense of her gung-ho attitude. "What's your angle in all of this?"

"I want it to stop, that's all. The taking advantage of innocent people, the bogus seminars, the baby switching and now extorting for money. Most of all, I don't want a bunch of misguided people to keep being bilked out of their life savings with some vague promises of a better version of themselves."

Leigh recoiled. "Is that really what you think of us?"

"I'm locked up in a basement cell with a broken ankle," Fiona replied. "From what I saw, Jake was beaten to within an inch of his life. Even though he's back in the cell next to me, I still don't know if he's received any kind of medical care. How about you let a doctor take a look at my ankle, maybe put a brace or a boot or a cast on it? Then maybe I'll be a tiny bit more inclined to think better of you."

But Leigh had already started backing away, eyeing Fiona as if she was something she'd found living under a rock.

Once Leigh had gone, Underhill chuckled, a dry, rasping sound. "She's never going to believe the truth," he said. "None of them do. That's why Micheline picks them. She knows how to zero in on the neediest ones."

"What about you?" she asked, genuinely curious. "Why work here?"

"I needed a job," he said. "They hired me for security. It was a decent gig, until I got greedy. When I realized what kind of moneymaking scheme Micheline had going here, I decided to try and get some of that cash for myself. I'd been pretty successful at it for a while, shaking down the newbies."

"Until I caught you."

"Yeah." He went quiet for a moment, and then started coughing. "She didn't like me beating up that kid. I was just shaking him down for cash. You turning me in was a death sentence, you know."

"Why?" she asked. "You don't think she'll let you go?"

He laughed, or tried to. It turned into a bout of coughing. "Nobody gets to leave here. This is Micheline's death row. Anybody she throws in one of these cells knows too much to ever see the light of day."

A chill skittered down Fiona's spine.

"Most die of something else. Like you, with your broken bone. Maybe infection will set in. Me, I got some kind of cold that moved to my chest. Bronchitis now, maybe. Eventually pneumonia. They don't treat you for anything. Hell, they barely even feed you, and some of the slop they bring isn't even edible."

"Except Jake," she pointed out. "They took him for medical help."

"Yes, they did. Which means Micheline has some use for him. Otherwise, she'd have left him there to rot in his own blood." His next fit of coughing left him gasping for air.

The bleakness in Underhill's voice gave Fiona pause. The FBI would be looking for her, she knew. However, they wouldn't be aware anything had gone wrong until it was too late. She had to figure out a way to get out of here on her own. She had to stop Micheline's rebirth gathering before it was too late for all the poor souls she'd managed to dupe.

Chapter 13

When Jake next stirred, he swore he heard Fiona's sweet voice, calling his name over and over. Dream? Or reality? Opening his eyes, he tried to sit up and the entire room spun. What the…? Then, everything that had happened came rushing back. Whatever had been in that shot that woman had given him had done a number on his equilibrium. Among other things.

Where was he? Squinting, he tried to make out his surroundings. Sore and nauseated, he realized they'd taken him back to his small cell down in the basement.

"Jake, are you okay?" Fiona's voice, sounding as if it was coming from the cell next to him, which most likely meant he was hallucinating, too.

"Jake?" Her voice broke as she tried again. "Please, answer me."

He frowned, not sure if what he heard was genuine or

a product of his drug-addled imagination. "Fiona? Is that really you? What are you doing down here?"

"It's me," she replied. "And they locked me up right after they beat the crap out of you. I've been trying forever to wake you up."

It took him a moment to process her words. Locked up. Fiona had been put into a cell, too. His gut clenched.

"I was so afraid they'd killed you," she continued. "Especially when you wouldn't respond no matter how many times I called your name."

"They drugged me. Not sure with what. How long was I out?" He glanced around, taking in the off-color artificial lighting. "I imagine it's hard to tell time down here."

"It is. The lack of natural lighting makes it impossible to even guess if it's day or night." She sighed. "Still, I'd have to say you were unconscious for several hours. What did the nurse say? How do you feel?"

He told her everything that had occurred while he was up in the sick bay, or whatever they called it here.

"Micheline came to see me," she said. "She's decided not to go with the fake-baby plan after all. She says she has someone inside Colton Oil who is going to tell them that I've convinced you to join in on the mass suicide. She'll offer to stop the scheme if they wire ten million dollars to an offshore account."

"Ten million?" He winced. "That's a lot of money. And why is she making you out to be the bad guy in all of this?"

"My cover is blown. She wants to make damn sure the Coltons won't want to rescue me. She even said something about making me be the first one to die."

Heart racing, he cursed. "We've got to get you out of here."

"My ankle is broken," she said, her voice steady, which made him love her even more. "They won't let me have any medical attention, so even if I could unlock this cell door and crawl my way up the stairs, I'd be moving so slow even a grandmother with a walker could catch me. I'm pretty sure escaping is out of the question."

"Then what?" he asked. "What's the plan?"

"I don't have one," she finally admitted. "Of course, I'd love it if the FBI magically realized I was in trouble, but honestly, by the time that happens, it will be too late. The Gathering for Rebirth is Friday."

"How many days?" he asked.

"Two."

"Two days?" Horrified, he tried to push past the mind fog from whatever drug they'd given him.

"Yes. And they've got something like seventy-five people signed up. My only hope is Leigh. She came down here to question me after Micheline. Leigh's gullible and a bit naive. I pushed her to really think about what she was doing. Though she still denies that she's involved in a cult, I'm hoping she'll take a long look at what's going on and figure it out."

In another cell, someone started to laugh, a raspy, wheezing sound that quickly turned into a breath-choking cough.

"That's Underhill," Fiona explained. "The guy who was beating up the college student. Apparently, Micheline locked him up here and he got sick."

"Really sick," Underhill clarified, in between bouts of gasping for air. "I think I have pneumonia. In fact, I'll probably be dead before she even gets a chance to force me to drink her poison."

"I believe him," Fiona said quietly. "He sounds pretty

ill. And that poor woman in the back cell. I wouldn't be surprised if she isn't already gone."

Jake felt in his pants pockets. No phone. Of course they'd taken it.

"There's no cell service down here anyway," Fiona said when he told her. "Believe me, I tried. If I could have called out, the FBI would already be storming the place."

Still trying to clear the last of the cobwebs from his brain, he thought for a moment. "There's got to be a way out of here," he finally said, wondering why he seemed to be slurring his words. "We've simply got to come up with a plan."

Fiona didn't respond. He could guess what she must be thinking. They were both injured, and even if they could figure out a way to unlock their cells, they wouldn't get very far.

While he knew Fiona well enough to know she'd put up a hell of a fight when they came for her, that broken ankle would hinder her abilities.

A wave of dizziness hit him, so strong he had to close his eyes and lower his head in case he passed out.

He must have briefly lost consciousness, because the next thing he heard was Fiona's voice, once again calling his name. He tried opening his mouth to answer, but he couldn't get his vocal cords to respond. Instead he found himself sliding back to the dark oblivion. He wanted to fight but didn't seem to be able to summon up enough strength.

Despite Jake's worrying lack of response to her requests for him to answer her, Fiona refused to give up hope. Most likely, whatever drugs they'd injected into Jake were causing his lapses from consciousness. She refused to consider the very real possibility that the severity of his head injury might be the cause. She knew head wounds were prone to bleeding a lot, so Jake's definitely could have looked worse than it actually was.

They were in dire straits, but she had to believe they'd make it out. She wasn't about to die, not now, especially not at the hand of a narcissistic psychopath like Micheline. Holden would try to reach her and when he couldn't, realize something was wrong.

Time locked up in her cell passed slowly, but her best guesstimate would be that at least one day had passed since they'd brought back an unconscious Jake. He seemed lucid now, though he still slept a lot, which worried her. From what she'd been able to see, he'd received some sort of head injury, and with a lack of any real competent medical attention, that could go south fast.

At least her ankle had stopped swelling, though the pain remained at an eight out of ten. She could only hope moving around on the broken bone didn't make it worse, but since she had little choice, she kept it off the floor as much as she could.

At least Micheline had put little toilets and sinks in the corner of each cell. Trying not to think of what might be on the floor, Fiona crawled back there only when strictly necessary. Mostly, she lay with her back to the wall, facing the front of her cell, so she could at least be ready whenever they came for her.

As if she'd summoned someone, the door finally opened. Luckily, it was Randall rather than Bart. As usual, he seemed awkward and uncomfortable, barely able to make even the smallest bit of eye contact.

"T-minus twenty-seven," he announced to no one in particular.

Twenty-seven what? Hours?

"Are you talking about the mass suicide?" Fiona asked, deciding to be direct rather than talking in euphemisms.

Randall flinched. "Wow. I'm not sure I'd call it that, but yeah. The Gathering for Rebirth is in twenty-seven hours."

"Are you going to take part in it, too, Randall?" Fiona asked, holding on to the bars as she struggled to stand. She finally managed to get up, using only her uninjured leg, keeping the broken ankle up off the floor.

He didn't answer. Still avoiding eye contact, he busied himself with checking some storage bins on a long, metal table.

"You don't seem to be the gullible type," Fiona pressed. "More of a thinking man, at least that's how I see you. Why would you want to ingest poison, just because some egotistical blowhard of a woman told you to?"

Randall snapped his head up at that. "Don't talk about Micheline like that," he ordered. "She's a good person."

"Is she? Are you aware that she doesn't even intend to be anywhere near here when all her poor followers die? She'll be hoofing it to the Caribbean, along with the ten million dollars she asked the Coltons to wire her."

"What?" Randall blinked. "No, you're wrong. She's going to pass out the elixir herself. She told me so."

"Really? Because when she visited me, she made it clear that she planned on bugging out of here long before the big gathering went down. She'll leave the rest of you holding the bag, Randall. If you live, you and Bart and Leigh will be accessories to murder. You'll spend the rest of your lives in prison."

Slowly, he shook his head. "Micheline wouldn't let that happen. She promised to always take care of us."

Before Fiona could respond, Randall's walkie-talkie squawked. At the familiar sound, Fiona instinctively looked for hers, but it had apparently been taken when they'd grabbed her cell phone.

Randall pressed the button and answered. "Code red, code red," Bart screamed. "Get up here now!"

"What the…?" Randall paled. He glanced at Fiona, then took off running for the stairs. Judging by the way he slammed the door, he'd left it unlocked.

"Too bad we can't get out of our cells," Jake said. "I'd love to see whatever is going on up there."

"I can only hope it's law enforcement," she muttered. "Who else could cause Bart to react like that?"

Due to the double set of steel doors, no noise from the house above reached them.

"I hate not knowing what's going on," Jake finally said.

"Me, too," she admitted.

She'd barely gotten the words out of her mouth when the door smashed open, so hard it slammed into the wall.

"FBI," a voice hollered. Holden St. Clair.

While she had no idea how they'd known to come here, the relief made her legs go weak. "Down here," she yelled. "They have me and three others locked up in individual cells."

The sound of more feet clattering down the stairs. Three more FBI agents, two men and a woman, came in, walking Randall and Bart, both in handcuffs, in front of them.

"We're going to need medical assistance," she told Holden once he'd retrieved the keys from Randall and unlocked her cell.

"How badly are you hurt?" Holden asked, pulling her to her feet and letting her lean on him.

"Broken ankle," she said. "But Jake has a head injury and probably broken ribs. There are two others in cells that way." She pointed. "The man most likely has pneumonia, but it's the woman I'm really worried about."

Holden nodded, signaling one of the other agents, who went back upstairs so he could call for help. Assisting Fiona so she could walk, they went to Jake's cell and unlocked it. Immediately, Fiona went to him.

"Are you okay?" she asked, falling to her knees next to him.

Attempting to smile at her, he nodded. "A bit woozy. Slipping in and out of consciousness. But I'll survive."

"Wait here," Holden ordered. "I'm going to check on the other two."

A moment later, he returned. "The man with the pneumonia is very ill. I'll have the paramedics take him out first."

"What about the woman in the last cell?" Fiona asked.

Slowly, Holden shook his head. "She didn't make it. No idea how long ago she died, but she's gone. I double-checked to make sure. She has no pulse."

Fiona didn't bother to hide her fury. "Micheline did this. When she's charged, you need to add this woman's death to the list."

"Oh, we will." Grim faced, Holden glanced from her to Jake, who remained woozy. "Luckily, we caught Micheline just as she was about to leave. She seemed stunned that we actually had a search warrant. And we've rounded up her closest followers, including Miss Mustang Valley."

"Leigh." Fiona nodded. "I warned her. I refuse to feel sorry for her now."

"We've got a full search going on of this entire building. We got a tip that all the poison Micheline intended to feed her followers had been delivered."

"A tip?" Fiona eyed him. "Is that how you found us?"

"As a matter of fact, yes. Dee Walton, Payne Colton's administrative assistant, called us. Apparently, Micheline asked her to not only extort her boss but to join in the mass suicide." He shrugged. "Pretty hard to believe, but she claimed she'd never realized she was part of a cult until then."

"I get it," Fiona said. "I tried to talk to Leigh about that, and she refused to believe the AAG is a cult. I'm not entirely sure why."

"Micheline had honed the fine art of brainwashing," Jake said. "She's always been good at convincing others to do what she wanted."

"The paramedics are here," one of the other FBI agents announced. "We've got enough ambulances to transport all four of the injured."

"One is already deceased," Holden informed him.

The agent winced. "Also, we need someone to make a statement to the other AAG members. They're demanding to know what's going on."

"I can do that," Fiona said. "Most of them know me anyway." She looked from Holden to the other agents. "I'll just need a lot of help getting up the stairs."

With one agent on each side, leaning on them heavily and hopping on one foot, she made it out. Someone located a wheelchair and brought it to her.

"We've asked them to gather in that amphitheater in

the back," the female agent said. "My name is Bonnie. If you'd like, I can push you there."

Grateful, Fiona accepted her help.

When she was wheeled into the large arena where Micheline had held her most intense seminars, the noisy room gradually fell quiet as people realized she was there.

She wouldn't have thought addressing these people, with whom she'd interacted on a daily basis, would be so difficult. Heart in her throat, she looked around, seeing their open, trusting faces, bracing herself for the disbelief and disappointment that was sure to follow.

Since she couldn't stand to reach the microphone on the podium, Bonnie unhooked it from the stand and brought it down to her.

Fiona swallowed, looking out at the group assembled, making eye contact with as many people as she could. "Good afternoon, everyone," she said. "Many of you know me as one of the AAG's newest recruits. In reality, I'm an FBI agent who has been working here undercover." And then she told them why. All of it, leaving out nothing.

As she spoke, she saw the ripple of shock and disbelief spread through the crowd. Many expressions turned mutinous, as if the instant she stopped speaking, they meant to stand up and accuse her of spreading falsehoods about their beloved Micheline.

She wrapped things up with the worst transgression of all—the born-again gathering, a blithe name for a horrible mass suicide. "We believe Micheline had a secret, offshore bank account, blackmailed the Coltons for ten million and had ordered a private plane to take her somewhere, likely in the Caribbean, like Grand Cayman. At this point, we can only speculate as to her reasons for doing such a thing. She is currently in FBI custody and facing numerous criminal charges."

At this last sentence, the room erupted in sound. Shouts of denial, some cursing her, calling her names. Some people cried, wailing loudly as if grief stricken, now that the woman they'd revered as a prophet had been proven false. There would be some, Fiona knew, who'd discount what she'd told them, who'd refuse to believe even the slightest stain on Micheline's character.

There wasn't anything she could do about that. All she could hope for was in the coming days, as the story played out on both the local and national media, the doubters would come to a gradual realization that maybe everything wasn't exactly as it had seemed in the AAG. She wondered if they'd ever truly understand how close they'd come to losing their lives. Would they someday look back on all this and wonder how they could have been so foolish?

Since the entire AAG center was now considered a crime scene, she'd pleaded her case and would be allowed to stay and work out of the room she'd been occupying while working undercover. Which was good, since the alternative would have meant going back to the field office and trying to work remotely.

She'd done well. Micheline had been stopped, pure evil taken down. Her supervisor had commended her and this would look good in her file.

As always when a case concluded, there were statements to make and reports to fill out. But first, she had to get her ankle looked at. Holden drove her to the same ER where Jake had been taken.

Jake. Just thinking about him had her stomach doing somersaults. More than anything, she wanted to explore a relationship with him, to see if the hot intensity of these feelings might do well as a slow simmer. She hoped he felt the same way.

X-rays proved conclusively that her ankle had been fractured. They gave her a pill for the pain, along with instructions not to drive for twenty-four hours. Then the doctor put a boot on her foot and handed her crutches, urging her to see an orthopedic surgeon as soon as possible.

"I want to go check on Jake," she told Holden, who only rolled his eyes, though he agreed to accompany her.

Jake had been admitted, she learned. Though they cited HIPAA laws and refused to release any information about his condition, she got his room number.

Moving awkwardly on the crutches, she and Holden rode the elevator to the third floor. She hobbled slowly down the seemingly endless hall, brushing off Holden's repeated attempts to help. "There," she said, relieved when she finally saw his room number.

Moving as quietly as crutches would allow, she went inside. Jake lay unconscious in the hospital bed, hooked up to an IV and various machines. He seemed pale, she thought, hobbling over to stand at the edge of his bed. His head hadn't been bandaged, so she took that as a good sign.

"You really care about this guy, don't you?" Holden asked quietly.

She nodded. "It caught me by surprise, but yes. I do."

"Does he feel the same way?"

"I think so." She gave Holden a tiny smile. "I'm hoping to get a chance to find out."

"Let's get you back to the AAG center," Holden said.

"You need to rest, and I've got to get back to work. There's a lot of evidence to process."

With one last lingering look at Jake, Fiona turned to go.

The efficiency and competence with which the medical personnel checked him out made Jake's head ache even more. While he drifted in and out, they took X-rays and blood, examined and cleaned his various wounds and abrasions, and hooked him up to an IV drip to provide him with fluids and who knew what else.

He couldn't tell how much time had passed—it could have been minutes or hours or days. Though no one had any idea what kind of drug he might have been given, they told him they were monitoring him to make sure he would be all right until it left his system.

Comforting, those assurances. Now all he wanted was Fiona. He was dimly aware of hearing that various Colton family members had stopped by to check on him, and he remembered seeing Fiona's face once or twice.

During one of his more lucid moments, he tried to locate his cell phone, intending to call her. But after a frantic search in his bed linens, he remembered the phone had been taken from him.

Surely, she'd come to see him as soon as she was able. Clinging to this certainty, he allowed himself to slide back into the darkness, even though he didn't want to miss seeing her.

When he next opened his eyes, he felt more like himself. Surrounded by the steady beeping of medical machines, he sat up slowly, bracing himself for pain. Instead, he felt only a dull ache.

And the fog had left his brain, which meant the drugs

had finally been flushed from his system. He stretched, tentative with his movement at first, then gradually allowing himself more confidence.

A doctor finally stopped by, letting Jake know he was actually in pretty good shape, all things considered. Aside from several messed-up ribs—bruised, not broken—he had a concussion and some nasty cuts and bruises. They'd been more concerned about the drug they'd injected into his bloodstream. Though the FBI had seized control of the entire AAG center, including the medical facility area, analyzing everything they'd found was going to take time. And since he clearly appeared to be recovering, that had removed any level of urgency in them getting rush results.

Once the doctor left, Jake sat back in bed, relieved. Now that all of this was finally over—Micheline had been arrested, the empire she'd built on lies and scams in the process of being dismantled—Jake had thought he'd feel more…satisfaction? Relief?

Instead, he couldn't help but feel sorry for all the innocent lives Micheline had ruined, including his own. He'd bet a lot of her followers still refused to believe that they'd been duped. He'd seen it over and over growing up. Somehow, Micheline managed to make people believe in her.

Not anymore. Though he wouldn't put it past her to try and start up some kind of cult following in prison once she got there.

Hell of a situation. And to think he almost hadn't come back. Just that tiny, remote possibility that Micheline might have really been dying of cancer had been enough to lure him in. And as usual, everything she'd done had been calculated as to how it could benefit her.

Now, Micheline's reign would finally be over. And a

lot of the people whose lives she touched would never be the same.

For him, a few good things had come of it all. He'd not only learned his true identity, but he'd met Fiona, the woman he suspected he could love. And he'd finally gotten started getting to know the family he should have grown up with.

"Hey, there." Ace Colton strolled into the hospital room, almost as if Jake's thoughts had summoned him. "Glad to hear you're going to live," he said, smiling.

Jake found himself grinning back at the other man. "Me, too," he said. "For a while there, I wondered."

Ace pulled a chair up next to the hospital bed and took a seat. "At least it's just a concussion, not a skull fracture. Fiona was really worried, you know."

Simply hearing her name brought warmth to Jake's heart. "How is she?" he asked.

"I was worried about her, too." Ace smiled. "Luckily, she won't have to have surgery on that ankle. They put her in a soft cast inside a boot. She's been up here twice."

Jake groaned. "She has? I wish someone would have woken me so I could have talked to her. How much time has passed?"

"Two days," Ace informed him. "Sorry, man."

"Do you have any idea when Fiona is coming back?"

"Oh, she's here now. I drove her. You should see her getting around on that knee scooter." Ace smiled. "She hates it."

"You would, too," Fiona said, wheeling herself into the room. "Good news, Jake. You're being released to go home today."

Home. For him, that would be his ranch, 120 miles to the north. Way too far away from Fiona.

Something of his mixed emotions must have shown on his face.

"You can stay with us," Ace invited. "One of our guest bedrooms is yours for as long as you need."

Relieved, he thanked the other man, then eyed Fiona. "What about you? Where are you going?"

"I'll be hanging out at the AAG center for a few more days, gathering evidence," she said, smiling. "I'd love to see you when I'm not working, if you'd like."

Ace laughed, startling them both. Jake realized he'd managed to briefly forget the other man was there.

"I have an idea," Ace said. "How about we have you over for dinner again, Fiona? Everyone enjoyed meeting you last time."

"Sounds great." She rolled over to Jake's other side and leaned in to kiss his cheek. If Ace hadn't been there, Jake would have turned his face toward her for a real kiss instead.

He could have sworn disappointment flashed across her expressive face.

"I'd better get back to it. I've got work to do," Fiona told them. "I wrote my number on a slip of paper, Jake. Use the room phone and give me a call once they have you sign discharge papers. They said it would be later this afternoon. I'll see who I can finagle a ride with."

"Will do."

"I can give him a ride," Ace volunteered. "Since he'll be coming to the Triple R anyway."

"Perfect." With a jaunty wave, Fiona wheeled herself out of the room.

After she'd left, Ace turned back to Jake. "My dad's assistant is beside herself," he said. "When Dee finally realized the truth about Micheline, she took it hard."

"At least she did the right thing and notified the authorities. Fiona said it was awful when she told the AAG members, too. Apparently, most of them didn't want to learn the woman they'd idolized had feet of clay."

Ace regarded him steadily. "We would have paid the money, you know. If it came down to that."

"What?" Jake stared. "Ten million? That's a lot of cash. Surely, you didn't believe I'd be foolish enough to even consider ingesting poison in some bizarre attempt to die and be reborn."

"Of course not. Dee let us all in on Micheline's scheme. Did you know when they caught her, she had a one-way ticket to Grand Cayman? That must have been where she set up her untraceable bank account. She would have disappeared by the time her followers started to die."

Shaking his head, Jake winced as a quick flash of pain hit him. "I don't know what's worse. The fact that she'd actually talked a bunch of gullible people into dying for false hopes and promises, or that she intended to leave them alone while they did it."

Ace grimaced. "I can't believe I'm actually related to her."

"My condolences," Jake replied. "Believe me when I say I know how it feels. At least neither of us will have to deal with her again. She'll be locked up for the rest of her life, most likely."

"I think so," Ace agreed. "I hear there are so many charges."

They talked about a few other things, including Ace's desire to show him around Colton Oil. "I used to be CEO there," Ace said, his tone rueful.

"This all has been a lot to deal with."

"True. But one good thing came of it. I met the woman

I'm going to marry. You met her. Sierra. She was a bounty hunter looking for me."

"Wow." Jake tried to wrap his mind around that. "She doesn't look the slightest bit dangerous."

For whatever reason, this caused Ace to laugh. "Oh, she is, believe me," he said. "She's the best thing that ever happened to me."

Jake nodded. He could definitely understand that. Because Fiona was exactly the same to him. Glancing over at Ace, he realized meeting his new family and getting to know this man, in particular, ranked right up there too.

Chapter 14

Getting around on the knee scooter was a royal pain. Though she had to struggle not to show her frustration, Fiona found the entire process way too cumbersome and slow. Patience had never been one of Fiona's virtues, and though it was something she constantly tried to work on, she realized twenty minutes into trying to navigate through life on one knee that she still had a long way to go. It didn't help that this broken ankle had happened at the worst possible time—the biggest bust of her career.

Micheline Anderson was going down. Though the FBI already had enough to charge her with to put her away for years, especially with Ainsley having direct experience of Micheline's Marriage Institute, Holden working with Spencer, and Spencer already investigating the AAG with Katrina, they wanted more. Fiona did, too, with a furious sort of passion that consumed nearly every waking moment. Because she wanted justice. Retribution for what Micheline had done to Jake Anderson, one of the finest men Fiona had ever known. And for all the poor, gullible or desperate souls she'd taken in with her quasi-affirmation hocus-pocus. The college students she'd swindled, the elderly people who'd gladly handed over their life savings and everyone in between. Including the Colton family, who'd suffered their share of bizarre events already. Learning their eldest son and heir wasn't actually related by blood had to rank up there as one of the worst. Having Micheline try to extort them for ten million dollars must have been the final straw.

Righting injustice had been one of the main reasons she'd chosen a career in law enforcement. The training she'd received at Quantico had underscored her certainty that she'd been born for this kind of work. Taking this undercover assignment had been more difficult than she'd expected, especially since so many of the things she'd been expected to do went deeply against her beliefs. She was glad it was over, happy that they'd been able to end it with an arrest and numerous, serious charges.

And because of it, she'd met Jake. While they hadn't known each other very long at all, the connection they'd made hinted at the possibility of a long and happy future as a couple. If she allowed herself to be optimistic—something she rarely did, since she considered herself a realist—she'd come to believe he might just be the one. Once this case was closed, she planned to take some time off and find out.

Meanwhile, the formidable fact-finding machine that was the FBI had gotten hard at work obtaining information. The AAG center swarmed with agents. Since they'd obtained a far more detailed search warrant, the Bureau had brought in teams, who all conducted an intensive search. This went on from sunup to sundown. As soon as one team left to get some rest, another showed up to take their place.

For her part, Fiona tried to stay out of their way. Though she hadn't been removed from the case, she hadn't been assigned to a particular team, either. The special agent in charge allowed Fiona and Holden to stay and do as they pleased, as long as they didn't interfere with anyone else. Fiona had claimed Leigh's suite as her own search area and took a certain satisfaction in taking apart the room piece by piece.

Thus far she'd found nothing substantial. But then, Leigh clearly had been coached not to leave any kind of paper trail. She'd kept only a few paper files—one with handouts touting the miracle seminars that AAG offered, and another with printouts and newspaper clippings regarding her Miss Mustang Valley win. The rest had to be stored on a computer or in the cloud.

Fiona itched to get a look at her laptop. But of course, she'd had to turn the computer over to the FBI's IT department, who would thoroughly examine its contents. Right now, she was kneeling on the floor going through the bottom drawer of a mostly empty filing cabinet, just hoping Leigh had been careless one time.

A quiet tap on the door made her look up. Holden St. Clair stood in the doorway, eyeing her. "Did you find anything?" he asked.

"Not really." Struggling to pull herself up without putting weight on her ankle, she gratefully accepted Holden's help getting on her knee scooter. "I have to say, I'm really disappointed. I honestly believed Leigh knew a lot more secrets than she let on. Now I'm wondering if Micheline kept her mostly in the dark and told her only what she wanted her to hear."

"I wouldn't put it past her," Holden replied. "Micheline was a master at manipulating people. And Leigh Dennings seemed a naive and trusting sort. By the way, speaking of her... Leigh has been asking for you. She keeps saying she doesn't belong in jail. She's been telling everyone who will listen that you will vouch for her character."

Momentarily taken aback, Fiona shook her head. "She's wrong. I gave her the opportunity to get out before it all hit the fan. I asked her to do the right thing. She refused. She left me lying in the tiny basement cell, injured, determined not to hear anything bad about Micheline or the AAG. She made her choice. Now she's going to have to live with it."

"I agree." Holden walked around the room, one brow raised. "She decorated this place like a Pottery Barn store," he said.

His comment made Fiona laugh. "Good analysis. Stylish, cozy and expensive." She eyed the other agent. "What about you? Is there something you're not telling me?"

"That's why I'm here now." Holden flashed a quick smile. "We've got some new information," he said. "A while back, we rounded up a guy named Harley Watts. He did all of Micheline's dark web work and took care of helping her set up a new identity for when she took off. Once he'd had a little taste of jail, he said he was willing to talk if the prosecutor would hammer out a plea deal."

Fiona perked up. "Did you get that worked out?"

"We did. And let me tell you, it was worth it. This Watts guy bugged Micheline's office. He recorded everything and hung on to it all. Once he told us where to find it, we sent a couple of agents over to get it. We've got people listening to it all now. My hunch says we'll have a ton of evidence of even more crimes. Enough to put Micheline away for a long, long time."

"I'd like to see the transcript when it's finished," Fiona said. "I want to throw the book at that woman."

"I agree. Anyone awful enough to plan for all her followers to commit suicide needs to go away for a long, long time." Holden shook his head. "It never ceases to amaze me how people can be so evil and yet manage to convince so many others to believe in them."

"At least we got her." Her knee had started aching, as it usually did when she spent too much time on the scooter. "I'd better get back to it."

"Let me know if you need any help," Holden replied, turning to go. "And please, give me a holler if you find anything good."

Even though she privately didn't think she would at this point, Fiona agreed. Back to work, she told herself, but she remained on her knee scooter rather than lowering herself to the floor. What she really wanted, she realized with some disbelief, was to be with Jake. This seemed so out of character for a woman whose work always, always came first, she had to sit still and consider.

She really had it bad for him. Jake was never far from her thoughts. She found herself wondering at odd moments during the day what he might be doing right then, if he felt okay, how his new Colton family was treating him.

Pushing thoughts of him away, she returned her focus to where it belonged right now—her search. She'd give Jake a call later, once she was off duty.

* * *

Though Jake had wondered if he'd feel awkward, walking into the huge house at the Triple R felt almost like coming home. Part of that feeling might have been the warm welcome everyone gave him, from Payne and his wife, Genevieve, who actually hugged him this time, to Ainsley, Grayson, the twins Marlowe and Callum, as well as Asher, and a host of other family members. Jake did wonder how Ace had managed to coordinate everything, but he definitely appreciated their kindness.

"I feel like one of the family," Jake mused to Ace after Ace had shown him his room.

Ace laughed. "You *are* one of the family," he said. "Actually more than I am."

Studying the other man, who appeared both confident and relaxed, Jake decided he might as well ask, especially since they were all going to be in such close quarters. "How are you feeling about all this, Ace? I definitely don't want to be encroaching on your…"

"Territory?" Ace grinned even wider. "You couldn't. They love me like a son. Hell, I *was* their son for forty years. I still am. As are you, now. Believe me, the Colton family has enough room in their hearts for one more." His smile faded. Stepping forward, he clasped Jake's shoulder. "I never, ever want you to feel uncomfortable or awkward around any of us, understand? None of what happened was your fault."

Slightly embarrassed, Jake nodded. "I know. I just wondered if it felt weird."

"Yes, of course it does." Ace released him, going to the window and pulling aside the drapes so he could see out. "At first, I questioned my own identity. I mean, Micheline is a pretty awful woman. Anyone would have issues learning they were actually related to her."

Now Jake had to laugh. "I know, believe me. I lived with that for forty years. It was hell."

Ace's cell phone rang. Glancing at the screen, he glanced at Jake. "Sorry, I need to take this." Answering, he walked out into the hallway to listen.

Jake placed his suitcase on the bed, debating unpacking. He decided he might as well. He hadn't brought a lot of clothes since originally he hadn't planned on staying long. Since then, he'd bought a few things, but he really needed to go shopping again. Maybe he and Fiona could make plans to do that when she was off work.

"Wow." Returning, Ace grinned at Jake, his expression both bemused and excited. "I'm officially a grandfather."

"What?" Stunned, Jake eyed the other man. Since they were the exact same age, he could hardly imagine. "I didn't even know you had kids."

"One—I just found out, to be honest. Her name is Nova. She just gave birth to her daughter, Clara, with her boyfriend, Nikolas, by her side." Ace shook his head. "He's a great guy. The baby isn't even biologically his, but he loves Clara so much, he's planning to raise her as his own daughter." A single tear leaked from one eye. Ace wiped it away with one finger. "I knew her due date was coming up, but I wish someone had called me when Nova went into labor."

"Congratulations." Jake held out his hand.

Ace gripped it, still grinning. "I've got to head up to the hospital. I want to see my granddaughter. And make sure Nova is doing okay."

"How about I take you?" Jake offered. "You seem a bit too shook up to drive."

Expression still a potent mixture of joy and bewilderment, Ace shook his head. "Thanks for the offer, but I'm fine. Just a bit…overcome, I guess." He snapped his fingers. "I need to stop and get some flowers or something. A teddy bear for the baby. I'll see you later back here."

He started to walk off, but then turned. "Oh, before I forget, Ainsley is planning a get-together so the entire family—cousins and all—can meet you. Bring Fiona, too, of course. I'm sure Ainsley will get you details as soon as she finalizes everything."

Ace rushed off, still muttering to himself under his breath.

After unpacking, Jake debated going into town alone and doing some shopping. But since buying clothes was a task he despised, he decided to wait and see if Fiona wouldn't mind joining him.

He wandered downstairs, still feeling pretty self-conscious, thinking he might go out to the barn and check out the horses. With Ace gone and the rest of the Colton family busy with their jobs or their daily routines, the massive house seemed empty.

As he headed into the kitchen to see if he could rustle up another cup of coffee, he found Payne sitting alone at the kitchen table. The older man still appeared weak, though he seemed to be gradually recovering.

"Pull up a chair," Payne invited, his fingers wrapped around a steaming mug of his own coffee. "Grab a cup. I just made a fresh pot."

Jake did. The coffee tasted strong, just the way he liked it.

Payne talked mostly about generalities, the ranch, his livestock and how much he loved Mustang Valley. Genevieve drifted in, wearing yoga clothes, smiled at Jake and kissed Payne's cheek before drifting back out. "I'll be home in an hour or so," she said, and left.

She'd barely left for her yoga class when Payne leaned forward, his intense gaze fixed on Jake. "I'm going to have to ask you to take a DNA test you know."

Jake nodded. "I've expected that. And I've already done one and sent it in. I'm just waiting on the results. Honestly, I don't blame you. That's the only way to make sure."

"Good, good." Payne exhaled, clearly relieved. "We'll get that done as soon as possible. That way there's no room for doubt."

"I agree." Jake smiled at the older man.

"So many years wasted. All because of that awful woman."

Fighting the urge to apologize, Jake nodded instead. "I really appreciate how welcoming everyone here has been."

"Welcoming?" Payne's brows rose. "Son, even though we don't have the DNA results, I can tell you're one of us. It might have taken you forty years to find your way back, but you're a Colton. Don't you ever forget that."

"I won't." Feeling absurdly relieved, Jake took another drink of his coffee. "I just wish I could have met my mother."

"Me, too. I loved your mother," Payne said. "I've been married three times. Tessa's been gone just a little over thirty-five years, but I've never stopped missing her."

Jake nodded. "You seem happy now, though. Genevieve seems nice."

"Oh, she is. And I am happy," Payne declared. "The only relationship mistake I ever made was marrying

Selina. And now I can't get away from her. Damn woman is even on the board at Colton Oil."

Jake wasn't sure how to respond to that, so he simply sipped his coffee and said nothing.

"Wait here." Getting up slowly, Payne disappeared for a moment. When he returned, he carried a large, faded photo album. "Come into the living room," he said, leaving his cup on the table.

Jake did the same. Payne grunted, lowering himself onto the couch. "Sit beside me. This is a photo album, one of many. Though Tessa was the photographer in most of the others, all the pictures in this one were taken by other people, so she's in them. Let's take a little walk down memory lane."

Once Jake had taken a seat, Payne opened the album. There, in the first photograph, a beautiful woman smiled at the camera, her face alight with love. She held a baby in her arms, whom Jake guessed must have been Ace. He felt a pang, well aware that this might have been him. Though he'd never wish to take that experience away from Ace, he couldn't help but feel envious. Not once in his forty years had he known a mother's unconditional love.

Payne turned the pages slowly, giving Jake time to study each picture. In all of them, Tessa's love of her family shone through. She positively glowed with it.

And there, on the last page, Tessa and Payne. Gazing into each other's eyes.

Swallowing hard, Payne closed the book. "Still gets me," he said. "Even after all these years. She was a good woman."

"Thank you for sharing that with me," Jake told him. "I really appreciate it."

"No problem." Payne yawned, covering his mouth with his hand. "Sorry, son," he said. "I need to go lie down. Colton Oil has a board meeting this afternoon, and I need to rest up for that."

The way Payne casually called him *son* made Jake's chest ache. He managed a nod. "A nap sounds like a great idea," he said. "Do you need any help getting to your room?"

"No, thanks." Payne waved him away. "I'm getting stronger bit by bit. The walk will do my legs good."

As Payne pushed to his feet, Jake did, too. "At least let me walk with you. It's always good to have company, just in case."

"Am I that wobbly?" Payne shot him an amused grin. "Don't answer that. You're not much better yourself, you know. Come on then. You can escort me to my room."

Once they'd reached the doorway, Payne turned and put his hand on Jake's shoulder. "I know I can never make up to you all the years we lost. We can only move forward. You understand that, right?"

"I do."

"You're welcome to attend the board meeting this afternoon," Payne said. "As my guest. I think it will do you some good to learn about our company." And he went inside his room, closing the door without waiting for Jake to answer.

Jake took himself outside, slowly walking the grounds around the ranch. The Triple R was well maintained in addition to being beautiful. He admired the livestock, their coats gleaming with health, took in the clean barn, the outdoor ring with its freshly raked surface. Pride of ownership shone here, making him miss his own ranch. Though not nearly as large or prosperous as the Triple R, he'd worked damn hard to get it and keep it running. He'd built it from the ground up, and while the ranch was still a work in progress, it was his.

Turning slowly, he took it all in. The massive house, designed to blend in with the landscape. The barns, the acres of fenced pastures and the mountains in the distance. This place was now part of his life, too. He couldn't imagine simply returning to his ranch and never seeing the Triple R or the Colton family again.

Or Fiona. The thought of going back to his old life—where he'd been a rancher with no real family—made his gut hurt. These people, each and every one of them, were important to him. Especially Fiona. He could see himself spending the rest of his life with her.

He'd simply have to figure out a way to make this work.

Ace arrived back home shortly after lunch. He sent Jake a text asking if he could meet him in the kitchen. Since Jake had been thinking about rustling up something for lunch, he texted back that he was on his way.

When he reached the kitchen, he found Ace munching on a sandwich. "I had the chef make one for you," Ace said, sliding the plate toward him, along with a can of diet cola.

"Thanks." Grateful, Jake pulled up a chair and dug in.

The two men ate in silence. When they'd finished, Jake eyed the man he'd come to think of as his brother. "How was your grandbaby?"

Ace's eyes sparkled. "Beautiful. Smaller than I imagined, but I'm told that's how newborns are."

"I can only imagine," Jake replied. "Want to do something this afternoon?"

"We're having a board meeting today," Ace said, his

tone apologetic. "Since you might someday be part of this company, I thought you might want to sit in."

"Payne invited me earlier, and I've been thinking about it. Won't they mind?" Jake asked. "The rest of the board?"

"Nope. I've already cleared it with them. And since I'm no longer CEO, I'll just be there as an observer anyway."

Jake shrugged. "Sounds good." He shifted his weight from one side to the other, trying to stretch and wincing at the sharp stab of pain. "As long as I can sit down. My ribs are really hurting me."

"There are chairs." Grinning, Ace checked his watch. "You have just under thirty minutes to get cleaned up and ready to go. Did you bring a suit?"

"A suit?" Jake looked at him as if he'd suggested going in costume. "I only own one suit that I wear to funerals or weddings. It's hanging in my closet back home at my ranch."

Ace laughed. "I don't think we're the same size, but I've probably got a pair of slacks and a dress shirt you can borrow. And I'll let you choose the tie."

The slacks were a little loose, but a belt took care of that. The shirt felt a little tight, though it would do. Since Jake and Ace had completely different shoe sizes, Jake had to wear his best set of boots. He chose a dark blue, nondescript tie.

When he made it downstairs, Payne was also waiting, since Ace would be driving him as well. He smiled when he saw Jake. "Glad you decided to come," he said, leaning on an elaborately carved cane. "Ace wanted me to use a wheelchair, but I'm perfectly capable of walking."

"As long as you promise to use that cane," Ace interjected. "The last thing you need right now is a fall."

Payne shook his head, but he didn't argue.

This time, they were taking one of Payne's vehicles, a large, black Mercedes. Ace drove, and Payne took shotgun, leaving Jake to ride in the back. He didn't mind. He was just glad they were letting him participate.

Ace dropped Payne off at the front entrance before parking in a spot marked Reserved for P. Colton. "I used to have my own spot," he commented. "I'm really hoping that the reason Payne asked me to come today is because he's planning to ask the board to give me my job back. Especially since I was cleared of any crime."

Jake had read up on how Ace had been accused of shooting his own father and gone on the run. "Makes sense," he agreed. "That must have been hell."

"It was a nightmare. But the one good thing that came out of it made it all worthwhile. I'd never have met Sierra otherwise."

They walked inside. Ace nodded to the receptionist before striding to the elevator. He punched the up button, and the doors immediately opened.

"Are you nervous?" Ace asked.

"Not really. I thought I might be, but I'm actually looking forward to seeing how these kinds of things work."

"They're never boring, that's for sure." The doors opened and they stepped out. "Come on."

Several people were already seated at a long, highly polished wooden table. Jake recognized Payne and Selina, Ace's ex-stepmother, along with Marlowe, Ainsley, and Rafe. Jake was glad he'd met them.

"Ace," Payne boomed. "I'm glad you're here. And welcome, Jake. So good to see you." As if he hadn't ridden in with them.

All of the others echoed his welcome. Except Selina, who simply eyed him with one brow raised.

Once Ace and Jake had taken seats in a grouping of chairs away from the table, Payne got down to business.

"I called this meeting the minute my doctor released me to get a little work done," Payne said. "I want Ace reinstated as CEO, if the board will vote to rescind the blood Colton clause. If not, I will dismantle the company."

Several people shifted in their seats, but no one dissented.

"We'll take this to a vote. All those in favor, raise your hands and say aye."

One by one, every single person at that table raised their hands and agreed. Save one. Selina. Mouth tight, eyes flashing, she pushed to her feet.

"Don't you see what he is doing?" she cried. "Each and every one of you? He's going to take away your birthrights and give it to that no-good son of his. Even worse, Ace isn't really even his! He's not a Colton by blood. I see no reason why he should be allowed to have anything at all to do with this company. Stand up for what is right," she entreated. "Because this is absolute nonsense."

No one spoke. In fact, they all sat frozen, appearing uncomfortable, watching Payne for his reaction.

"You're finished, Selina," Payne said. "I'm ousting you. From the board, from the company and our lives. I want you to go to your office, pack your things and get out of my building. I'll have my attorneys draw up papers immediately with your severance package."

Instead of surprise, fury darkened her eyes. "You

won't dare, Payne Colton. Because you know damn well I'll reveal your little secret. The one I've kept for way too long. It will destroy you." With a self-confident smirk, she dared him to contradict her.

Payne took a deep breath. Jake saw the barest hint of nerves in the way the old man's fingers trembled. But he lifted his chin and met Selina's gaze. "Go ahead. My family has already been to hell and back, and we're still strong. We've survived everything else, and we'll damn sure survive you and the blackmail you've levied against me for years."

"You'll be sent away to prison for life," she warned. "And you'll never see that precious family of yours. Remember, there's no statute of limitations on murder."

Murder? Jake started. Next to him, he heard Ace suck in his breath.

"It was self-defense," Payne declared, looking around the room. "I swear to you."

Selina snorted. "He told me he shot and killed a man at the mansion during his marriage to Tessa. Turned out the guy was a well-known enemy of his and he was afraid to report it, so he buried the body himself and told no one."

"When was this?" Ace asked.

"Thirty-five years ago," Payne replied. "You first three kids were small. It was right before Tessa got sick and died."

A long time to carry such an awful secret, Jake thought. This entire thing felt intensely private, and Jake really wished he were somewhere else—anywhere else instead of there.

"I'll give you twenty-four hours to change your mind," Selina announced. "If I don't hear from you before then, I'll go to the police. And I know exactly where you buried the body, remember? I'm sure the Mustang Valley Police Department will happy to reopen a cold case like this, especially with such a high-profile killer."

Snatching up her designer alligator-skin briefcase, Selina sailed out the door. She paused at the last moment and turned. "You can all go to hell," she said. A moment later, she roared off in her Porsche. They all wanted to cheer that she was finally out of their lives, but the gravity of her accusations made that impossible.

Only once she'd left did Payne's impassive expression crumble. "I'm so screwed," he said, covering his face with both his hands. "Everything she said was true, except it really was self-defense."

Ace went to him and clasped his shoulder. "There's got to be a way to prove that. We'll do whatever it takes."

"I'll help, too." Jake pushed to his feet and joined Ace. He exchanged a troubled look with the man he'd come to regard as a brother. "Somehow, we'll figure something out."

Chapter 15

After the meeting broke up, Jake and Ace collected a visibly shaken Payne and left Colton Oil. The somber mood felt heavy, much different than the one they'd driven out with. As they drove back to the Triple R, Jake watched the two in the front seats, worried. Neither man spoke much, each lost in his own thoughts.

"Mustang Valley sure is a dramatic place," Jake finally said, hoping to lighten the mood.

Ace shot him a surprised look, but then he smiled. "It has been lately," he agreed. "So much craziness going on, we could be an episode of one of those television soap operas."

Once they arrived at the ranch, Jake went up to his new digs and called Fiona. Rather than sit around and brood in the unfamiliar room, he wanted to find out what time she'd be finished with work. Maybe they could go out for dinner or take a walk.

"I'm just wrapping things up now," she said, sounding delighted to hear from him. "Since it's too early to eat yet, maybe we can figure out something else to do."

The husky invitation in her voice made his body stir. "I'm on my way to pick you up," he said. "I'll be there in ten."

As he pulled up in front of the AAG center, he knew for him, the rustic beauty of the huge house would forever be tainted. Micheline might be safely behind bars, but he'd always feel her presence in this location. Always.

The instant Fiona climbed into Jake's pickup, she somehow knew that something had gone wrong. "Are you all right?" she asked sharply.

He told her all about his visit to Colton Oil, the board meeting and Selina's threats.

Fiona frowned. "If this is true and he really did kill someone and hide the body on the Triple R, it's not going to look good, to put it mildly. Self-defense is his only hope."

"But how would he even prove that?" Jake asked, refusing to allow the utter hopelessness of the situation to creep into his voice. "That was long before the days of modern technology. It would simply be his word against the evidence."

Fiona didn't comment. He figured he knew why. Sometimes, if there was nothing good to say, it was better not to speak at all.

"I just learned I had a father," he said. "I've barely even begun to get to know him. If he goes to prison now…" He couldn't finish the sentence. Since his mother had died so long ago, he'd never get the chance to develop a relationship with her. The Coltons were the family he'd never known he had.

"Are you sure you're in the mood for company?" she asked. "If you'd rather have some time alone, I get it."

Incredulous, he shook his head. "I need to be with you. I was hoping we could go for a long walk. Fresh air helps me think. There are a lot of trails out at the Triple R, if you don't mind going back to the ranch with me."

"Trails?" she asked. "Do you ride? I'm betting Ace wouldn't mind loaning us a couple of horses. The Triple R has some amazing riding trails, or so I've heard. We could ask one of the ranch hands."

He liked that idea. If his still-healing ribs could take it. Which, as long as they kept the pace slow, he felt confident they could. Before he could think too hard about it, he pulled over to the shoulder of the road and dialed Ace's cell. As soon as he relayed his request, Ace agreed.

"We've got several horses we use just for taking guests on trail rides," he said. "I'll have Jarvis or one of the ranch hands get them saddled up for you two. He can give you some info about where to go. Sierra and I would join you, but we've already made other plans. We'll be going out in about an hour." He gave instructions as to where they should go and promised to have the horses brought up and ready immediately.

"Thank you so much," Jake said. "We should be there in about ten minutes or so."

"Perfect. When you pull in, drive straight to the big white barn. The horses will be tied up inside. When you're done riding, a couple of the ranch hands will come get them."

Ace hung up. Jake passed along all he'd said to Fiona while he drove.

"I haven't been riding since I was a teenager," Fiona said. "Is it weird that I'm really looking forward to this?"

"Not at all." He smiled at her, right before they turned onto the road that led to the Triple R. The enormous house sat high on a hill, surrounded by acres of fenced land and well-maintained barns and storage sheds. A beautiful and prosperous ranch, with the mountains as scenic backdrop. Sometimes he wanted to pinch himself.

All the years he'd missed... But then again, he wouldn't wish his actual childhood on anyone, especially not Ace.

"I wonder if my mother liked to ride," he said. "It feels awful not to know anything about her, other than the photo album Payne shared with me."

"Maybe you should ask Ace to share some of the photos she took," she suggested. "Didn't Payne mention she was some sort of amateur photographer? If so, I bet there are a ton of pictures. You might see a lot of her in the way she framed her images."

Her insight made him love her even more. Swallowing past the sudden lump in his throat, he nodded. "Good idea. I'll ask him later tonight or tomorrow."

When they drove around to the barn and parked, Jake saw that Ace had been true to his word. Two ranch employees waited with two horses, already saddled.

But just as Jake and Fiona got out of the truck, the sound of several vehicles driving too fast on the gravel road had them turn to look back in the direction from which they'd come.

Several Mustang Valley patrol vehicles pulled up in front of the house. Jake cursed. "Selina must have gone to the police." He took off running, then remembered Fiona couldn't keep up due to her knee injury. Instead, he motioned for her to get back in the passenger seat, and they drove back.

They reached the house just as Ace opened the door.

Clearly dressed for his night out, he wore a dark blue suit and tie. He glanced back at Jake and Fiona before focusing on the police. "Can I help you, Officers?"

"We have a search warrant." The man in front ceremoniously handed it over, waiting while Ace read it.

"You want to search the house?" Ace asked, clearly taken by surprise.

"No." The detective, an older, graying man, scratched his head. "Sorry, but we're just going to do some digging on your property."

Digging. Jake met Ace's gaze and swallowed. Fiona took his arm and held on tight.

"Have at it," Ace finally said. Sierra came up behind him, her expression troubled. Behind her, Ainsley frowned. Ace filled them in. Then they all stood watching while the police officers got in their cars and drove over to a small, unused pasture near the edge of the property.

"Exactly where Selina told them to dig," Ace said. "Payne showed me the spot earlier."

"Hush," Ainsley chided sharply. "I'm putting on my attorney hat now. No more discussion of any of that, do you hear me?"

They all nodded, even Jake. The more time he spent around these people, the more welcome they made him feel. Like part of the family. *His* family.

Though everyone wore the same worried expression, they all clearly didn't want to look away. Side by side, they kept watching. Standing on the sidewalk, near the circular drive, with a clear view of all the activity taking place below them.

Only Payne was absent. He'd taken to his bed shortly after the confrontation with Selina, worried that he was too newly recovered to deal with so much stress.

"This is too much," Ainsley finally muttered. "Let's go back inside. They'll come and tell us if they find anything."

Not *if,* Jake thought. But *when.*

"Come on." Ace punched his arm, a light, brotherly type of gesture. "When Ainsley speaks, the rest of us listen."

Which earned him a glare from his attorney sister.

They trooped back into the kitchen, got cups of coffee and took seats around the large table.

The knock on the door came exactly thirty-seven minutes later.

"I'll get it," Ainsley said. No one argued.

A moment later, she returned, her face ashen. "They found a body. They're going to arrest Dad."

Of course everyone insisted on standing in solidarity when the police read Payne his rights. Though the older man kept muttering that it had been self-defense, he didn't argue. Instead, he held out his hands for the cuffs, his expression resolute.

"We're going to beat this," Ace reassured him.

But how? Jake wondered silently. Right now, all they had was Payne's claim, no proof. And his actions after killing the man pointed more toward someone guilty.

Once the police had driven off with Payne, Ainsley had immediately gotten on the phone, rustling up help from Santiago, who specialized in criminal defense. "He'll meet them at the jail," she announced once she'd ended the call. "Meanwhile, we've got to get busy finding some sort of proof to back up Dad's claim of self-defense." She eyed Fiona. "Is any of this your area of expertise?"

Slowly, Fiona shook her head. "Not really. But I'll do everything I can to help you."

Ainsley nodded. "Jarvis had done quite a bit of searching the property already. At the very least, he can tell us where not to look."

"We need to find proof," Ace declared. "There's got to be something. We'll just have to find it." But how were they going to do that? No one asked the question out loud, especially not Jake. He'd barely spent any time with his birth father, certainly not enough to understand what made Payne Colton tick.

Ace, on the other hand, was an open book. Despite his previous plans with Sierra, he canceled them, saying he wanted nothing to distract him from focusing on clearing Payne. Talking to him, Jake could see hints of the ruthless CEO he'd once been, though he'd clearly mellowed. He was also leaner than he'd been in the old photographs Jake had seen online.

"Don't you think if Payne had evidence to back him up, he would have produced it by now?" Fiona asked softly.

Though Ainsley shot her a quick look, she nodded. "My thoughts exactly. Unless he isn't aware that there even *is* evidence."

And there might not be. Jake knew better than to voice this thought out loud.

"There's got to be something we're overlooking," Ace announced, pacing the length of the kitchen and back. "It's got to be right there in front of us. Got to be."

"Sometimes when you try too hard to find something, it stays just around the corner of your vision," Jake pointed out. "We need to take a break, look at something else for a little while. Maybe then, something will come to us."

At first, Ace shot an impatient look his way. But then he apparently reconsidered. "You may be right. How about this? Earlier, you were asking for information about your birth mother. Payne stored all of her photography stuff and her journals in one of the unused bedrooms. When we were younger, we all spent some heavy-duty time in there, going through the pictures. I think it might help you get a feel as to what kind of woman she was."

Jake nodded, feeling a flicker of interest. "I'd like that," he responded quietly. "Plus it might be a good distraction right now." He turned to Fiona. "Want to come?"

"Sure."

Sierra chimed in that she'd take a look, too. "I've always been a huge photography fan."

"You guys go," Ainsley said, waving them away. "I've got some case law I want to study before I head downtown to see what I can do to get a judge to allow me to get Dad out on bond."

Instantly, Ace declared he wanted to go, too.

"We'll see," Ainsley replied, not appearing convinced. "Actually, I think it would be better if I just went. We want to try and keep this small, quiet and contained. Since I work with these people, I'm the best candidate. I promise to fill everyone in as soon as I know anything."

Ace looked like he wanted to argue, but he clearly thought better of it.

"Now shoo." Ainsley returned her attention to her book. "I've got a lot of ground to cover in a short period of time."

Fiona and Sierra followed the two men down a long hall, up a flight of stairs and into another part of the house. She couldn't help but admire the way the decor and furniture worked together and looked both elegant and comfortable.

Her heart ached for this family. They'd been through so much already, and now this. So many people erroneously believed the simple act of being wealthy ensured an easy life. In Fiona's opinion, great wealth seemed to bring even greater challenges.

Ace paused at a closed door, turning to face the rest of them. "No one is usually allowed in here," he said. "Dad keeps this room as sort of Tessa's shrine."

Jake glanced over his shoulder at Fiona, who shrugged. "Maybe this isn't the right time," Jake said, looking as if he wished he were anywhere else but there.

"It's the perfect time," Ace responded. "Honestly, I think Dad would want me to show you this. We'll let Ainsley do her thing, clear our heads and go back to brainstorming in a little while."

"I thought you and Sierra had plans." Jake tried again. Fiona wasn't sure why he appeared to be so hesitant.

"We canceled them." Ace raised a brow. "Do you not want to learn about Tessa? Sorry, it never occurred to me to ask first."

Fiona moved to Jake's side and took his arm, offering her silent support.

"Naturally, I want to learn about my birth mother." Jake's tone was wry. "Actually, I ache for it, with every fiber of my being. But my birth father has been arrested, might be charged with murder and has been hauled off to jail after recently awakening from a coma and being released from the hospital." He shook his head. "Honestly, Ace. After reading up on everything on the internet, I found himself wondering if the Colton family had been cursed."

Ace's mouth twisted. "I hear you. If not cursed, we've certainly had a rather spectacular run of bad luck." He eyed Jake. "Say the word. If you don't want to do this right now, we won't."

Fiona found herself holding her breath. She caught Sierra watching Jake, too, a similar look of anticipation on her face.

Jake turned and caught Fiona watching him. "Let's check it out. I think we could all use a small distraction right now."

Small distraction? Either way, Fiona breathed a sigh of relief. Personally, she thought Ace was right. If they all sat around wringing their hands and bemoaning Payne's fate, they'd have trouble thinking up any kind of solution.

Ace turned the knob and opened the door. He flipped the light switch, and they all stepped inside.

It wasn't a bedroom, as Jake had expected. Instead, the room appeared to be some sort of studio, with photographs rather than paintings.

There were trays of negatives, labeled by date, and a neat row of photo albums stood on one long shelf. Her favorite prints had been blown up and hung on the wall, the subjects ranging from landscapes to people and animals. They were all good, some spectacularly so. One or two made Jake catch his breath.

"She really was talented," Fiona breathed, catching at Jake's arm. "I'm surprised she didn't have a career as a professional photographer."

"Remember, some of these were taken over thirty-five years ago," Ace interjected. "Think about how different things were when we were kids. Since there are two entire photo albums filled with baby pictures of me, Ainsley and Grayson, I'd venture a guess that most of these pictures are at least thirty-six years old, many older."

Jake stood frozen, taking it all in. Still holding his arm, Fiona moved them forward. "Look," she said, pointing. A couple of vintage cameras sat in a glass-fronted cabinet. She spied a Pentax, a Nikon and even an ancient Polaroid.

"Back when everyone used actual film," Ace said. "Since photographers often have to take tons of shots to get one good one, I imagine she burned through a lot of film." He pulled open a drawer. "See. Here's a bunch she hadn't developed yet."

"Interesting." Jake came closer. "Did she have her own darkroom?"

"Yep. In the closet." Ace walked across the room and opened the door. "We were all too young to remember, but I'm betting this entire area was off-limits to us kids."

Fiona hung back, letting Jake set the pace. She could only imagine how he must feel, seeing his real mother's art—an expression of herself—for the first time.

As Jake picked up one of the albums and began leafing through it, Ace's phone chimed. "It's Ainsley," he said. "She'd like us all back downstairs right now."

With what could have been a sigh of relief, Jake placed the photo album back on the shelf. They all filed out, Ace carefully closing the door behind them.

Ainsley waited, tapping her foot impatiently, making a drumming sound with the heel of her shoe. "One of my colleagues is at the jail, waiting to see Dad. He's trying to expedite a bail hearing so we can get Dad home before he gets sick."

"Can we go see him?" Ace wanted to know.

"Right now, they aren't allowing any visitors other

than his lawyer," Ainsley replied. "If we can get bail set, we'll be able to post bond and bring him home."

Impressed with the younger woman's efficiency and optimism, Fiona kept her mouth shut. In her experience, the legal system moved at a snail's pace and wouldn't be hurried along by anyone. She could only hope that in this case, Ainsley was right.

Sierra offered to give Fiona a ride back to the AAG center, most likely because she felt as out of place as Fiona did. Fiona accepted, kissing Jake on the cheek and asking him to keep her posted.

The two women kept the chatter light and inconsequential on the drive. Fiona had met a bounty hunter or two in the past, and Sierra did not fit her preconceived notions of individuals in that profession at all.

Once they reached the AAG center, Sierra dropped her off and waved a cheerful goodbye. As she got out of the car, Fiona impulsively turned. "You and I should get together sometime when things aren't this crazy," she said. "Talk over a drink and get to know one another."

Sierra grinned. "I'd like that. Let's plan on it."

As they'd all feared and as their cousin Bella had warned them, the story hit the newspaper the next day. "Body Found on Rattlesnake Ridge Ranch!" the headline screamed. "Prominent citizen Payne Colton arrested and charged with murder."

Fiona's stomach clenched when she read the story. Selina had gone ahead and leaked the information to the paper. It didn't escape Fiona's attention that since the woman had clearly known about this for years and helped cover it up, she could also be named as an accessory. Though Fiona wouldn't put it past her to have worked up some sort of plea agreement in advance. Fiona itched to check in with the Mustang Valley Police Department and see what she could learn, but felt doing so officially would be unethical since the FBI wasn't involved in the case at all.

She just needed to put her head down and work. The sooner they'd gone through every square foot of the AAG center, the better case they'd have built against Micheline.

Still, the day crawled slowly past. Fiona helped catalog and bag evidence, trying to keep her mind on the task despite being unable to stop thinking about Jake.

She must have pulled out her phone a dozen times with the intention of calling Jake. Each time, she reconsidered. No doubt he, and the entire Colton family, were already aware of this. She needed to wait until he called her. He'd found himself in a unique and awkward position, just getting to know his new family while under the shadow of a major investigation.

When he finally called, he wanted to know if she'd like to come over and look at Tessa's photographs with him again. "I'm going to spend a couple hours in there tonight, and I could use your professional help?"

This surprised her. "Professional? What do you mean?"

"Going through things," he replied, making her wonder if he deliberately chose to sound vague. "I'm more of an outdoor guy, not a paper pusher. Just the thought of trying to see my mother by flipping through tons of photographs is overwhelming to me." His voice softened. "Plus, I'd like to see you. I'd enjoy your company."

She laughed. "I'll be there in twenty minutes. Do you want me to bring anything?"

"Just yourself. We'll grab dinner here. Ace had the cook make a bunch of sandwiches since everything is so crazy right now. They're stored in the fridge."

"Is Payne out yet?"

"Not yet. Ainsley is up there now posting bond. She said she's not leaving until she has him with her."

"I really like her," Fiona told him.

"Me, too. I really hit the jackpot when it comes to family," Jake said. "Both Ace and I got lucky. See you soon."

She hung up, thinking she'd also lucked out in meeting him. While she didn't know where this relationship might be going, she couldn't wait to find out.

Chapter 16

After ending the call, Jake walked downstairs and went out to sit on the front porch and wait for Fiona. He'd felt weird all day, as if there was something vitally important he'd managed to overlook. Though he had no idea what that might be or even what it might relate to, he'd learned from past experience that sitting outside in nature and clearing his mind often helped him figure out a solution to whatever problem he had.

The Triple R had several oversize rocking chairs on one side of the house. He took a seat in one, taking in the breathtaking view of land and livestock and mountains. A sense of calm, of peace, stole over him. With all the recent turmoil, it felt good to sit and breathe, to simply *exist*.

In one of the pastures below him, a horse reared up, kicking up a clump of dirt before taking off running, tail streaming high behind him. Soon another horse joined him, and then another, galloping just for the sheer joy of it.

By the time Fiona pulled up, driving a government-issued dark sedan instead of the old junker she'd used before, he felt calm and centered. And hopeful—more hopeful than he'd been in forever.

"Hey!" He stood, moving down the steps to greet her. The instant she swung her long legs out of the car, he pulled her close and held on tight. "You smell good," he told her, trying to identify the scent and failing.

"Lavender and vanilla body lotion," she said, smiling up at him.

He kissed her then, unable to help himself. Right there, on the front porch of the Triple R, where anyone could see. When they finally broke apart, they both were breathing heavily.

"Whoa, cowboy," she said, smiling.

"I've missed you," he replied, aching to kiss her again. "Let's go inside."

She slipped her slender hand in his. Together they walked through the front doors.

"It's sure quiet in here today," she commented. "Are you the only one home?"

He liked that she used the word *home*. It wasn't yet, but he knew it could be if he wanted. The entire family had been hinting about that. "Right now, yes. But Ace knows I've been planning to spend some more time in Tessa's studio, so it's all good." As long as Payne didn't mind. No one had exactly been clear about that.

Once they'd reached the room, he turned on the light and stood in the doorway for a moment, marveling at how it seemed untouched by time.

"Someone cleans in here regularly," Fiona said when he spoke that thought out loud. "Otherwise there would be dust everywhere."

She had a point. He wondered if Payne took on that particular task himself or if he had household staff do it.

They spent the next hour going through photo albums, most of them of Tessa's children, Payne and a beautiful border collie who must have been the family pet.

After they'd gone through the tenth album, Jake pushed to his feet and stretched. "I think I've had enough photo albums for now. Maybe we should check out some of the more artistic shots she took."

"Where?" Fiona asked, sweeping a wayward strand of hair back from her face as she too stood.

"I think she filed them in those large portfolio things." Moving toward them, he eyed the assortment of cameras. One of them, a big, bulky, rectangular thing, didn't look like a camera at all.

"Look." Jake pointed. "Is that...?"

"A Sony BMC-100. One of the very first personal camcorders." Fiona moved closer. "Look how freaking huge it is!"

Jake carefully picked it up. "Heavy, too. If I remember right, these guys recorded to those old clunky video tapes." He pushed a button, and a compartment on the side slowly opened. "There's still one in here."

"I wonder if there's anything on it?" Fiona smiled. "Wouldn't it be awesome to be able to actually see your mother's face and hear her voice?"

"It would." Carefully, Jake closed the camcorder door. "Though if she were the one using it, I doubt she'll be on any of the recordings. Still, it wouldn't hurt to look.

I wonder if Payne happens to have an old VCR sitting around so we could watch it. I'll ask Ace later."

A quick tap on the door had them turning in unison.

"Hey," Ainsley said, smiling tiredly. "I got Payne released and he's home. He's exhausted, so he's gone to his room to try and get some rest."

"That's understandable," Jake said, relieved. "I'm so glad you were able to get him out of there."

"It wasn't easy. I had to do some serious convincing. I mean, come on. He's elderly, no prior record, and it's not like he's a flight risk or danger to society. Luckily, the judge took all that into consideration and set a reasonable bail amount."

Jake didn't want to ask what she thought was reasonable.

"Do you happen to know if there's a working VCR in this house?" Fiona asked, explaining why.

"Seriously, a video tape?" Ainsley appeared intrigued. "That'd be cool if something really was on it. I know Payne has a DVR, but maybe he might have hung on to one of those old VCRs. Ace would probably know for sure."

By the time Ace returned home, both Ainsley and Grayson had gotten excited about the tape and wanted to find a VCR. The instant he strolled through the door, Ainsley immediately grabbed him, demanding to know if he had any idea where they might find one.

"A VCR?" he asked, incredulous. "Why on earth would anyone need one of those? Did you find an old stash of videotapes or something?"

As soon as they explained, his eyes lit up. "I'd love to see that. Honestly, though, I don't remember her ever using a video camera."

"Probably because you were so young," Ainsley shot back. "Duh."

Ace laughed. "Good point." He thought for a moment. "Did any of you look for one?"

"Not yet," Ainsley chimed in. "We wanted to wait for you."

Jake envied the easy camaraderie between brother and sister. "We actually figured if anyone would know, you would," he said.

This made Ace grin. "You guys didn't even try, did you? Because I'm pretty sure Dad still has a VCR hooked up to the big flat-screen television in the media room. Along with his DVR and Blu-ray player."

"Seriously?" Fiona looked both flabbergasted and intrigued.

"Yep," Ace replied. "He has a huge cabinet in there full of videotapes, DVDs, etc. There's a ton of old movies, along with newer ones."

Jake cleared his throat. "Does Payne know we've been in Tessa's room?"

The three siblings exchanged looks. Ainsley shrugged. "I didn't say anything. I figured he had enough on his mind already."

"I didn't, either," Ace added, his expression rueful. "To be honest, I was afraid he'd say no, and I really wanted you to learn about your mother, Jake."

Fiona crossed to his side, once again slipping her fingers through his. Grateful, Jake smiled at her before eyeing the others. "I was just thinking Payne might like to see whatever is on the video."

"Let's wait and see what it is first," Ace suggested. "For all we know, it might be a blank."

A sobering thought, but Jake knew Ace was right. No

sense in stirring up Payne without good cause. The poor man had already been through enough.

"Come on, let's go see." Ace led the way. They all trooped upstairs to the media room, a large, windowless area with theater-style seating and a huge flat screen hung on the wall.

"There it is," Ace said, pointing. "Let me make sure it's still hooked up." When he pressed a button, a light came on.

"Yep." Jake handed Ace the remote so he could power up the TV. "From what I remember, I think you have to change the input."

Finally, once Ace had everything ready, Jake handed him the videotape. Once he'd inserted it, he pressed Play.

"Here we are." A woman's voice. *Tessa*, Jake thought, his heart skipping a beat. His mother. A quick glance at the others revealed similar expressions of wonder. Just then, he realized none of them had actually truly known their mother. They'd all been so young when she died.

The video showed the interior of the Triple R house, looking much newer, with totally different furniture, of course. Tessa continued to narrate, naming each room as she filmed it.

Jake struggled not to show his disappointment. He didn't want to look at the others, aware they probably felt the same. Fiona squeezed his hand, offering her silent support.

Finally, Tessa stepped outside. She filmed one of the barns, a few horses frolicking in an outside paddock, still speaking in her soft, pleasant voice.

As she rounded the corner of the house, she froze, still recording video. Two men came into view. One of them, a much younger Payne, appeared to be arguing with the other.

"Damn it," Tessa cursed, still quietly. "That's Randy Stanford. Payne fired him last week. I'm not sure what he's doing here, but it can't be anything good."

While trying to keep the camcorder focused on the two men, Tessa took pains to stay out of their line of sight. She ducked back behind the house, which briefly sent the video feed swerving crazily, showing sky and dirt and brick before she got herself situated and finally turned the lens back on her husband and the intruder. They still appeared to be arguing. Because of the distance, no one could make out what exactly about.

When Randy pulled a gun on Payne, the entire room gasped out loud.

A second later, Payne pulled his own gun and shot the other man, so quickly he didn't have time to react and fire his own weapon. A clean shot right to the chest.

Tessa gasped, muttered something and took off running, forgetting to turn off the camcorder in her haste. Because the thing was so heavy, she lugged it along with her, recording all the way until she got back to her room.

Breathing hard, she finally pressed the button to power it off. The recording ended.

For a second longer, everyone simply sat in stunned silence. Then they all started talking at once.

"Was that…?"

"Clear case of self-defense."

"But if Tessa had this all along," Jake asked, "why wouldn't she have shown it to Payne so he could be exonerated?"

No one knew.

"Maybe they never discussed it," Ace said. "We can't ask her and clearly Payne had no idea this tape existed."

"I need to get that to the prosecutor immediately. We'll request a meeting with the district attorney's office." Ainsley marched to the front of the room and extracted the videotape from the VCR.

"What if they don't have anything to play it?" Fiona suggested. "I'd run it again, and this time, record the relevant part with your phone."

"Good idea." Ainsley smiled. Then she did exactly that.

Once she'd finished, she handed the tape to Jake. "Keep this safe, please."

He nodded, absurdly pleased. "Will do."

"This should be enough to get them to drop the charges," she announced, smiling. "We'll deal with the media once that's done." And then, to Jake's complete and utter shock, she strode over and hugged him. When she finished, she hugged Fiona, too.

"This would never have come to light without you two," she said, her voice breaking. "Thank you, from the bottom of my heart."

Once Ainsley left, Ace came over and slung his arm over Jake's shoulder. "Good job," he said. From his seat, Grayson echoed the sentiment.

True to Ainsley's prediction, once the video evidence had been reviewed, backing up Payne's claim of self-defense, the DA refused to prosecute. And the media covered the story, the headlines stating Payne Colton had been cleared of any wrongdoing.

Payne, too relieved to mind that Jake and Fiona had been in Tessa's room, took a particular delight in phoning Selina to let her know. He reported she told him to go to hell before ending the call.

The FBI wrapped up its investigation into Micheline and the AAG. The government would seize the property, which would soon be locked down until it was auctioned off. Jake figured Fiona would have to leave Mustang Valley—and Jake—soon. Part of him wanted to ask her to get a room at the Dales Inn there in town, just to stay close.

The DNA test came back. He'd had it sent to Payne, who phoned him with the results. The match proved beyond a shadow of a doubt what everyone already knew: Jake was a Colton.

Finally, Fiona called and asked him to meet. When he pulled up, he saw her suitcase in the back of her car, along with a few other belongings that she'd accumulated since arriving in town.

"We're done," she said simply. "After all this time, all this work, what happens next is out of our hands. I'm not sure when, but multiple indictments will soon be handed down. I don't think Micheline will be getting out of prison in her lifetime."

"Good." He pulled her into his arms and held her, breathing in the scent of her hair. "Good job, Fiona."

She tightened her arms around him, though she didn't speak. "Where are you going to go now?" she asked, her voice muffled since she'd pressed her face against his chest. "Back to your ranch?"

"No. I'm staying here," Jake said, pulling back a little so he could watch Fiona's face for a hint of how that might make her feel. "At the Triple R, with my family."

She nodded, her expression neutral. "What about your ranch? Are you going to sell it?"

"No. I worked too damn hard getting that ranch up and running. I'm proud of it, especially since I did it on my own. I've got capable people taking care of it for me and keeping it going. I'll just drop in and check on things from time to time." He smiled. "Ace says once Nova and Clara are up to it, we're going to have a big shindig, even if we have to have two parties. It'll be huge, since I hear the Colton Oil branch of the family and the Colton triplets are all much closer now."

Fiona nodded. "That's a lot of people to get to know. It must be pretty awesome," she commented. "Finding out you have an entire family you never even knew about."

"It is," he replied, still unable to tear his gaze away from her. "I consider myself lucky that they're all so welcoming and generous with their love."

His comment made her blink. Was that sheen in her dark eyes from unshed tears? "They've even asked me to consider changing my last name legally from Anderson to Colton."

"Wow." She smiled then, though her gaze remained serious. "Are you going to?"

"I think so. Yes." He hadn't been certain until that very moment. "Micheline and her fake last name never should have been a part of me. I'm a Colton by blood, and I'm honored that the entire family wants me to make that official."

"How does Ace feel about that?" she asked. "It must be difficult for him, knowing he's the interloper here."

"He's not, nor will he ever be." Heart full, Jake couldn't suppress a grin. "The family is throwing a big party for both Ace Coltons, as they call it. We're both Coltons, no matter what."

"Wow." She blinked again. Now he was almost positive she was keeping back tears. His precious, wonderful Fiona. Was she wondering what place in his life would be left for her? "Will you be spending the summer holidays with them?"

"I am. How about you?" he asked. "Are you close to your family?" Testing the waters, to see if she'd be willing to spend time with him.

"No siblings—I'm an only child." Her smile wavered a little.

"I hate that," Jake began.

"Don't." She shook her head. "Don't pity me. It's all right. I'm used to being alone." Then, clearly trying to change the subject, she told him she'd heard that some of Micheline's followers had turned against her, particularly after having learned she kept people in a basement. "They're willing to testify against her," she said. "Including Harley Watts, who sent the original email to the board about the baby switch."

"That's great," he replied, refusing to be deterred. "But I don't pity you, Fiona." He shook his head. "Never that. I was used to being alone, too. I told myself that I didn't even mind it. But being accustomed to something doesn't mean you have to like it."

Did she get the hint? Heart pounding, he waited for her response.

"Of course." Now she wouldn't look at him. "And I envy you that. But how do you think it would be for me, knowing you dragged me to your family's celebrations, just because you didn't want me to be by myself?"

He took a step closer. "That's not why I want to spend more time with you," he said. "I want to be with the person I love the most in the entire world. You."

Now she got it. She froze. "Do you really mean that?" she whispered, her gaze locking on his.

"I do." Now he went to her, pulling her into his arms. "From the moment we first met, I knew there was something special. A connection. I know you felt it, too."

Face against his chest, she nodded. "I like how you let me be vulnerable," she said, her arms wrapped around him as she held on tight. "Being strong all the time can be tiring."

"I know. We've been through hell and back in the last few weeks. You're the strongest person I know. That's one of the many things I love about you."

She sniffed and started trembling. Stunned, he realized she actually was crying now. "Please don't cry," he said, helpless in the face of feminine tears.

"I'm trying not to." Lifting her head, she angrily swiped at her face. "It's just that's the nicest thing anyone has ever said to me."

"That you're strong? I find it hard to believe no one's ever remarked on that before."

"No." She gave him a watery smile. "That you love me. I love you, too, you know."

He debated pretending shock but settled for kissing her instead.

* * * * *

Available now from Harlequin Romantic Suspense!

WE HOPE YOU ENJOYED THIS BOOK FROM

HARLEQUIN
ROMANTIC SUSPENSE

Danger. Passion. Drama.

These heart-racing page-turners will keep you guessing to the very end. Experience the thrill of unexpected plot twists and irresistible chemistry.

4 NEW BOOKS AVAILABLE EVERY MONTH!

What could she tell him? Her situation was horrid.
Frightening. Desperate. And that was why she had to
keep Luke out of it. She had to protect him from the
ugliness that her life had become and the danger Joseph
posed.

But he was standing there, all devastatingly handsome,
earnest and worried about her. She had to tell him
something. The lies she'd told friends for years to hide
the truth tasted all the more sour as they formed on her
tongue, so she discarded them for one that was more
palatable.

"A few years back I made some…poor choices," she
began slowly, picking her words carefully. "And I'm

trying to correct those mistakes. Until I get my life back on track, my finances are going to be tight. But I can't make the fresh start I need if I accept money from you or anyone else. I need to do this by myself. To be truly independent and self-sufficient."

"Poor choices, huh?" A hum rumbled from his throat, and he twisted his lips. "We all make those at some point in our lives, don't we?"

With his gaze still locked on her, he inched his palms from her shoulders to her neck, and his thumbs now reached the bottom edge of her chin. His work-roughened hands were paradoxically gentle. The skimming strokes of his calloused fingers against her skin pooled a honeyed lethargy inside her. Reason told her to pull away, but some competing force inside her rooted her to the spot to bask in the tenderness she'd had far too little of in her adult life.

Luke is the kind of man you should be with, the kind of man you deserve.

Don't miss
In the Rancher's Protection *by Beth Cornelison,*
available July 2020 wherever
Harlequin Romantic Suspense
books and ebooks are sold.

Harlequin.com